# Back Where You Belong

Ivy Beck

# Contents

# Prologue

A jerk on an electric scooter turned Emerson Taylor's not-so-great day into an even shittier one when he bumped her elbow, upending her half-finished green drink all over her fresh-from-the-cleaners suit jacket.

Shocked, Emerson froze. Her mouth hung open, but no sound came out. It only took a second before she was impeding traffic and began to get jostled and grumbled at for being in the way.

Holding back a growl of irritation, she swiped at the thick green liquid with a napkin while juggling the half-full cup and her monstrous purse that could double as luggage. Taking a deep breath as she began walking again, merging back into the flow of the foot traffic on Hanover Street, she tried to bring back the Zen she'd been searching for on this quick lunch break. The calendar said that it was spring. But from her perspective there wasn't a budding tree in sight, and the only birds around were die-hard pigeons who'd survived the harsh winter. She was hopeful, thinking she could sense it in the air and maybe even feel a little warmth in the breeze.

After taking in a deep breath, she sneezed. Not from spring allergens, but from the stench of the overflowing dumpster in the alley she'd just passed.

Glancing at her watch, she picked up the pace in her pumps, seeing that she only had ten minutes to get to her afternoon meeting. She'd barely had time to come down to the corner to get a liquid lunch since the meeting that morning had run over. Tossing the remains of her drink and her soiled napkin in the nearest trash can, she secured her bag close to her side. At the corner, she turned left onto Wall Street and hot-footed it to her office building.

She could have had lunch delivered to her, but she'd needed to step outside and take a breath of fresh—well, air, at least. Her colleagues had gotten into a screaming match this morning, causing her head to pound. She tried to be the mediator, but sometimes she thought they just needed to duke it out.

She meant that figuratively.

Although, on second thought...

New York City's lunchtime crowd cruised along the sidewalk, jostling her from time to time, but she stayed sturdy on her three-inch heels, focused on her goal. The ringing of her phone was nearly drowned out by the honking cabbies racing down the street, jockeying for position. Reaching into her purse, she pulled out her phone and couldn't help the sigh that escaped when she saw the name of the caller.

She really didn't have time for this now.

If she ignored it and let it go to voicemail, she'd only catch more grief for it the next time. With more than a little regret over her reaction to seeing her sister's name on the screen she pushed the answer button. "Hello, Sidney."

"Emmie!"

The tears in her sister's voice instantly grabbed her full attention, stopping her dead on the sidewalk. Several people ran into her back, telling her to "watch out" and "get out of the way."

"What is it? What's happened?" Was this the phone call she'd always dreaded receiving? Was this about her mother?

"Emmie, it's Mom." Sidney sniffed, partially confirming her fears. "She's sick and we need you to come home."

At once, her thoughts immediately went to her work schedule. When could she find time to go home for a visit? But the sadness in her sister's voice brought her around.

*What the hell am I thinking?*

"What's wrong? Did she fall? Was it a stroke?" Her mind raced with the possibilities.

Sidney sniffled a time or two more before explaining, "It's Parkinson's, Emmie. The tremors are only slight, that's what caused her to go to the doctor. She's been losing her balance some."

Emerson closed her eyes and took several deep breaths to get her mind to focus on all that her sister had just told her. "Is there medication for it?" She didn't know anything about Parkinson's. Just that people had tremors and that there was no cure.

"Yes. She's already been prescribed some."

She couldn't believe her mother was sick. The strong woman who had raised her and her two older siblings mostly on her own since Emerson's father died when she was six. A famous artist, who resided in a sleepy little artsy village on the Eastern Shore of Mobile Bay.

Parkinson's? This brought the world around her to a screeching halt. She no longer heard the traffic noise as the cars pushed their way through the busy downtown streets, or the chatter from the people walking past her.

"Emmie? Are you there?"

Emerson shook her head to bring herself out of this trance. "Yeah, I'm here. Tell me how she's doing. How she's dealing with this." She began to pace back and forth outside her office building, in a narrow space between a row of planters and the wall of windows.

Sidney laughed. But it was more of an exasperated laugh than a joyful one. "Oh, the usual, she's going about her daily life, ignoring the doctor's recommendations, totally in denial about the changes her life is about to take."

Emerson held back tears. She loved her mother—for her strength, for her kind heart, but also for her stubbornness.

"I'll be there as soon as I can." She glanced at her watch and groaned. She was late. "Sid, I have to go, I'm late for a meeting—"

"You're always late for a meeting, Em. That's all your life consists of. Take some time for your family without having to worry about your schedule," she huffed. Then added in a softer voice, "Mom needs you, sis."

Emerson sighed and closed her eyes, knowing Sidney was right. She hadn't had much spare time for her family lately. Sidney's youngest was nearly one and she hadn't seen her since the day of her birth. Well, actually, the day after. "I know. Look, I'll let you know when I have a plane ticket, okay? Hug her for me."

Emerson couldn't imagine a world that didn't have Carolyn Taylor in it. Her strength had been passed on to each of her children. Emerson had taken hers and fled to Wall Street, to make something of herself, leaving behind her family who were scattered around the south for the Big Apple and the big bucks. Her brother Logan was a firefighter in Pensacola, married with three kids and living a happy life. Her sister Sidney was an artist like their mother. She and her husband Dave lived on a barrier island on the other side of Mobile Bay with their two kids.

Sighing, she wiped the tears from her cheeks and pulled open the front door. She didn't look forward to rearranging her schedule, but she knew she needed to. Her mother was important to her, and she couldn't neglect her any longer.

# Chapter One

"So, are there really alligators living in the sewers of New York City?"

"What?" Emerson looked up from the phone in her hands, blinking at her cousin, Callie Henley, across the table from her. Tuning back in—trying to leave the finance world she'd immediately gotten sucked into after only a glance at the text from her colleague—she followed Callie's gaze and caught the tail of the alligator fifteen feet below as it slipped beneath the murky surface of the marshy creek beside the restaurant. Excited calls from the kayakers nearby could be heard from the outdoor seating area on the deck. She and Callie were seated at a high-top next to the bar that ran the entire length of the covered deck.

"Not that I know of," she laughed. Blinking her eyes, she shifted her gaze from the kayakers to the Live Oaks draped in Spanish moss across to the waves washing onto the shore. "Wow, this is really pretty."

"Yes, it is. Put your phone down, Em," Callie admonished, "and take in the scenery."

Emerson released a deep breath as she put her phone face down on the table. Before her hand was even off the phone another text came through, beeping its alert. Glancing at Callie, noticing her disproving eighth-grade-teacher-raised-eyebrow stare, she pulled her hand back and with a sheepish smile she took another minute to focus on the sights around her. The sun near the horizon across the bay cast a reddish-orange glow on the tall marsh grasses bordering the creek and shimmered on the water that moved with the incoming waves. Besides the alligator there were numerous shore birds walking about the shallow water looking for a fishy dinner.

She had missed these scenic views of Mobile Bay when she'd moved to New York City. The only nature she saw there was when she stepped into Central Park and breathed in the trees. Otherwise, it was a concrete jungle where she lived and worked, and she didn't take the time to notice much about the scenery around her.

This was one of her favorite things to do when she did manage to make it home for a visit.

Although, this wasn't just for a visit.

Emerson absently picked up her phone and scrolled through the incoming texts, her fingers flying in response to the multitude of questions and complaints from colleagues and clients. She didn't know how long she'd spent back in her work world, but a glance up at Callie told her it had been too long.

Hoping to get herself mentally away from work and back into the present, she cleared her throat as well as her mind. "Sorry, Cal."

Callie tilted her head, her long blonde hair sliding forward over her shoulders. "How's your mom doing?" she asked, as if she knew what was also going on in Emerson's mind. Worry about her mother was tussling for control in the thought department with everything she'd left behind in New York.

She and Callie had always been able to read each other's minds and hearts. They were called the "twin cousins" having been born only three days apart. They had matching eyes—a beautiful blue green that changed with their emotions and the color of the clothes they wore—a color all the cousins shared, as well as their moms. Their biggest difference was their hair color. Emerson's was red like her father's side of the family. Callie's was blonde like her mother's side.

Their moms were sisters and had lived only a few miles apart their whole lives. Callie didn't have any brothers or sisters, so she practically lived with Emerson and her crew when they were growing up.

"She's getting tired easily, but you know Mom, she's stubborn. If you ask her, nothing's changed and nothing will. She plans to out-stubborn this disease, I guess."

"If anyone could, it's your mom." Callie laughed and squeezed Emerson's hand on the tabletop, offering comfort but at the same time swiping the phone that Emerson couldn't seem to break away from.

"Hey!"

"It's for your own good," Callie said, putting the phone in her purse hanging from the back of her chair.

Sighing, disgusted with herself, Emerson closed her eyes briefly. "Again, I'm sorry. Work is just such a part of me, that I can't seem to let it go. Not even for a dinner date with my favorite cousin."

"Flattery will not get your phone back." Callie laughed after saying that with a straight face. "I've missed you, Em."

"I've missed you too. More than I realized. You look good, Cal." Emerson waved a hand at her outfit, hoping to change the subject. The capped sleeves of her emerald-green blouse showed off her fit arms. "You've toned up since I last saw you, huh?"

"Yes, ma'am. Finally realized I can't eat like the middle schoolers I teach. It started staying put instead of working itself off, so I had to up my exercise game." Callie eyed Emerson over the top of her menu. "You look too damn skinny, Em."

Emerson nodded and looked out at the kayakers who were banking their boats and getting out. She was too skinny. She hadn't taken the time in New York to realize it though. There'd always been a meeting to attend, a lunch date to get to where she'd spent more time looking over her notes and stock market numbers than the menu. After her last breakup, she'd focused whole-heartedly on work so there wasn't time to grieve and that didn't allow much room in her schedule for food.

Maybe this trip home would help her change that.

Scanning the menu, Emerson's stomach began to grumble in appreciation. Just like the views, she hadn't sampled a fare like this in quite some time either. She decided on a dinner of grilled fish. She couldn't resist ordering cheese grits and corn on the cob to go with it. Her colleagues in New York would be appalled at her choices.

Callie decided on the seafood gumbo and asked for fried blue crab claws as an appetizer.

"So, tell me all about the big city. Where did you go on your last date? Describe what you were wearing, the restaurant and most especially, the man," Callie ordered with a chuckle.

Emerson's smile in response didn't match the wattage of Callie's. Work had been so all-consuming, as well as this worry about her mother, that Emerson hadn't realized that she'd buried the hurt she'd experienced after the breakup with Evan.

She tried to stay in the moment, right here on this beautiful spring evening with Callie, and not think about the pain of her breakup. But her mind didn't listen. Emerson was transported back to her last date, which had been a total disaster. It had been the night Evan had told her their relationship was over, and that he'd already moved on. She'd been so busy with work that she hadn't even noticed how distant he'd become.

Emerson could see the scene clearly in her mind, but she didn't want to share that memory with anyone, not even her cousin.

She glanced around at the other patrons while she thought about her answer, her eye snagging on the bartender as he wiped a glass dry. He looked up at her, somehow sensing her gaze on him.

And she couldn't look away.

Caught in the trance created by his amazing whiskey-colored eyes twinkling beneath the overhead lights. His lips curved up on one side, and he offered her a nod, causing his shaggy, sandy-brown hair to fall over his forehead.

Emerson could hear Callie clearing her throat in the distance. Like she was much farther away than just across the high-top. But quickly the haze of fog clogging her ears evaporated when she realized Callie wasn't clearing her throat but instead, she was choking.

Hearing Callie's choking cough as she recovered from what must have been a miss-sip brought her out of her trance. She blinked, breaking eye contact, which in turn released the restriction the trance had put on her lungs. She drew in a choppy breath. Her gaze shot to her cousin, who was clutching her throat and coughing, holding her glass in her other hand.

She quickly realized that Callie was choking more on laughter than sweet tea, thankfully.

"Are you okay?" Emerson sat up in her chair and leaned forward across the table. *Lock it in, Em, no more gawking at the bartender!*

Callie set her glass down as she cleared her throat again, then wiped the tears from under her eyes and took a deep, cleansing breath. "I'm fine. Whew, that was rough. I practically snorted sweet tea through my nose when I realized why you hadn't answered me!"

Emerson blushed a little at getting caught checking out the bartender.

"But, hey, I don't blame you. He's hunky," Callie whispered with a wink. "So back to my 'last-date question.'"

"I haven't been on many dates lately. Work has been a demon," Emerson quickly explained instead of getting into any details about Evan. "Are you still dating Tim?"

Callie guffawed. "No. All that man liked to do was fish," she explained, her eyebrows furrowed. "When he chose to take part in the tenth fishing tournament already this year instead of spending a Saturday hiking in Blakeley State Park with Goose and me, I gave him the heave-ho."

Emerson laughed at both her cousin's expression and the name of her beloved yellow lab. The dog looked nothing like a goose, nor did he live up to his heritage as a retriever. Callie had a hard time explaining the connection between the lovable pup and his name, so everyone just accepted it, and him, with loving arms.

Emerson's lips pulled up into a partial frown. "I'm sorry, Cal. I know how much you liked him."

Callie shrugged and spun the saltshaker on the table. "I guess I liked the idea of being in a relationship more than being in one with him."

As soon as their waitress set a steamy basket of fried blue crab claws in front of them, they reached in. Emerson closed her eyes, enjoying the savory taste. Callie set about adding ketchup to the little tub of horseradish available on the table to make the cocktail sauce to their liking.

Both liked it with a kick.

Emerson licked sauce from the tip of her finger before asking, "Have you dated anyone else since Tim?" She looked up in time to see Callie's face flush. She didn't think it was from the tangy horseradish. "What?"

"Well, you're gonna laugh, but I signed up on one of those online dating sites."

Emerson's hand paused in route to her mouth. "Online dating? Really?"

Callie nodded, her hair sliding easily over the satiny material of her blouse. "I knew you'd be shocked, but it's actually been kind of fun. You shouldn't knock it until you try it," she said as their food arrived. Callie waited until the waitress left before saying, "Actually, I think you should try it while you're here. Maybe you could meet a hunky man like him."

Emerson followed Callie's pointed gaze over to the bar. Her heart started thumping when she took in the sight before her. The bartender faced them, balanced on a barstool. Stretching overhead to one of the top shelves situated high above the bar top, his shirt had come up with his reach. Tight muscles and tanned skin were exposed in the gap between his T-shirt and his jeans. Instantly, her mouth watered.

Afraid she might be drooling she quickly snapped her mouth closed and averted her eyes.

Callie was biting her lip, holding back a chuckle when Emerson met her gaze. She suddenly felt hot and had the need to shift in her seat. "See. Hunky."

"He's just a bartender, Cal—"

"When did you become such a snob, Em?" Callie reprimanded, her brows furrowed.

Emerson closed her eyes and sighed, wondering the same thing. "I'm sorry. I shouldn't have said that. It's just—"

"I know you're used to a fast-paced world in New York and being involved with financial guys and making big-money deals, but that isn't all there is to life, Emerson."

"All valid points," Emerson conceded and picked up her silverware. Quickly the conversation turned to shopping. Emerson smiled. Now that she could talk about for hours. She shared with Callie all the shops she'd been to lately and had her cousin groaning with envy.

"Just like old times, I'll give you free rein over my wardrobe. You can have one item and only one. No outfits this time, missy." Last year when she'd been home for her niece's birth, she'd let Callie look through her things. Callie had gone overboard and taken a top as well as her favorite slacks.

This time she would put a time limit on her cousin's shopping spree too.

"You're the best."

***

Emerson finished the last email for the night to her newest client. The man was outraged that she wasn't in New York working on his portfolio 24/7. She tried to explain that she'd taken a leave of absence, and her colleague Don Westbrook would be handling his portfolio until her return. She reported her client's discontent to her boss, who reassured her that Don would take care of the gentleman.

The next thing her boss said practically blew her workaholic mind—he actually told her to turn her phone and computer off and...Try. To. Relax.

And not just off for the night. Off for the duration of her leave time.

Impossible. Emerson had no idea how to do that.

Her phone was on twenty-four hours a day and she was active on it, most days, for at least eighteen to twenty hours. Her job didn't stop. She had clients all over the world and she needed to be available. Her laptop was on and open nearly the same length of time.

She'd gotten an entry-level position at Lawson Financial straight out of college and had worked her way up the ranks. After eight years she held an esteemed senior position as a financial analyst and was the first woman to do so. It had not been an easy route, but she'd fought hard, and she was proud of all that she'd achieved in such a short time.

She found it exhilarating but if she was truly honest with herself, she also found it exhausting.

She hadn't really had a chance to stop and think about it much. When she'd been in the thick of living the life, completely immersed in that fast-paced world, she hadn't taken time to consider what that pace was doing to her.

Physically.

Mentally.

Emotionally.

But her life was exhausting. The pace she put herself through, from the second the alarm sounded in the morning until the very last minute before her head finally hit the pillow at night, she was *on*. And by on, she really meant on.

On the phone. On task. On point at every meeting.

But tonight, she was trying to reconcile with the fact that she didn't have to be as *on* as she was in New York. That she could sit down. She could relax a bit. Maybe even put her phone down for extended periods of time. Take a step back from the world she lived in and see what was going on around her.

Dinner with Callie had been fun, enlightening and so therapeutic. She'd needed to have her phone removed from her hand and her sight. Spending time with her "twin cousin" was one of her favorite things and she'd needed that time to make the transition from crazy, hectic chaos, to slowed down, quiet peace.

Thinking back to their conversation, she found her thoughts revolving around her family. And how the recent events of her life had unfolded the instant she'd gotten the call from her sister.

She was home again.

If she allowed herself to admit her feelings to her family, she'd have to tell them that it was good to be home. For more than one reason.

She was glad that she was here for her mother, because she enjoyed spending time with her. But also, it was good for her own health.

She hadn't realized how much she enjoyed the sounds of gulls fighting over breakfast just outside her bedroom window. Or the scent of all the flowers scattered throughout the terraced backyard.

Emerson had grown up in this house on the bay. It was an old, two-story home, with tall, robust columns on the front porch. It backed up to Mobile Bay. The house sat uphill from the water with large, three-hundred-year-old Live Oak trees draped in Spanish moss framing their yard.

On the day she arrived, Emerson's ears had still been ringing from the chaotic world of New York City. There, her blood seemed to pump at the rate of the movement and noise surrounding her. And in New York, it was always fast paced. From the racing traffic jockeying for position in the crowded streets to the loud calls of the street vendors trying to sell their wares.

After greeting her mother with an enormous hug where she spent time holding back tears, she ventured out in the backyard to her favorite spot. A long, thin board, roomy enough for two to sit, with thick ropes still hung from a sturdy branch of the Live Oak closest to the water. She loved to sit on that swing for hours. As a kid, when she'd really gotten her feet pumping it would seem like she was flying over the water.

Sitting in that swing on her first night, she felt that dull roar transform from the persistent noises in her hectic world to the deafening silence of life on the bay. *The silence was so loud.* It took multiple deep breaths and plenty of time focusing on the steady movement of the gentle waves pushing onshore to clear the intensity of that loud silence.

After more than thirty minutes of sitting motionless on that swing, she felt the silence simmer. Her ears gradually began to pick up the quieter sounds around her. The wind rustling through the oak leaves above her head. A testy squirrel arguing with a Blue Jay two branches up from where the swing was attached. The rush of the waves hitting the sandy beach in front of her. The distant sound of a Jet Ski on the water.

Eventually, the loudly chirping crickets drew her out of her trance and sent her back inside the house to check on her mother.

A beep alerted her of another text coming through, startling her back to the present. Sighing, she set the phone down and looked around the kitchen of her childhood.

The dining table still sat against the wall of windows looking out at the water. She'd automatically sat in her unofficial assigned seat from the time she'd gotten out of her highchair to the present. Her kindergarten artwork hung on the wall beside the refrigerator next to her brother's and sister's. Though her art was nowhere near the caliber of her mother's and sister's back in kindergarten she'd held her own.

But then numbers became more important to her than art.

The space around her was so familiar, so comforting, that even after being away for nearly a year, she knew where everything was.

It was reassuring to know that not much had changed.

Except her.

And her mother's illness.

Taking a few deep breaths, Emerson realized she was going to have to change up her routine and most definitely her expectations on a daily basis. No longer would she be waking at 4:30 a.m. and getting a quick sweat in on her Peloton. Then popping in to pick up a green smoothie breakfast at the corner store before heading to her first meeting by six a.m.

Here, her mother woke around seven and started the day off much slower than Emerson. Maybe she'd have to start running when she woke up early to get her day started. It would give her a chance to take in the sights of what she'd always thought of as her "nowhere hometown."

Just in the time she'd taken to drive around a little over the last two days while taking Carolyn to her doctors' appointments, she was surprised to see this sleepy southern coastal town she couldn't wait to get out of as a kid was actually a thriving community.

She hadn't been old enough the last time she'd lived there to appreciate its uniqueness. Artsy lawn ornaments in the shape of dolphins, fish, and herons adorned manicured lawns of old homes shrouded by old Live Oaks. And, most especially, the slow, friendly pace of the people of Sweetgum, Alabama.

When she'd been a teenager, she'd developed this itch, this need, to break free of this place, to get away from the peaceful, the normal, the everyday. She wanted to experience something bigger, something better, and something more meaningful than working at the local CVS to pay for school like her friends were planning.

So she'd worked hard, studied hard, and it paid off with a full ride on an academic scholarship. The instant she'd arrived at Columbia University she tried to convince herself that what she was feeling was the sense of coming home. Instead, it had been trepidation at being so far from home, from family, from everything that was familiar. Her mother had never discouraged any of her dreams or took any offense at her daughter's ideals that south Alabama was a nowhere-kind-of-place.

What a fool she'd been to overlook all that this place had to offer.

Emerson also became aware of a strong hunger that was taking up space in her middle. After being here for just two days, she'd felt like she'd put back on some of the weight that she'd lost due to the stress of her job and her determination not to feel anything after her breakup with Evan.

Thoughts of Evan brought her attention back to the computer in front of her. Her fingers, seemingly with a mind of their own, began typing in the web address that Callie had mentioned at dinner.

Its happy, friendly web page drew her in. Emerson couldn't believe she was even contemplating online dating. Since she was going to be here for four weeks, she didn't want to spend all that time sitting around. Even with the responsibilities she had with caring for her mother, she would have some free time.

What the hell. She clicked on the "sign up now" icon. Why not go ahead and have some fun for a few weeks. *It's not like I'm looking to marry and settle down here, right?*

Emerson was amazed at all the questions she had to answer to fill out her profile. Once she'd written her autobiography, she typed in her zip code.

She likened the experience of looking at all the men before her to browsing a menu, looking carefully to find out what she was hungry for. The idea of a menu brought her dinner experience from earlier to mind and her mind's eye couldn't help itself as it immediately flashed to the view of the bartender that she'd been awarded with when he'd reached overhead. That man had abs for days and thinking about them made her own stomach muscles tighten and even quiver a little.

Clearing her throat, she hoped that would help clear her mind of his image. Shaking her head, she focused on the screen before her. Clicking randomly, she was amazed at the photos that were displayed of these guys.

"Who allowed this photo to be taken or used as his primary?" she muttered as she looked at a man who had obviously taken the photo of himself. It was too close, too out of focus, and downright creepy looking. Wasn't this guy looking to get a date? Maybe someone should tell him that he wouldn't be getting many with that photo.

Another photo showed a man in a suit with stained-glass behind him. Stained-glass that was probably from a church. "Was this picture taken at his wedding? Geesh," she grumbled, quickly scrolling past.

After reading some of the other profiles of the available men in the area, she was somewhat discouraged. She wasn't sure exactly what she'd been hoping for, but she didn't think this was it. Again, her mind flashed her a pic of the hottie from the bar today. *Nope.*

She broadened her search area to include Mobile and Pensacola, the major metropolises in the area. The man she was hoping to meet would hopefully be in finance and could quote the stock market values at a moment's notice.

Her idea of the perfect man was one with similar goals as her. He didn't have to be Fortune 500 material, just damn close. Her grin quickly turned.

Sighing, disgusted with herself, she logged out and turned off her computer for the night. She'd look at it again tomorrow, in the bright light of a new day. Hopefully, more eligible men would sign up overnight to expand her options.

Because if that was all that was on the menu, she'd rather go hungry.

# Chapter Two

The ringing of his cell woke Nick Valentino from a deep sleep. Prying his eyes open, he blinked against the bright sunlight coming through his blinds. Ugh. *These late nights are killing me.*

He'd always been an early riser but tended to go to bed at a reasonable hour. Filling in for his brother at Keel & Rudder was about to do him in.

Nick stretched before grabbing his phone off the nightstand. "Hey."

"Good morning, sunshine! You sound like you're still in bed," Tony said, laughter in his voice. "I thought you were always awake to greet the sun."

"I usually am but tending your bar has kept me up past my bedtime," he finished around a yawn. Nick slid his legs over the side of the bed and rose, stretching his whole body before leaving the bedroom for the kitchen. The smell of coffee brewing hit his senses the second he rounded the corner.

"How's that going?" Tony asked.

Nick could hear windy static in the background. "It's going well, no issues so far. Just a ton of people asking where you are and when you're coming back."

"I always knew I was the more likable of the two of us," Tony chuckled. Tony was only three minutes and twenty-seven seconds older than Nick. They probably wrestled in the womb to decide who was coming out first. They were identical, except for the length of their hair. Tony went for a close cut while Nick kept his shaggier.

"Hah. In your dreams, T." Nick poured a steaming cup of coffee, taking a sip before he stepped out onto his deck. He was greeted with the calls of songbirds. Then a grumpy-ass garble from a Great Blue Heron that took off from his dock at the sound of the French door opening. "How goes your trip? When's the regatta again?"

Like he'd forgotten. It was all his brother had been talking about for over a year now. Tony had sailed his boat down to the Caribbean for a two-week vacation and a chance to final this year in a regatta he'd participated in five years running. Nick was covering for him at the bar while he was away.

"Thursday, knucklehead."

Nick took a seat on a deck chair and propped his bare feet on the railing. "Did all your crew show up?"

"Yep. Chip got in last night. Asshole. Nearly caused me to have to forfeit or sail without him." Tony spoke to someone else, then was back on the phone. "Gotta go, brother. There's a captain's meeting starting shortly."

"Best of luck to you, Tony." Nick raised his coffee mug in salute and said goodbye. After another ten minutes of listening to the sweet spring sounds of life along Blue Bottle Creek, he finished his first cup of coffee and headed back inside.

Another ten minutes and he was showered and out the door with his second cup of joe to go. He drove with his truck windows down along the winding neighborhood road that followed the creek. Spanish moss dripped from large Live Oaks alongside the road. His bungalow was nestled between three of them. He could literally build a treehouse if he wanted. These trees were abundant all over southern Alabama. And had been there for centuries.

Nick loved the history of the local flora and fauna. He'd fallen in love with it about the same time he'd fallen in love with high school senior Emerson Taylor. Nick's family had moved from inner-city New Jersey and settled here along the Eastern Shore of Mobile Bay to open a pizza joint. It turned out to be the best one in town.

His parents still ran it. They were very active for being in their late fifties.

Nick and Tony grew up in the business and much to their parents' dismay, both had wanted nothing to do with it. Both boys had fallen in love with the water and decided to spend their life on or near it.

Nick worked for the gentleman who ran Paddlers Paradise while he was in high school. When Nick was in college, the man started making noise about wanting to move to Michigan. Nick let him know that he was interested in taking the business off his hands.

He loved being on the water and getting others out there also. He'd taken to it right away, learning to kayak, fish, sail, snorkel, and scuba dive all in the first year that they were here. Over the years he'd loved learning about the history of the area, and found tourists really enjoyed hearing about it when he led guided kayak tours on Blue Bottle Creek.

His shop rented and sold kayaks, sunbirds, paddle boards, canoes, boogie boards, you name it. If it can float on the water or get you out in the water or frolic along the shores of the bay, he'd rent it or sell it to you. He sold all kinds of gear. His wasn't a fishing gear store, but he did have a small sampling of items that you could use when fishing from a kayak.

Nick parked out front of the shop and waved a greeting to the woman who owned the flower shop next door. She was setting a barrel of flowers outside her shop door. Spring had definitely sprung. The air temps were warming each day, and the sun was full-on shining. Nick couldn't wait to get on the water. He hoped there was a tour he could lead, or someone to give a lesson to.

"Good morning, sunshine!"

"That's the second time I've heard that this morning," Nick grumbled as he entered the shop, a bell jingling overhead. "I'm not that late."

"Well, you weren't here before me, so yeah, you're late." Amber gave him a wrinkled-up-nose grin, her glasses rising with the movement.

"Guilty then. How's it going here? Where's Terry?" Nick walked behind the counter and set his to-go mug down. He noted there were two folks in the store now, both browsing in the camping gear section. Man, he couldn't wait to lead a camping/kayaking trip soon.

"Terry's out back loading up a couple kayaks for these two," Amber said, pointing at the couple. "They are visiting from Tennessee."

"Nice. Is he going to give them a lesson, or are they skilled?"

"Skilled. Avid kayakers on their waterways. They are eager to tour along the shoreline here and bird watch." Amber leaned back against the front counter and crossed her arms. He knew that look. And he knew he wasn't going to like what she said next. "So, how's the job hunt going? You know I'm leaving at the end of May."

"I know. I know. Graduation is coming up." Nick couldn't share anything good about the job hunt, because he hadn't even started looking for a new accountant/bookkeeper/payroll employee. Amber had been working for him for six years, ever since she was a freshman. She was almost finished with her Master's program and would be leaving at the end of May. He had no skills at doing her job and was in denial of her leaving, so he was putting off the search for a replacement. Yep, he knew that was a dumb move, but there it was.

"If you hire someone now, I can train them before I leave," she reminded him. He knew this, he was just really good at letting things slide. Especially things that caused change or an interruption to how things were moving along smoothly in his world. He liked it just the way it was and didn't want anything to disrupt the flow.

But Amber was leaving, and he needed to face it and make the move to replace her.

"There are plenty of online companies that can do all the work for you." She smiled at him, encouragingly. "They can do payroll; they can balance the books—"

Nick was already shaking his head at her first statement. "Nope. Not gonna happen."

"Your distrust in technology is stunning," she said, her voice dripping with sarcasm. Luckily, he was saved by Terry entering the back door. "Hey, boss. How goes it?"

"Going great, Terry. Got everything handled?" Nick nodded to the couple.

"Yes, sir. Kayaks and paddles are on the beach. I'm going to lead them down there and check if they've got any questions. I've already got all the paperwork and payment from them."

"Good. Offer them some sunscreen and bug spray if they don't have it."

"Yes, sir." Terry nodded then walked around the counter over to the couple. They were all smiles as they followed Terry out the back door and down the steps that led underneath the building.

Terry was a great kid. His grandparents lived two houses down from Nick on the creek and had asked last month if he had any work for him to do. Terry was eighteen and taking classes at the local community college part time. He wanted to save money to go away to college next year. Nick hired him right away. Now that spring was here business would be picking up big time.

He had three part-time employees, including Amber. He needed to fill her position immediately, so he wasn't without someone to do the books after she graduated and moved out of state to her career job.

"I'll be in my office," he grumbled, depressed now from Amber's gentle reminder about getting started with the job search. He didn't even know where to start. Hating computers, hating the online world that seemed so immense and foreboding to him, really hindered this part of his job. He was a people person. He loved face-to-face conversations and interactions, but technology was his downfall.

He really needed some help here, but there was no one to ask. Suddenly a pair of the prettiest blue green eyes he'd ever seen popped into his head. An image of long, red-gold hair sliding over bare shoulders took up residence in his mind.

Emerson Taylor. Emmie to her friends and family.

Damn. He couldn't believe she was back in town. He wondered if it was for a short visit and what the occasion was.

Nick was pulled from his daydream about Emerson when his office door opened. Amber stuck her head in. "Jazzy is here, so I'm going to come help you for a few minutes. That is, if you want my help." Amber placed her hands on her hips and tilted her head, her dark brown hair shifting across her cheek. "Since you've got your feet on your desk and you're staring out the window, I'm guessing you haven't started listing my job yet."

Amber shut the door and ambled over to his desk, pulled up a folding chair and pushed his legs down. Nick was thankful for her assistance. He nodded to her when she raised a brow over her glasses, silently questioning him about getting started. She pulled the keyboard closer to her and began typing at a speed that he could barely comprehend. *Wow.* Her fingers were flying over the keys, and she wasn't even looking at the keyboard. You'd think a thirty-year-old man would have seen this before, but he tended to stick to the great outdoors instead of inside around computers.

Within ten minutes, Amber had opened an account with an online job search website. She'd filled out the position requirements, salary and date ready to hire, all with him only giving minimal input. She was definitely the one to know what the job entailed, so she was the best person to fill all that out.

"Done. It's posted on as many job search sites as I know. Hopefully, you'll be hearing from people within a few days. Maybe even hours," Amber said confidently. She straightened her glasses as well as her position, leaning back in her chair with a satisfied smile.

Nick nodded. "Thank you, Amber. I didn't even know where to start."

"You're welcome. Happy to help." She hopped up from the chair, slid it back to the corner and skirted the desk ready to head back out into the shop. At the door she turned with her hand braced on the edge. "I'm going to be sad leaving here. I've loved working for you all these years. I've learned so many things and have had so many amazing opportunities—kayaking, camping, sailing. It's been a dream. I'll miss it when I move inland."

Nick followed her through the door. "Atlanta is going to be so different. Night and day, from here. I know you'll do great at your new job."

***

"You're in my light."

Emerson held her sigh but couldn't keep her hands from fisting at her hips. She assumed a fighter's stance and faced Carolyn. "Mom, you're supposed to be resting."

"I've always found painting to be restful, dear," Carolyn said as she dabbed golden ocher onto her brush. Before her on a table easel sat a half-full canvas. Beautiful springtime flowers, begonias, gerbera daisies, black-eyed Susans, and salvia had found a home there on her canvas. Carolyn was using her own garden as a model. She'd spent the morning weeding it so it would be perfect for her to paint it this afternoon, and she told her daughter just that.

"Exactly my point. You haven't rested today." Emerson stepped back out of her mother's light at the raised-eyebrow look she got in response. Frustration was mounting inside her. The stubbornness that she'd said she loved once upon a time was taking its toll on her. She handled know-it-all businessmen on a daily basis with more ease than she seemed to be handling her own mother.

Emerson decided to let it go for now and stepped off the deck into the lush, green grass. The flowers were gorgeous and smelled amazing. What was more amazing was that they were just getting started. By mid-summer the whole garden would be in bloom with no room to spare around all the bursting buds. It was definitely show-worthy then.

There were stronger waves today in Mobile Bay. Murky brown water pounded onto the sand, washing away a lot of their meager beachfront. This place had survived many weather events, from tropical storms to hurricanes in summer and fall, to bitter-cold north winds in the winter. The sand would get washed away but then deposited again at another time. The push and pull were mesmerizing to watch.

Emerson felt her heartbeat slow to the rhythm of the moving water. She took a couple deep breaths and coughed.

Eeww. There had to be a dead fish on the beach somewhere.

That kind of killed the peaceful mood she'd been achieving. Stepping out on the dock, she strolled to the end, her eyes focused on the surface of the water. In New York City, whenever she'd start to feel overwhelmed with work or life, she'd have to find a place that had very little going on so she could do some meditation to calm her erratic heartbeat. But there weren't many places that had little action or were quiet there.

It was so much easier to do that here. And she found herself doing it a lot less often surrounded by all this soothing nature. There wasn't as much to be stressed out about. She was still struggling internally to let work go for a while. The need to check the market and respond to any text or email sent her way was overwhelming.

But she was trying.

A fish splashed leaving radiating rings flowing outward on the surface. Emerson's eyes lost focus as she watched the energy dissipate.

Her mother's stubbornness was not something to stress over. She was a grown woman who had a life of her own before this disease came about and Emerson showed up to be boss. She had to remember that her mental faculties were fully functioning. Her unwillingness to rest was typical of not wanting to let go of the lifestyle she'd been enjoying up until recently.

Emerson needed to respond with more patience and understanding.

Needed to.

But it was a hard thing to do.

Good thing Emerson was just as stubborn and was determined to treat her with patience and understanding, but also get her to follow some directions that would only benefit her in the long run.

It took another hour, but Emerson was patient, and her mother finally gave in. Sitting beside her bed, Emerson held back tears. This strong, radiant, albeit stubborn woman was getting weaker. Emerson tried to hide her emotions in front of her mother but let them go in private. She didn't want her to see Emerson's tears as a means of acceptance of her disease. She wanted to be strong for her. Emerson wanted to deny that her mother's body was changing without her permission just as strongly as her mother was hell-bent on doing.

The only reason Carolyn had given in and was sleeping now was because after painting for a couple hours she'd hardly been able to hold firmly to her paintbrush for more than a minute or two at a time. The doctor prescribed pills for her to take on a regular basis to keep the trembling to a minimum, but the drug didn't last the entire length of time between dosages.

Numerous questions flooded Emerson's mind. Was the medication going to work? Was she going to have another five or ten or twenty good years of life? Would she be able to keep painting? It was her life, and she knew no other way to live. Painting to her was as much a dose of daily medication as were the pills she was now forced to take several times a day.

Emerson's gaze moved from her mother's resting form to the large picture window facing the bay, pulled by the sounds of gulls squabbling with each other. The sun glinting off a sailboat catching wind caught her eye and she watched it until it was out of view. Her mind flashed back to her younger years when Carolyn was strong and amazing and so in love with Emerson's father. Even as a young kid she could see that and knew how special it was.

They always did everything together as a family. Bowling, camping, hiking, riding bikes. They spent a lot of time in the water right there on their waterfront. Her father had a thirty-foot sailboat that he loved to be on during the weekends. He'd take the whole family and sail across the bay or down the coast.

Emerson had been so young, probably five, the last time she'd sailed on it, so she hadn't been much help. She just liked to lie back on the bow, her body rising and falling with the waves. Her family had been so happy, so full of love, laughter and good times.

The family photos hanging on the walls and positioned on the dresser were evidence of those good times. Her father's pictures always showed him smiling. There were so many of her mother and father smiling at each other, their love on full display. Emerson's eyes slowly carried over each of those pictures, taking in all the details, and her heart felt heavy.

She missed her father dearly.

When he suddenly died from a heart attack at the age of thirty-seven, it devastated the family. It was unexpected. It was awful. It was crushing to them as a family unit. But their mother's strength shone through. She was an amazing woman. She pulled their family back together and made them even stronger.

Now, Emerson needed to be strong for her. She needed to be the one to pull them together as a family and rally around to help her get through what were expected to be tough times ahead.

But it was going to be harder than she had thought. When she'd scheduled that one-way ticket, she had hoped that she would arrive, find out her mother wasn't as ill as suspected, and would heal quickly with the prescribed medication, allowing her to be back in New York City, back in her world, in no time.

At that time, she hadn't looked up Parkinson's yet and didn't have a full understanding of what was happening to her mother's body. There would be no "healing quickly."

Would she even be able to return to New York? Only time would tell.

****

"I don't think I can decide on just one," Callie groaned from in front of the floor-length mirror on Emerson's closet door.

Her adorable five-year-old lab, Goose, lay on the floor near her feet snoring. He was totally unaffected by Callie's excitement. His eyebrows twitched every so often. Emerson didn't know if he was attuned to his person or if he was just dreaming.

"Only five minutes left," Emerson said flipping the pages of the latest Garden & Gun magazine. She was grinning, enjoying the sight of her cousin so frazzled. Callie's shoulder-length blonde hair had come out of her braid from repeatedly pulling shirts over her head and tossing them behind her on the end of the bed.

Emerson had given her twenty minutes to look through her wardrobe this time and stipulated once again that she could only have one item.

Callie had it narrowed down to a small pile consisting of a Kate Spade handbag, a stunning emerald Donna Karan blazer, and her newest pair of Jimmy Choo pumps. The tissue-thin top she'd just pulled over her head got dropped into the discard pile before she pulled the blazer on once more, buttoning it up minus a shirt underneath.

Slipping the shoes on, she grabbed the handbag and stood in front of the mirror, turning left and right. "Are you sure?" she whined.

Emerson tossed the magazine onto the pile of discarded clothing and stepped up behind her. She pulled her cousin's shoulders back, smoothing the lines of the blazer across the back. "I like this on you. I'm not sure it's appropriate to wear it as is in front of eighth grade boys busting at the seams with raging hormones though." Emerson chuckled at the image that brought forward. "Maybe if you catch me at a weak moment before I head back up north, I might give in to your demands."

Callie met her gaze in the mirror and grinned. She whirled around and slung her arms around

Emerson. "Thank you. I really miss having you close by."

Emerson hugged her and laughed. "You just miss my clothes."

Goose jumped up to join in the excitement, nosing his way into the hug. He let out a happy bark when they both petted him. Callie ruffled his floppy ears then slipped the shoes off and placed them back in the closet. She set about straightening up the disaster she'd created. "Did you check out the online site yet?"

Emerson cringed as she slipped a hanger inside a purple blouse. Callie saw her reaction and called her on it.

"You did!"

"Yes, I did. I actually signed up for it and browsed a little the other night."

"That's great," Callie exclaimed. "Did you see anyone you liked?"

Emerson thought back to her menu analogy and shook her head. "I didn't see anyone my type."

"Just keep looking. Someone will stand out, I promise." Callie turned back from the closet with a bashful grin on her face. "I have a date for Thursday night."

"Really? That's great, Cal. Tell me about him." Emerson flopped down on the bed, thinking about when they used to sit around in high school and talk about boys. Not much had changed, it seemed.

Goose leaned against the end of the bed, his head resting on Emerson's comforter. His eyebrows twitched as his eyes shifted back and forth between them. Callie sat on the bed beside him and stroked his head. "He's a teacher—wait, do you have your computer handy? I'll just show you instead. That way I can check out the selection from your point of view."

Emerson wasn't too thrilled to look online again but she reached across to the bedside table and grabbed her laptop. Booting it up, she asked Callie where they were going on their date.

"We're meeting at Keel & Rudder. There's usually a good band playing, so I won't have to make too much small talk if he's a bore."

Emerson let Callie sign in first so she could look up her profile and click on the guy who'd thought "she was interesting, as well as beautiful." Callie said she was impressed with the order in which he said that. She pulled up John's picture and turned the screen so Emerson could see it.

"Cal, he's cute. Thirty-three, a high school baseball coach, teaches physics, loves fishing—" Emerson broke off with a grimace. "Uh-oh, hope that's not a bad sign."

Callie laughed but agreed.

"He sounds great. Do you feel safe meeting him alone?"

"Yeah, I think so. That's why I'm meeting him there instead of letting him know where I live.

I'll be okay. Now, enough stalling, sign in and let me see it," she instructed, setting the laptop in front of Emerson.

Begrudgingly, Emerson typed in her username and password. She was surprised to find that she had three emails. Clicking on the first one, she cringed outwardly at the poor grammar used by the sender. He was trying to tell her how impressed he was with her beauty, but she wasn't impressed with his writing skills.

*Next.* She clicked on the second one.

She was met with a marriage proposal in the first sentence. *Delete!*

The third email didn't sound so bad in relation to the other two. She browsed the photos he had on the site and thought he was handsome. When she saw one of him smiling a goofy, pleased-with-himself grin and holding a large fish, she skimmed over the rest, down to what he was looking for in life.

Callie fidgeted beside her. Goose's eyes popped open at her movements. "I'm sorry, Em, I just can't sit here quietly. Email him back. Just do it."

Emerson looked up from the screen, her eyebrow raised in response.

"Em, remember you're not going to find any Wall-Street types here, but there are plenty of decent guys, you just have to work hard to find them."

"But he's a dentist! What if we go to dinner and all he talks about is teeth? I won't be able to eat a thing, worrying that I have food stuck on my gums!"

Callie laughed. So did Emerson. "Okay, so I'm overreacting a little bit. I just don't know."

"It's just an email. You don't have to go out with him. Let's look at some others before we decide."

Emerson turned to her, gave her the raised-eyebrow look again. "We?"

"Yes, we. You'll never do anything if you're not pushed. So I'm here to give you the little shove that you need. We're going to find you a guy to email tonight. Maybe you can make a date for tomorrow night."

"That's moving a little fast, don't you think?" Emerson's eyes widened. She felt a flush rise on her cheeks.

"It could work," Callie said, already focused on the images displayed on the screen. She scrolled through some photos, stopping when she thought someone was particularly good-looking. Emerson hunched down next to her and had to agree with her choices so far.

"Looks aren't everything," Emerson reminded her. "I have to be able to have a conversation with this guy. And it can't be about fishing!" she added with a laugh.

"Here! This is the guy you have to email tonight," Callie exclaimed, moving the computer closer to her. Goose lifted a large paw onto the bed and barked. "See, Goose agrees with me."

Emerson squinted at the photo before her. "Well, he isn't exactly ugly..."

"You just said looks aren't everything," Callie pointed out. "Look here, he's in finance, he likes computers, it says nothing about fishing." Callie looked up at her. "Give it a shot. What have you got to lose? A couple hours of your life, right? You could meet him for drinks only, no dinner necessary. You could do the same with the dentist, too."

Emerson sighed heavily, knowing her cousin was right. What did she have to lose? She missed being in a relationship, missed the friendship, the time spent together, eating a meal with company...but was she ready to get into another relationship, here in Sweetgum, Alabama?

"Come on," Callie encouraged. She clicked on the "email now" icon and pushed the laptop closer to Emerson.

Emerson sighed once more and gave in. She sent Mr. "Funluvinguy" a quick email asking if he would be interested in meeting for drinks tomorrow night. She kept it short and somewhat sweet. She felt so odd sending out an invitation like that to a complete stranger.

Never before had she been on a blind date or even been set up with a friend of a friend. The only men she'd ever dated were ones that she'd met personally, whether at the gym, in line at her favorite coffee shop or at the office.

"Great!"

Emerson wasn't so sure that she felt the same. "Now, where should we meet for drinks?"

Callie thought about it a minute, then said, "Meet at Keel & Rudder. We had a great meal the other night. You know they have a bar, so plenty of good drink options. They have music a couple nights a week. That could limit your interaction time with the guy if he's completely boring, especially if the music is loud."

"Sounds good," Emerson said, this time her smile was sincere. "Thanks, Cal. You're right, I did need the push."

Callie looked up at her from under her lashes and grinned. "So, is this a weak moment?"

# Chapter Three

Emerson ran her fingers through the ends of her hair for the fifth time since entering the restaurant, tossing her silky-straight locks back over her shoulder. Straightening her blouse again, she fussed at herself for being, well, fussy. She couldn't believe she'd let Callie talk her into wearing this blouse. Yes, it was part of her wardrobe, but she didn't think it was a good "first date" top. She was proud of her cleavage, but she wasn't sure it was appropriate to put it all out there this soon.

She was early, on purpose, so she could scout out the place. Music played from speakers at one end of the room, but instruments were set up there also. The band must be waiting for the after-dinner crowd to show before revving up. Taking a deep breath to calm her nerves, she leaned against the deck railing and took in the view. Pelicans flew low over the water and gulls cried out, chasing the one in the lead carrying a shiny silver fish in his beak.

Several patrons occupied the bar, as well as the tables scattered around. She chose an empty spot at the bar, sitting a few spaces over from a burly man who looked as if the beer stein he was holding had been made to fit the shape of his palm.

Emerson gave him a half-hearted smile when he glanced her way. Geesh. *What if that guy's my date?* What if people put fake pictures on their site? Or pictures of them ten years and twenty pounds ago? She shook off the thought and looked at the people sitting on her other side, scanning each face for her date. He might have shown up early too.

She was so into her search that she didn't hear the bartender. He had to knock on the bar in front of her to get her attention. Emerson jumped at the sound and glanced over at him. She immediately forgot to breathe. Her pulse picked up speed as she took in the gorgeous sight before her. She'd been hoping that he wouldn't be on shift tonight, knowing that his half-smile could make her heart skip a beat.

His grin continued to grow wider the longer she stared at him. Clearing her throat, she blinked and pulled her lips into a semblance of a smile. Thinking as quickly as she could on her fumbling feet, metaphorically speaking, she said, "Club soda with lime, please."

NICK COULDN'T BELIEVE it. Twice in just a few days. The love of his life—well, his life at age seventeen—was sitting before him. Looking just as beautiful as she'd looked the day he'd first seen her walking down the hall at Sweetgum High. Her long, silky, shiny red hair was still down past her shoulders.

He'd thought he was dreaming when he spotted her at one of the high-tops the other day. Seeing her had taken his breath and he'd had trouble keeping his eyes off her.

Nick's heart beat erratically. He'd always had that problem whenever she was around. It wasn't because she'd talk to him and he'd get all tongue-tied, too shy to respond. In fact, he couldn't remember her ever talking to him—outside of his dreams anyway. She'd barely even looked at him when they were in school together.

He'd moved to Sweetgum with his family his senior year and she'd been raised here all her life, so she had already been settled into the high school atmosphere, and he hadn't. He'd generally kept to himself and just watched her from afar. He wouldn't go as far as to say he'd stalked her because he hadn't. She just happened to be going to a class on the same hall as him or, if he got lucky, she would be in the lunchroom when he was.

Nick chuckled at the expression on her beautiful face as he pulled a glass from the rack. He wondered if she recognized him and that's what had her staring. It had been only a fantasy that he'd run into her again someday and she'd immediately call out his name and ask him what he'd been doing with his life.

But that's why it was called a fantasy—it wasn't likely to happen.

"I'm Nick, by the way." Loading the glass up with a splash of club soda and a squeeze of lime juice, he held it aloft, sending a questioning glance her way. "Sure you don't want me to add anything to it?"

Emerson cleared her throat again before answering. "Emerson, and thank you, no, ice is all." He stared an extra second as her throat muscles moved. She had a slender, elegant-looking throat and if he let his eyes wander down just a few inches more he'd get a stunning view of her very sexy cleavage.

Something he'd only been able to dream about as a teenager, never having even seen a glimpse of it back then. She hadn't worn any tops this revealing at that age. Thank God. He never would have been able to handle it when he was just a horny teenager.

Nick shrugged his shoulders, trying to ease some of the tension, and slid the glass her way. She took a sip then quickly averted her eyes, scanning the crowd once again.

EMERSON FIGURED THE laughter she saw in Nick's sparkling amber eyes was directed at her. He probably had women drooling over him every waking second, and then some.

Emerson stole a peek at her watch and continued looking for Brent in the sea of faces. Since she'd sat down about twenty more people had entered the bar. In the corner of the deck, the band sat, tuning their instruments.

She felt someone staring at her and looked back over her shoulder. The bartender, Nick, was standing there, his wide hands braced on the bar, blatantly staring at her. Of all the nerve. Turning back to face the door, she tried to brush off the heated sensation flushing through her body.

"Is he late or are you early?"

As much as she wanted to think he was talking to someone else and wait him out with silence, she had a feeling he was a talker, and wouldn't let up until she turned back around and spoke to him.

Emerson stole another peek at her watch. Only a minute had passed. Brent wasn't due to show for another ten. *What am I doing?* With an internal groan, she fought hard to control an eye roll as she swiveled back to belly up to the bar.

"I'm early," she finally admitted. "Just wanted to get a feel for the place."

Nick leaned forward, his head lowered, and he spoke in a conspiratorial whisper. "There's a back exit by the restrooms." Then he grinned wide once more and resumed his full height. "Blind date?"

Emerson thought he asked too many questions. Weren't bartenders supposed to be good listeners? "Thanks for the heads up, and yes," she said and took another swallow of her drink. Now she wished she'd asked for a shot of whiskey instead.

First, she was here to meet a guy from the Internet.

Now, she had to deal with this guy.

Gorgeous or not, he was too nosy for her liking.

She couldn't help the involuntary shiver that danced across her skin when he laughed though. Glancing around, she pushed all thoughts of the nosy, frustratingly sexy bartender away and scanned the faces once more, ready to get on with this date.

"Emerson?"

Emerson set her drink down, took a fortifying breath then turned on her stool, ignoring the bartender's watchful eyes. She was happy to see that Brent, aka Mr. Funluvinguy, had posted up-to-date photos of himself. Holding out her hand, she introduced herself. He had a nice smile, but she didn't feel the same zing she'd felt moments ago when the bartender had directed his glowing grin at her.

She felt irrationally disappointed.

"Good to meet you," he said after shaking her hand, his grip on the strong side. "How about a drink?"

She turned back to the bar and noticed a new drink filled with something pink and fizzy sat beside her old drink. Looking closer, she saw a cherry on top and thought the pink must be grenadine. Rolling her eyes at the bartender's interference, she gestured toward her drink, and offered to get him one. Stepping up closer to her, he called out to the bartender and said he needed something more manly to drink. Emerson watched as Nick ambled down the bar to them but avoided his eye.

Brent asked, "Would you like to get a table?"

"Yes." Unsure which drink to pick up, she just grabbed both, and followed him to one of the few tables left. It was far enough away from the band that they would be able to talk, at least until the band started playing all out. Walking behind him, she had an opportunity to check him out. He wasn't too tall, maybe an inch taller than her. His gray suit pants fit nicely, as well as his blue button-down shirt. No tie.

The man had manners too, she noticed, when he held her chair out for her. She thought that was very southern. Very few men in New York had the idea of this concept.

"So," Brent began as soon as he sat down. "Your profile said you live in New York. What are you doing here?" Brent drank from his glass and held her gaze. His eyes were brown, as well as his hair, which was thinning a little on top. He had a nice face though, well proportioned. Sipping her new drink, she hated to admit that it tasted better with the added dose of sugar.

Huh, she should never have told the truth on that one because she was dreading this discussion. She decided then not to be too honest. "I grew up around here and am back for an extended visit," she explained, then changed the subject. "Tell me about yourself. Something you didn't put on your profile that is important about who you are." Emerson leaned forward in her seat and forced herself to act interested. She wasn't sure what it was about him exactly, but she wasn't feeling it.

And if she had to define "it" she wasn't sure what she would say.

But she would know it when she saw it.

Brent grinned at her, but just as he started to speak the guitarist broke out with a squealing guitar solo, straight from a Metallica concert. All heads turned toward the band and conversations around them faded into the noise. Emerson shrugged at him then settled back in her chair to listen to the local cover band.

Brent surprised her when he moved his chair around to her side of the table and draped his arm across the back of her chair. Leaning his head close to hers, he answered her question. She could hardly hear him over the music and wasn't sure she was too comfortable with where his hand had moved. Instead of resting on the back of her chair, it was now cupped around her shoulder. It might have been an innocent move, but she decided she'd shrug him off if he got too handsy.

There was no innocent "boob brushing" going to happen on this first date, of that she was certain.

"These guys are really great!" she said, trying to encourage him to listen rather than talk.

After the first set, Brent got her attention and gestured to his drink. "Would you like another?" he shouted into her ear. Emerson tried to hold back a cringe as she shook her head, thanking him with a smile that quickly vanished as soon as he'd turned his back. When he got up from the table, she allowed herself a second to close her eyes and release a sigh that she'd been holding in ever since they'd sat down.

*What am I doing here?*

So far, she wasn't too impressed. The man talked too much, when one should be enjoying the music, and he was too handsy. She didn't have a problem with being touched. Loved it, actually, but it had to be the right man putting his hands on her.

She still couldn't believe she was here meeting some total stranger from the Internet. Even if his profile was three pages full of information, it could all be made up. Being truthful with herself, she wasn't feeling any sparks for this guy, but it was still early in the game.

She'd made herself read the dating tips the website offered before leaving the house tonight, and it stressed that most people don't know at first sight if the person will be their love match. One needed to go on at least three dates in order to find out a person's true self. On the first two dates people were usually too anxious and out to impress the other, but by the third they might be more comfortable and able to be more expressive about who they are. Emerson wasn't sure she would be able to make the effort for date number two with this guy.

Plus, she wasn't looking for a love match, anyway, right?

She felt someone looking at her. Thinking it might be Brent she turned toward the bar and wasn't thrilled to see it was Nick.

Though her body felt otherwise.

He leaned back against a counter, arms folded, his T-shirt stretched across his impressive chest, his muscular forearms standing out at her, the navy-blue material pulling tight around his biceps. She had a feeling he stood like that a lot to impress the ladies. Suppressing a groan and another eye roll, she turned back around and tried to focus on the music again.

Brent returned with two drinks, telling her he'd ordered her a "real" drink this time. Emerson kept her eyebrows from rising at his high-handedness and tried for a polite nod. Then he proceeded to ask her more questions about New York and why she was back visiting.

Emerson tried once again to deter him from that line of questioning and responded with a brief synopsis of her family. She used her nieces and nephews as her excuse to come back. Then she steered the loud discussion they were having over the beat of the drums to his job.

"What do you do for a living?" she asked, feeling stupid for shouting over the music.

Brent took a drink from his glass, leaned into her ear, bumping it with his nose. Pulling back, he chuckled and apologized with a grin. "I work for an orthopedic company, in the accounting department."

Then without any other encouragement from her he proceeded to tell her all about the work he does. When he paused for a breath, Emerson jumped to her feet. In the process, she nearly upended his beer on the table and popped his jaw with her shoulder. She offered him a brief smile as an apology and gestured to the bathrooms.

Clutching her purse to her side, she wound her way through the crowd, keeping her gaze averted from the bar as she made her way to the ladies' room. Inside, she leaned against the counter to stare in the mirror but thought better of it as she touched something sticky. Public restrooms were not her favorite places, especially after living in New York.

Staring into the mirror as she washed her hands, she was pleased to see that her reflection revealed none of her frustration. Her hair still hung down straight around her shoulders, her lipstick still covered her full lips, and her eyes still looked normal, hiding the craziness she felt inside. This wasn't what she was looking for or had expected.

She groaned, thinking ahead to how the night would end.

*There's always the back exit.*

That thought made her grin. It brought the image of the bartender to mind, his gorgeous lips curved up in a lop-sided smile. Once again, there was that little shiver, just a brief flutter that moved around in her stomach.

Just as she stepped outside the bathroom door, she heard a deep voice say, "The bathroom window unlocks on the left side."

She suppressed a groan. Of all the people she had to run into in the bathroom hallway. Emerson turned to find the sexy bartender leaning against the wall between the men's and women's restroom doors, his arms crossed over his chest, a knowing grin on his face. Emerson frowned and couldn't help but ask, "Hmm, are you following me?"

EMERSON MIGHT NOT have been aware that when she put her hands on her hips like that, her top pulled farther apart at the neckline offering him a delectable view, but Nick was. He had to swallow the saliva that had just pooled

in his mouth at receiving such a present before answering her. "No, I happened to be back
here using the facilities myself and just saw
you come out," he said with as much innocence
as he could muster. This was just like back in
high school. He'd always had a lie ready to cover his ass if she'd thought he'd been following
her around school like some sad, pathetic little
puppy.

She didn't look like she believed him, but he
wouldn't have fallen for her if she'd been stupid.
Well, yeah, he probably would have when he
was seventeen, because the things he'd thought
about hadn't involved her brain.

Most of the fantasies he still found himself
having from time to time didn't involve much
thinking or talking for that matter. Man, he still
had it bad for Emerson Taylor, even if she was
now an adult and a successful businesswoman.
And a New Yorker. He knew that his fantasies
from now on would revolve around this feisty
spirit he'd never known she had.

"I need to get back," she said, looking away but
not moving.

Nick wanted to tell her his thoughts about her
date but told himself to keep out of it. And what
the hell was she doing going out on blind dates?
That joker was nowhere near her caliber. She
must have been bored within ten seconds.

Just because she was back in town didn't
mean she was going to stay, so there was no
reason to get involved. He could just lust af-

ter her from afar like he'd done in high school. "Good seeing you again," he said, unable to keep the words in his mouth, nearly kicking himself when she looked at him like he was crazy. He offered her a nod as he brushed past her out into the main room. Her scent trailed along with him, tickling his senses, and keeping her locked firmly in his mind as he finished out the night.

EMERSON LOOKED AT Nick like he was crazy. *Good seeing you again?* Did he mean from just an hour before? She slowed her pace as she made her way back to her date. Now, how to end this not-so-delightful evening, she wondered as she sat back down in her chair.

The band members were taking a mid-set break, so Emerson decided to make a break for it while it was quiet enough to tell him goodbye. "Brent, I'm going to call it a night," she said rising to her feet. "Thanks for meeting me. This was fun," she said keeping it brief but pleasant. No promises.

"It was nice," he said, and she didn't know how to interpret that. *Nice* as in lovely, can't wait to do it again, or *nice* as in you're nice, but... "Let me close out my tab and I'll walk you out."

Brent walked her out to her car, told her he'd enjoyed the evening and hoped to hear from her soon. Brent squeezed her hand, said goodnight, and then headed off to his car.

Emerson was thrilled that he hadn't asked her out for another date. Realizing it was better not to get any further into a relationship with him, she decided to be happy about the evening. It hadn't been a total loss.

At least the music was great.

# Chapter Four

The welcoming bell jingled overhead as Nick entered his parents' pizzeria an hour before they opened for the lunch rush. The spicy scents of dough and tomato sauce mingled in the air, wrapping around him like a security blanket. This was home to him. A place where he cut his teeth on fresh crust. A place where he learned fractions by cutting the pies into slices.

It wasn't the same building he did those things in, but the atmosphere was the same. The red-checked tablecloths, the wine bottles lining the walls, the white dinnerware, were all the same. He and his brother were born in New Jersey, and grew up in their parents' pizzeria up there, where they lived in an apartment over the shop. They were always surrounded by these smells.

"Mamma!"

Nick's mother turned at the sound of his voice, clutching the wrapped silverware in her two hands. "Oh, *mio bambino*. It's so good to see you, my sweet Nicky!" She held her arms out to him, and he gladly walked into them, wrapping his around her small frame, his cheek resting on her short brown hair.

Both of his parents were small. He and his brother got their height from their father's father. He'd been a giant of a man to Nick when he'd been little. But he was actually just a little over six feet tall. The height gene skipped their father's generation, leaving him and his brothers and sisters squarely in the mid five-feet range.

She pulled back, then drew his shoulders down and kissed his cheeks. He returned the greeting. "Great to see you, Mamma. How are you doing?"

"Much better now that my boy's face is in my hands." She pinched his cheeks and smiled. The smile reaching her eyes; eyes that matched his and Tony's. "How are you doing? Are you getting any sleep?"

"I'm fine, Mamma. Working Tony's evening shift and my day shift has been hectic, but I'm managing. Where's Papà?" Nick looked over his shoulder at the kitchen. He could hear whistling coming from there, so he figured his father was preparing for the lunch hour. "Have you heard from Tony today?"

"No, we haven't. Did you hear how he did in the regatta?"

Nick held out his hand for hers and led the way to the kitchen in the back. "Yes. I'll tell you together." Nick pushed open the swinging door, pulling his mother behind him. The tangy scent of the sauce bubbling on the stove top hit him full force. Nick took in a deep breath, savoring the freshness of it. "Papà, good to see you."

Nick's father was elbow-deep in dough. He had three large balls of dough on the worktable in front of him and he was giving one chunk hell, massaging it into place on the pie pan. Flour drifted in the air around him. Another familiar sight and smell in Nick's life.

"Nicky." His father nodded, keeping his hands busy in the dough. "Happy you stopped in."

"Nicky says he heard from Tony," his mother blurted out. She was practically dancing, hopping from one foot to the other in anticipation.

"Tony called last night." Nick watched his father press out a second mound of dough into another pie pan before spooning sauce on top. "He finished third."

"*Meriviglioso!* Wonderful. He's a good boy," his mother said, tears gathering in her eyes. She'd always said that, about either one of them. And tears in her pretty eyes were commonplace. She was an emotional woman and unafraid to show it, especially about her boys.

"Proud," was all his father said. His face held a stern expression, that was commonplace for his father, but Nick knew that he was indeed proud of Tony. He might not show it with emotion like his mother did, but he did express it with words.

Even though sometimes they were succinct like this. But that was high praise coming from him.

Nick stepped to the side of the kitchen and washed his hands before picking up a knife on the cutting board opposite his father's workstation and began chopping tomatoes, green peppers and mushrooms. He tossed some toppings on the pizza closest to him, before placing the rest in the boxes that would go on the salad bar. He worked and chatted with his parents, telling them about his bartending experiences.

He didn't share about running into his high school love though, deciding it wasn't necessary. If he said her name out loud, there would be questions about weddings and babies immediately, so he thought it best to avoid all that.

Nick paused after slicing the last mushroom; he hadn't cringed when those words had just floated through his mind so easily.

He shook it off, because it really was too soon to be thinking about weddings and babies with a woman whom he'd seen as an adult all of two times and only spoken a handful of words with.

But a guy can dream, can't he?

The pizza Nick had topped was only minutes away from coming out of the oven. Per their routine they made the first pie of the day and enjoyed it for lunch, taste-testing to make sure the dough had the requisite taste and texture that the Valentinos were known for. Nick often popped over about this time when he was free.

Just to help out.

And to fill his stomach.

Grabbing the boxes to add to the salad bar, Nick pushed backwards through the swinging door and set them in the chilled cart in the same order that his mother had required him to do since he was five years old and tall enough to reach over the top. Wiping the crumbs from his hands he shifted and peered out the front windows. His heart lurched when he spotted Emerson across the street helping an elderly woman into a chair at the outdoor coffee shop.

His lips turned up of their own accord at seeing her smiling at the woman and the ladies that she'd joined at the table. Damn she was a vision. Her hair glowed a deep red, the sun shimmering off it like a spotlight. Sunglasses shaded her eyes. Her smile was radiant, almost glowing as bright as her hair.

He really wanted to get her to turn that smile on him.

"What has put such a handsome smile on my boy's face?"

Nick jerked at her voice. He hadn't even heard her enter the dining room carrying the large bowl of salad greens. He hurriedly took the bowl from her and placed it on the cart. "Nothing, Mamma. I'm just glad to be here with you and Papà."

She moved closer to the window and flipped the switch to illuminate the "open" sign. "Uh-huh. So, it wouldn't have anything to do with the Taylor girl standing across the street with her mother?"

Nick turned towards her, his brows furrowed, wondering what she was getting at. "What Taylor girl?"

"You know, the youngest one. The one you were so infatuated with in high school."

At his wide-eyed response she just laughed. "What? You don't think your mamma has eyes?"

She placed a work-roughened palm against his cheek and smiled a motherly smile at him. "Of course, I knew you were moony eyed over her. Every time she came in here with her friends or family, you'd be so awestruck by her that you weren't the least bit of help."

Nick's heart twisted. Hopefully it was just her that had been able to read him so well back then. And now. Nick straightened his posture, cleared his throat and his mind. "She's just home for a visit, Mamma."

Her hand moved from his cheek to his chest, right over his heart. "Then, *mio caro*, maybe you should give her a reason to stay."

***

"Oh, Mom, this one is beautiful," Emerson whispered for the twentieth time in the same number of minutes. She held up the 16x20 of a sailboat catching wind in the bay. The shade of the sun was radiant and the reflections of the boat shining in the rippling water. Carolyn had a true talent. One that completely passed Emerson by. Sidney was the lucky one there. She was an impeccable artist herself, focusing mainly on animals and sea life.

"Thank you, dear. That one should go," her mother directed, pointing toward the pile that they were sorting for the Art Festival taking place next week. Emerson handled them and Carolyn commented yay or nay. After leaning at least twenty-five of them against the back wall of the art studio to cover and load up later, Emerson turned back around and dusted her hands, preparing for battle.

"Okay, that's it for now. If there are more things to sort out, we can do it tomorrow." Emerson placed her hands on her hips and squared off with her mother, who, at the moment, was standing in the exact same position. Definitely a chip off the old block. But Emerson was trying to do her best to get her to rest as she adjusted to the new medications, and not overexert herself.

"Now, Emerson, I am doing nothing but saying yes or no here. I'm not overdoing it." Her blue green eyes took on a stubborn tone, but Emerson held her ground.

"Rest time, Mom. Let's go enjoy the sunshine on the back deck." Emerson moved towards her, ushering her through the doorway, down the hall to the back doors. "I'm thirsty. Would you like some lemonade? Aunt Deborah brought over some zucchini bread. How about a slice of that?"

Carolyn sighed deeply as she shuffled through the French doors. "Yes, dear, that sounds lovely."

Emerson knew that sigh meant the very opposite, but Carolyn was struggling with her new limitations. It was a hard adjustment for all of them. They were used to her being in charge, in control, at full throttle, her whole life. Seeing her weak and trembling was so out of character that it didn't seem real. Emerson knew it was even harder for Carolyn to accept that her body was changing and there wasn't a damn thing she could do about it.

Emerson carried a tray of lemonade and zucchini bread out onto the deck. She poured them each a full glass then sliced some pieces of bread and arranged them on two plates. Emerson sank her teeth into the sweet bread immediately. Her aunt made the best zucchini bread. It was something that she'd missed living up in New York City. She mostly spent her time drinking green drinks chock full of chia seeds and hemp hearts rather than eating sweets like this.

The gentle breeze off the water cooled them as they sat in the shade and breathed in the heady scent of the dramatic array of flowers that covered the backyard. Before this disease had started attacking her mother's nervous system, she'd been a force to be reckoned with. She was quite active in the arts community, giving lessons at the senior center, as well as for the children's art center.

She grew prized dahlias and gave cuttings away for free, just to spread the love of gardening and fresh flowers. The bees, butterflies and birds loved the backyard. It had been this grand display of colorful foliage for as long as Emerson could remember. As a child, she'd helped plant a lot of these hydrangeas, beauty berries and lilacs that bordered the south side of the yard. She had enjoyed getting her fingers dirty and spending time with her.

As an adult she was realizing how precious those moments were and how fragile the future was.

Emerson traced a bead of condensation on her glass. "I've always loved this yard, Mom. You've made it a beautiful space over the years, even with all the kids' toys that were here when we were growing up, and back again now that your grandkids visit a lot."

Carolyn took a sip of her lemonade, then said, "I love having my family close. And I love this home. Very much. Sitting here, looking out at the flowers, at the bay, brings me much joy. The only thing I'm missing is your father and," she turned to look her youngest daughter in the eye, "you being here fulltime." Carolyn noticed Emerson was about to object and raised a hand towards her, palm out to stop her from commenting. "Now, I know that can't be, it's just how I feel. I'm not going to pressure you about your job. I just want you to be happy. I also want you to know that I've loved having you here." Carolyn's smile was as bright as her blue green eyes when she looked over at Emerson across the table.

"I'm enjoying being here too, Mom. I've missed this place," she added in nearly a whisper, her eyes focused on the water beyond the grass. "I didn't realize it until this visit, being home now, with time on my hands to let all my surroundings soak in."

Carolyn nibbled on a bite of bread. "You were young when you left. Young and ambitious with bright, shiny stars—or dollar signs, if you will—in your eyes." Her wink took the sting out of that comment. "A lot has changed since you were eighteen years old. You've changed. You've grown. I hope that your time here helps you focus on what's important to you. To *you*," she emphasized with her tone and her direct gaze. "Not what I need, mind you. But what you need, Emmie."

***

*What you need.*

Her mother's words kept running through her head throughout the day. *What do I need?* Another first date with a total stranger? Probably not, but here she was, once again sitting at the bar, waiting for her date to show.

Emerson wasn't sure her nervous system could handle another encounter with Nick the bartender. His warm whiskey-colored eyes and delectable grin played havoc on her emotions, sending butterflies all aflutter in her stomach. Luckily, for her peace of mind, and her libido, he didn't appear to be here this evening. She needed to concentrate on the guy she was here to meet. She'd only chosen this place again because she was comfortable here.

Emerson let her mind wander and found that Nick's image was front and center even with her eyes open. She also couldn't help but wonder if she knew him from somewhere. He had said in the hallway to the bathrooms the other night—*It was great to see you again*. Had she met him before?

Suddenly, she was thinking each passing person was someone she'd either gone to high school with, saw here at this bar or was on the dating website. *Focus, girl*, Emerson scolded herself. The dentist could be here any minute. And she needed to stop thinking of him as *the dentist* and instead call him by his name. Joe Suggs. What kind of name was *Suggs*?

"Emerson?"

Emerson whipped her head around, her hair sliding over her shoulders at the movement. She put on a welcoming smile, not at all trying to show off her gleaming white teeth that she'd spent extra time on before coming here and held out her hand to shake his. Joe Suggs was shorter than her, she realized when she slid off the bar stool. His return smile was beaming, and his handshake was gentle.

"Hi, Joe. Great to meet you."

"Great to meet you too. Would you like to stay here at the bar or grab a table?"

"A table sounds great. One by the water, if possible."

Joe waited for her to lead and walked a step behind her with his hand on her lower back.

Emerson picked the table in the corner that had an amazing view of the sunset and the creek beside the restaurant. Joe held her chair for her, which was sweet. She gave him a smile of thanks. Wanting to forgo the inevitable questions about why she was here and not in New York, Emerson jumped in immediately after he was seated and asked, "Are you from here originally?"

Joe adjusted his chair out of the direct sunlight then answered, "No, I'm originally from Texas. Born and raised. I came here for college and stayed. I opened my own practice in the town north of here a few years ago." He leaned forward, resting his forearms on the table. "What about you? I saw something about New York."

*Saw something? As in, you didn't read the two paragraphs that I wrote? He wasn't showing* much interest in her character. Maybe he'd accepted this date proposal because of her looks. Huh. Shallow.

"I was born and raised here but left for the big city to attend Columbia and start my career on Wall Street."

"Damn. That's a big leap from here." Obviously. "What brought you back?"

Emerson shifted in her seat, but answered quickly, using her nieces and nephews again as her excuse to be back in town, with an open-ended return date. It wasn't the truth, but she just didn't want to share anything about her mother's disease. Especially with a stranger.

"Good evening, y'all."

Emerson jolted at that voice. She'd heard it a time or two in her dreams recently.

Its deep richness was hot enough to melt chocolate *and* her panties. Her eyes quickly shifted off Joe and onto the handsome, hunky bartender, whom she'd hoped was off tonight.

It took a few extra seconds to control her reaction than she was comfortable with. Taking a breath, she released it through a smile and returned his greeting. "Good evening." Her voice might have sounded a little strained, at least to her own ears, hopefully not to the two men before her.

Two men who were complete opposites.

Joe was well under six feet, where Nick stood a couple inches over. Joe had a soft handshake, where Nick's hands looked like they would likely sport some calluses on the undersides and were quite muscled and sleek. Joe's hair was black and straight, almost a military cut, where Nick's had more of a surfer, beach-bum shag to it, sandy brown with a bit of a curl to the ends.

Emerson tuned back in to hear Joe ordering a beer on tap. They were both looking at her, expectantly. She cleared her throat and said, "A hard cider, please."

Her heart thumped extra hard in her chest when Nick's lips shifted into that lop-sided smile she'd come to expect. He nodded, apparently pleased with her choice. Likely anything was better than club soda in his eyes. "Coming right up."

Emerson watched him walk away, admiring the way his jeans fit when she realized what she was doing and snapped her attention off him and back onto her date. Thankfully, Joe was looking down at the creek and didn't appear to notice her practically gawking at the man taking their order.

They spoke about hobbies and interests as they finished their drinks. The sun had sunk below the horizon and candles in hurricane lanterns securely lining the deck railing brought an intimate glow to the setting. Emerson realized she was having a nice time. Not a swoon-worthy event, but that was to be expected on a first date with a stranger.

After they'd ordered a second round, she excused herself to go to the bathroom. On the way out the door, she couldn't help but remember the last time she'd been in this hallway, and it brought a smile to her face as she exited the bathroom.

"Almost. But not quite."

Emerson stopped suddenly and put her hands out to lessen the impact of hitting the person standing there. The impact jolted a muffled cry from her. What she felt under her fingertips—hard muscles, heat—had her biting her lip. She thought she heard a groan from him and swiftly pushed back. "I'm sorry. Are you okay?" She straightened her purse on her shoulder and quickly asked, "Wait. What did you mean 'almost, but not quite'?"

Nick lowered his arms from where he'd held her elbows after impact. She still felt the heat his fingers had imprinted on her skin. "Your smile." He stepped back, giving her more room. "You might know this already, but I just can't help but share. That guy's much better than the first douche, but I'm not sure he's the one."

Emerson's eyebrows raised of their own accord. Well, that was pretty high-handed of him, but, what the hell, she'd bite. "And why do you think that?"

"I haven't seen your full-wattage smile yet tonight."

What? She tilted her head, thinking back to the conversations she and Joe had been tossing around. There wasn't anything terribly wrong with him, she just wasn't feeling it. "And when have you seen me smile like that to know what it looks like?"

Nick seemed to hesitate, then blinked and said, "Sunday night when you were here with your girlfriend. That's when the real you shone through."

"That was my cousin, Callie," she offered and took his words to heart. It likely was. She'd been happy and comfortable with her cousin, not so much with these two guys, so she could see where he was going with this. Just meant he'd been watching her more closely than she'd thought. But she'd have to admit, at least to herself, that she'd been checking him out an awful lot as well. Sneaking glances under her lashes at him periodically.

Nick's lips curved up and his eyes seemed to gleam in the dim light of the hallway. "I bet I could bring that smile out. It would only take me about ten seconds."

Well, that sure was cocky of him.

To her dismay and partial delight, she realized she really wanted to stick around and find out, but after a few too many seconds had gone by lost in that gleam and grin, it dawned on her that she'd been away from her date far too long. She could see Joe glancing at his watch now.

"As much as I'd like to see you try, I have to get back."

Nick winked at her, and she couldn't help the blush that rose on her cheeks. She looked away quickly so that full-wattage smile he spoke of wouldn't make a sudden appearance and prove him right.

# Chapter Five

"I can't believe you talked me into this," Emerson said when she hopped into Callie's SUV Saturday morning, just before eight. She tossed her backpack at her feet and sipped her to-go cup of coffee, savoring her second cup. She had her first one with her mother on the back deck before Callie arrived. Her brother Logan, sister-in-law Brenna, and their three kiddos were en route from Pensacola to spend the weekend, giving her some extra time off this morning. She looked forward to seeing them when she got back from this crazy adventure with her "twin cousin."

"It's going to be a blast. When was the last time you were on the water? Or in a kayak even?" Callie grinned at her as she backed out of the driveway. Her blonde hair was in a ponytail covered by a ballcap displaying the South Alabama Jags logo. She had on quick-dry shorts and a long-sleeved sun shirt. And she smelled like sunscreen.

"Exactly!" Emerson glanced down at her cut-off jean shorts and her tank top, thinking that maybe she hadn't dressed the right way for the day. "I'm not even dressed properly!"

"Relax," Callie reassured her. "You look great. I've got a rain jacket in the back. You can sit on it and cover your legs with it, so you don't get your shorts wet."

"Good thinking," Emerson said after another swallow. "Now, why are we doing this little adventure again? Besides it being a beautiful spring day and the sun is shining."

Callie turned out of the neighborhood and made her way north along the scenic drive. "I'm hoping to learn a lot about the natural history of Blue Bottle Creek as well as the 'people history' in this area. I'm thinking about bringing my students out here for an end-of-the-year field trip."

"That sounds like fun." Emerson didn't remember going on any fun trips like this when she was in eighth grade. But Callie did teach history at a private school, which provided a lot more perks and advantages for her students.

"Callie!" Emerson shifted in her seat, startling Callie, who gripped the steering wheel tighter. "I almost forgot. How did your date with John go?"

"Woman, you scared me!" Callie released a long breath, placing a hand over her heart. "It went great. We had a fun time talking. We found out we have a lot in common." Callie stopped at a red light. She turned to Emerson, her smile extra wide. "I found out he is a great kisser."

"Shut up!" Emerson swatted her arm and high-fived her. "That's awesome. Do you have another date planned?"

"We do." Callie accelerated when the light turned green, then signaled and turned into the parking lot of Paddlers Paradise.

Emerson ducked her head below the visor and looked closely at the sign by the road, then at the sign on the building. She spotted Keel & Rudder across the creek to the left. "This is it? Um, Cal, that's where we saw that alligator last weekend."

After putting her SUV into park, Callie turned her mega-watt smile on Emerson and said, "Isn't this going to be fun?!"

The brightness of Emerson's return smile was a little forced, but she made herself leave the vehicle. Callie handed her a rolled-up rain jacket that she placed on the top of her backpack. Taking her last sip of coffee, she left the cup in the back of Callie's Traverse and followed her cousin toward the entrance. From here Emerson could see the restaurant where she'd spent three evenings this last week. The "date" with her cousin had been the best of the three.

Her encounters with Nick the bartender outweighed both of her blind dates and she'd only spent a matter of minutes with him each time. She had to admit that he was sexy as sin and his smile brought heat as well as butterflies to her stomach. She remembered his parting words to her in the hallway last night—*I bet I could bring that smile out. It would only take me about ten seconds.* Emerson felt heat rise on her cheeks.

"What's got you smiling so?" Callie asked as she held the door open for Emerson to enter first.

Emerson wasn't going to share about her unconventional encounters with the bartender, but she realized she hadn't shared about going on another date last night. Just as the words were about to pop out of her mouth, her breath was cut off at the sight before her.

Nick stood behind the counter, his hand swiping a credit card, his smile directed at the woman paying. Emerson's breath caught in her throat and heat infiltrated her belly once again when he turned that smile her way. The second he recognized her, his smile widened, and Emerson thought she was going to have a heart attack right there as she stood inside the entrance to the shop. Her heart was beating wildly out of control.

Callie bumped into her, not seeing that she'd stopped and questioned, "What? Who—oh, I see."

Emerson quickly looked at her, shaking her head to clear it from the trance she'd been in the instant their eyes had locked. "What's he doing here?" she whispered.

"Um, Em, I forgot to tell you." Callie bit her lip and touched Emerson's hand. "But last weekend when we had dinner, I thought I recognized him and had to wrack my brain for a bit before it came to me. That's Nick Valentino. We went to high school with him. And his twin brother, Tony."

Emerson's brow wrinkled. She didn't recognize the name.

But her body recognized his, on a soul-deep level.

Emerson had never felt this way before. She'd only been in his presence, counting this one, four times. But her body had a mind of its own and his smile, his gleaming eyes, his powerful build did something to her insides.

Something warm and melty and delicious.

Emerson couldn't deny it any longer. She was attracted to Nick the bartender.

But what was he doing here?

"Let's go check in," Callie encouraged and led the way to the counter. She greeted Nick with a smile and a cheery hello.

Emerson was still in a daze but managed to blink her way out of it. She took a fortifying breath and pulled her southern manners out of a compartment long sealed and gave him a sunny smile. "Good morning. Fancy seeing you here." She took a moment to look around the shop, then back at him before asking, "Why are you here?"

Nick paused. His smile was just as strong and vivid as when he'd spotted her walking in the door. "I work here."

Emerson was stunned by his comment. What? He worked here and next door at the bar? "That's ambitious of you. When do you sleep?"

Nick chuckled. Emerson felt that deep sound rumble throughout her lady parts.

"I get by," he said and took the card Callie handed him to pay for their spot on the tour this morning. "It's a beautiful day for a kayak tour. I'm glad y'all are here this morning."

Nick pointed them in the direction of the back stairs that led to the meeting point. "Have a nice time."

Emerson stood there a couple extra seconds longer than necessary to admire the view one more time. She ducked her head and hid her smile as she turned away, following Callie.

IT WAS DEFINITELY his lucky day. Nick was going to get to see Emerson again, and without a douchebag date by her side. He was so glad he'd taken this morning's tour group from Jazzy, needing to have time on the water, and be back in his element. The bar business was entertaining, but this was the life he enjoyed. Interacting with humans in nature. His eyes couldn't help but follow her as she exited the main room of the shop.

And admire how those jeans shorts showed a whole lotta leg.

A throat clearing brought his attention back to the counter. Amber leaned against it, a knowing grin on her face, an eyebrow quirked. "You work here?"

Nick nodded. "I do. I just left out a minor detail," he said with a shrug. "She saw me this last week over at Tony's place, so I think she thinks I'm a bartender. Now, she'll just think I'm a really hard worker," he added with a wink.

"Starting any relationship off without being truthful—"

Nick jerked in response to that word. "What relationship?"

"I saw how you looked at her. And she you," she added with another knowing grin. This time she wiggled her eyebrows and caused him to laugh. "Even if it's an innocent one, starting off by misleading her might not sit well later on. If she's willing to stick with it and get involved with the likes of you."

"Hey!" Nick grunted and grabbed Amber's shoulders, pretending to strangle her. She was the closest thing he had to a sister. He was going to miss her like crazy when she was gone. "I'm glad you're joining me this morning. Packing in as many adventures as you can before you leave me, huh?"

With a tilt of her head, Amber grinned and said, "I'm going to miss you too. Speaking of leaving, have you checked to see if there are any job inquiries yet?"

Nick shrugged and looked at his watch. "We only posted it Tuesday. How could there be any already?"

Amber shook her head and made a *tut-tut-tut* sound with her mouth. "You haven't even checked your email? That was days ago!" When he shook his head, she added with a grumble, "I can't believe a man your age is so afraid of technology. It's just email. You push a button on your smartphone, and it shows you the emails you've received." She held out her hand and wiggled her fingers, looking at Nick expectantly.

"What?"

"Give me your phone." He slipped it from his pocket and put it in her hand. She easily got in and opened his email app. "You have three job inquiries. That's amazing!"

"Three? Really?" Nick couldn't believe it. And he was kinda ashamed to admit that his phone was smarter than him. He didn't do much on it except make phone calls and text. He glanced at his watch again. "Come on, we have to get down there and join the group."

Nick slid his phone inside a waterproof sleeve and attached it to his backpack. Pausing at the doorway, he grabbed a wide-brimmed hat off the sale rack. He led the way down the back steps outside to the meeting area. There were eight people going on the tour today. As he descended the stairs he scanned the crowd, counting them, then practically stumbled on the stairs when his eyes focused on Emerson immediately.

With her back to him, she was bent over at the waist, applying sunscreen to her legs. Her ass looked amazing in those short shorts. He knew those shorts would be featured in his dreams tonight. As well as her silky red hair that flew over her head, settling around her shoulders as she rose back to her full height. Nick gripped the railing and carried on down the stairs after his near miss-step. His heartbeat and breath were a little erratic.

"Good morning, folks!" he called out as he and Amber joined them at the picnic tables. "Terry has been hard at work this morning getting all the gear set out, so after y'all choose your life jackets and we do a quick lesson, we can be on our way. Any last-minute bathroom needs should be seen to now."

Terry had set out the number of sit-on-top kayaks ordered, along with seats and paddles. He was just heading back inside to man the shop while they were gone. He sent them a quick nod and said, "Have a good trip."

Nick focused on Emerson once again. She was done with her sunscreen—thank good- ness—and was chatting with her cousin. He to- tally hoped to impress her today, to get her to see him differently than the bartender she thought him to be. Smiling to himself, he walked over to her and plopped the hat he'd picked up inside on Emerson's head.

Damn she looked cute now. The blue brought out the color in her eyes. She had the most amazing eyes, with her subtly changing colors, they'd been a different shade each time he'd seen her this week.

"What's this for?" she asked with her hand on the top of it, looking up at the brim.

Nick tilted his head, wanting to return a smartass comment about the obvious function of a hat, but opted to instead say, "It'll keep the ticks out of your hair." He laughed when she cringed and grinned when she blushed through a "thank you." Next, he put his own hat on his head and dropped his backpack in his kayak. He picked up a paddle and returned to the assembled group.

"How many of y'all have paddled before?"

All but one raised their hands. Good. An easy start then. After demonstrating how to handle the paddle, he pulled his kayak closer to the group and reminded them how to get into and out of the kayak.

"Blue Bottle Creek is fairly shallow, with only a few deep spots. I'll be sure to point those out to you along the way. So, if you fall in, try standing up first before you panic," he added with a chuckle.

LORDY, THAT SOUND. Her insides just did a happy dance at that rumbling chuckle. And his smile did more than that to her. It brought heat to her lady parts. She'd been so shocked to see him when she'd entered the shop this morning. He worked two jobs? When did the man sleep? It was a legitimate question. She just couldn't imagine.

Emerson followed Callie's lead and chose the kayak next to hers. She took out Callie's rain jacket and laid it over the seat, then clipped her backpack to the mesh behind the seat, tucking it in. All the while Emerson was wracking her brain to remember the last time she'd been in a kayak. They'd had them growing up and she'd paddled close to shore, so this wouldn't be too different.

At least they weren't going into deep water. That kind of freaked her out. Always had.

Growing up on the bay in the murky brown water was fun but it held its unpleasant surprises—stingrays, oyster shells and blue crabs to name a few—that could stab, slice or pinch your bare toes. Her brother loved nothing more than putting baby blue crabs or slimy fish down his sisters' backs and watching them squeal and squirm. What a jerk he'd been, she thought with a reluctant grin.

Emerson was pulled from her memories when Nick yelled out, "Let's saddle up!" He was in the lead and there was a couple ahead of her and Callie. Emerson let Callie head out first, hoping she wasn't going to *tump* over.

*Lordy, where had that word come from? That was a blast from the past.*

*Tump* was a super-southern word spoken only by a true southerner and meant to dump or spill. Hah! Emerson nearly laughed out loud, her mind's eye immediately picturing her mother's cousin, Jenny, whom Emerson grew up thinking of as an aunt. Jenny was the sweetest soul and always had a sparkle in her bright blue eyes and the purest laugh she'd ever heard. She'd loved learning "southernisms" from Aunt Jenny.

Luckily, thinking of her Aunt Jenny had occupied her mind long enough that she got right into the kayak with nary a spill. *Whew, thank goodness.* She really didn't want to look like a fool today, especially with Nick nearby. She wanted to appear competent in this outdoorsy stuff, knowing now that he worked in an outdoorsy store. He probably lived and breathed nature and loved exploring it in every possible way.

Her idea of exploring nature was cutting through Central Park to get to an exercise class, a dinner meeting, or a sale. This was truly a new experience for her, at least in the last twelve years. She was most definitely out of her element, but she was going to give it her best shot and enjoy herself.

Callie was a natural. Always had been. She was always more enthusiastic about kayaking or paddle boarding when they were younger. Taking a deep breath, she decided to bring herself back to the present and tune in to what was going on around her.

The water was calm and a greenish brown. It had a little bit of a current that they were going against, but it wasn't too strong. Live Oaks and Magnolias lined the creek, their branches stretching out over the water, dripping Spanish moss and Resurrection ferns over their heads. Emerson was very thankful for the loan of the hat. The only thing she'd prepared for properly was her footwear. She'd found these sporty sandals in her bedroom closet and hadn't worn them since high school. They certainly hadn't made the cut for the move to NYC since there would never be an occasion up there to wear them. But today they were perfect.

A loud squawk startled her. Up ahead of the group a Great Blue Heron grumbled his displeasure about being disturbed and flew off ahead of them. In the silence, Emerson could hear several songbirds tweeting and the buzz of insects among the tall grass on the far side of the creek. Dragonflies and bees darted about. The scene before her was beautiful. Flower buds were just beginning to open on some of the plants low on the water. It was so peaceful here.

She realized Nick was talking so she tuned back in and heard him say, "Blue Bottle Creek was named because of the bottle factory that was about twenty miles upstream." Nick turned in his seat and looked at the group while he spoke. The muscles in his arms snagged her attention as he flexed his grip on the paddle. "They would dump their irregular bottles or broken pieces in the water. A lot of those pieces have found their way down here to the bay. It is a rare find to actually see a cobalt blue bottle or shard, but I've been lucky to find a couple over the years."

Nick paused when the man behind Emerson asked him a question. Emerson tried to muffle the squeak that wanted to escape when she realized the folks in front of her had stopped their kayaks. To avoid bumping into anyone, she might have bobbled a bit, but luckily didn't *tump* over. Callie reached out and grabbed the side of her kayak and pulled Emerson up against hers to steady her.

"We'll take a break here soon and get out to stretch our legs," Nick called out. "Y'all can search the shoreline for any shards of glass." He glanced over at Emerson; she could feel the heat of his stare from behind his sunglasses. "Everyone doing all right?"

There were shouts of affirmatives and head nods, so they decided to paddle on. Emerson noticed some of the docks and houses through the thick foliage lining the creek. There were a few sprawling mansions, some shacks and everything in between. Most had elaborate dock setups on or near the water, shack or not. She even saw a big screen TV under one cover and some lounge chairs facing it. Must be the perfect place for watching the game.

"Break time!"

Emerson prepared herself for stopping in advance and didn't bobble even a little bit this time. She executed a perfect parking job next to Callie's kayak on the shoreline, proud of herself for making it look easy. She was doing great, until she exited the kayak and her foot kicked something hidden under the murky water. The something had sharp edges that sliced the top of her foot not covered by her sandal and she yelped in surprise and pain.

Callie reached for her as Emerson hopped in the water but couldn't quite get to her fast enough before she fell backwards and plopped into the shallow water. The yelp and the splash drew everyone's attention, including Nick's, who rushed over to her side.

Emerson couldn't believe it. How embarrassing to fall on her ass when she'd been about to execute the most perfect landing and dismount off a kayak that she'd ever done.

"Emerson! Are you okay?"

Nick grabbed her elbows and helped her stand. Emerson shook her wet hands to remove as much water as she could before she reached up to straighten the hat he'd given her. Her jeans shorts were soaked clear through and molded to her butt and thighs. She had a wedgie but had absolutely no intention of rectifying that problem in Nick's presence. She'd just have to suffer.

Emerson lifted the hem of her tank and wrung out as much water as she could, then fluttered it in hopes that it would dry soon.

Nick asked again, "Are you okay?"

Emerson took stock and lifted her foot out of the water. Water dripped off the top of her foot, revealing a cut oozing blood.

"Ouch. That looks like it hurts. Probably an oyster cluster got you when you stepped out of your kayak." He led her to shore and motioned for her to sit on the sand. "I'll grab my pack and we'll get you fixed up."

Callie sat next to her and held her hand. "Em, how bad does it hurt? I've got some pain meds if you need them."

"I'm okay," Emerson reassured her, removing her hat so she could pull her hair up off her surprisingly hot neck. Heated from embarrass-ment, no doubt. "It's just a small cut. I'm more upset over the graceful landing I made."

Callie chuckled. "I'd give it a six. Because you only soaked the lower half of your top, and your head is still dry. Had you gone all the way, then it would have been a ten for sure."

"I'm glad you can find something funny about this." Emerson propped her elbows on her knees and covered her eyes with her hands and shook her head slightly. Taking a deep breath, she told herself to relax and go with it.

"Okay, folks. I'm going to need to put my expertise in first aid to use, so Amber is going to take over the shoreline walk and talk with you. Please, look around, and search for some bottles or fragments. Finders' keepers." Nick walked back to Emerson. "Good luck," he called out before squatting down by her foot.

Emerson had removed her shoe and was wiping off some of the sand around the perimeter of the wound. "Don't worry about that. I have water to rinse it off," Nick said.

Emerson noticed Callie was looking between her and the group. "Go. I'm okay. You need to hear the info and get your hands in the sand searching for bottles. Go," Emerson said again when Callie hesitated. "This is what we are here for."

Callie squeezed Emerson's hand again and hopped up to join the group on the hunt. Emerson watched her go then focused back in on the handsome man at her feet. "So, how much first aid experience do you have?"

"About twelve years' worth." Nick took a bottle of water out of his backpack and slowly poured it over the cut. It hadn't looked deep until he'd cleared away all the sand and blood. The jagged line crossed the top of her foot from side to side and looked to be an inch. Nothing major, but It would likely leave one interesting scar.

"How long have you been working here? Did you start after high school?" Emerson looked at his hands. One gently held her foot, and she could feel the heat from his skin soaking into hers. The other stroked lightly over the top of her foot removing any extra sand that hadn't been washed off with the water. For a big guy, with such callused hands, you'd think he'd be rough, but his touch was so soft, so tender. She couldn't help the shiver that coursed through her body as her thoughts went awry and she pictured his hands caressing the rest of her with the same softness, the same tenderness.

"I worked here while I was in high school. I was in Terry's position at that point." Nick looked up at her and she was caught in the heat of his gaze. He'd removed his sunglasses and his whiskey-colored eyes blazed into hers. She found she couldn't blink. Couldn't look away from the patterns of rich, dark swirls flowing through his irises. His eyes couldn't be called just brown, they had too many shades shifting around the pupil.

"And at what point are you now?" Emerson's voice was breathier than she'd like it to be.... must be the trance she was under. Finally, she blinked and shifted her gaze back to her foot where he'd applied some antibiotic cream. Now, he was placing a non-stick pad over the wound then started wrapping gauze around her foot to keep it in place.

Nick paused, glanced up, and then spoke as he started wrapping again. "I'm closer to management now."

They both lifted their heads and turned to see one of the group members raise his hand in the air and shout. Nick grinned. "Must have found one."

# Chapter Six

Nick finished packing his gear away and sat beside her on the sand. "How's that feel? Do you need any pain meds? I've got some here in my pack."

Emerson shook her head. "I'm fine. Cleaning it out helped."

"It'll get stiff and won't like it when you start to move it, so you're going to have to take it easy for a bit while it heals. I don't think it's deep enough for stitches. But maybe a steri-strip if you have one at home."

Emerson wrung her hands, then placed them behind her on the sand, leaning back. She looked like she was uncomfortable. He hoped it wasn't because of him sitting so close to her. "My brother's visiting and he's a firefighter. He'll probably have one in his kit in their vehicle."

"That's good." Nick glanced over at the group, checking on their progress.

"I'm fine sitting here by myself, if you need to go with the group."

Nick glanced back at her and grinned. "Nah, Amber's got it. She's been working with me for six years now. She's got the tour down and is great with answering questions on the spot." Nick stretched his legs out in front of him, crossing his ankles, and leaned back on his palms. "She's graduating next month and is leaving for Atlanta. The boss isn't too happy."

"Yeah? Why's that?"

"She handles all the accounts and payroll. The boss isn't excited about hiring someone new to do the job. Or having to do any of it himself. Numbers are not his game," Nick chuckled, feeling ridiculous for concealing that he was indeed the boss he spoke of, but he didn't think it would hurt anything.

"There are plenty of hiring sites that can help—"

"Amber's already on it. She's hoping to train her replacement before she goes."

"Well, that's good. Continuity in a workplace is extremely valuable."

"Speaking of workplace, what do you do—"

A group of loud voices heading their direction interrupted his question. He rose when he saw the group emerge from the brush along the creek. There were many smiling faces and a few glass shards to share with him and Emerson.

Nick jumped back into tour-guide mode and answered all the questions that his guests asked about the area. Emerson's cousin, Callie, had the most. He was happy to learn that she was a history teacher and wanted to bring her students out here for a field trip.

When it was time to get back in the kayaks, he turned to find Emerson shifting to lift herself up. He quickly crossed over to her and put his arms under her knees and around her back, picking her up off the sand. She let out a startled yelp and hit his back with her shoe that was gripped tightly in her hand as both her hands wound around his neck.

"Nick! You don't have to carry me!"

"It'll be easier this way," he assured her, shifting her easily in his hold. Damn she felt good in his arms. "We don't want sand in the dressing. You also have to keep this as dry as you can."

Callie helped by steadying the kayak on her side while Nick lowered Emerson onto the seat. She only wobbled a little when he let go. "Good?" He searched her eyes. He saw her release a quick breath and smiled when she offered him a small nod. "Good." Once the paddle was in her hands, he pushed her kayak back out into the water. Callie was already by her side.

Hurrying, he jumped into his kayak and pushed off, taking back the lead of the tour. He loved his job so much. This was where he was meant to be. Nick loved the sound of the water lapping against the kayak and the *thunk* of the paddle as it knocked into the hard plastic sides. He loved the birds, the insects, the grasses and trees. He loved sharing about the people who settled into these parts before names were given to the towns, cities, creeks and bay. He loved breathing in this sweet-scented spring air and the feel of the sunshine on his skin.

He had no idea what he was missing when he'd been growing up in Jersey. There was so much smog and grayness, snow and rain. Here, thankfully, there was no snow, and the air was so clear and crisp that he wanted to spend nearly every day outside.

And he was damn lucky to get to do that for a living.

The tour was over before he was ready. Seeing Emerson again was such a bonus. Nick couldn't believe his luck. He hated that she'd gotten hurt, but he sure hadn't hated getting to put his hands on her.

He needed to see her again.

Terry was onshore ready to help unload everyone. He started assisting the first to dock. Nick jumped out and immediately pulled Emerson's kayak onto the beach. "Just toss your paddle up here," he suggested, pointing farther up the beach. He moved to the side of her kayak and reached for her again.

"No, Nick, I can walk."

Nick stopped, his arms still outstretched. "How are you going to get out of here and not get water or sand in your bandage?"

Emerson bit her lip. Then shook her head in defeat. "I have no idea."

Nick stayed close but didn't pressure her. Instead, he kept his hands at his sides and asked, "Can I help you?"

She nodded and he reached for her again. This time she gracefully wrapped her arms around his shoulders and held on tight. Nick carried her up to the picnic tables and sat her down on the closest bench, stretching her leg out along the bench to keep her foot elevated. Squatting before her he forced himself to move his hand from her knee to the bench beneath it. She had felt so good in his arms. "All good?"

"Yes, thank you." Her gorgeous eyes gleamed at him, glowing from the bright sunlight. "Thank you for everything. I really enjoyed the experience." She sent him a wry grin. "Not so much the free souvenir, but hey, guess it could have been worse."

"That's the spirit," he chuckled. Her hands were still on his shoulders. He didn't think she realized that, but he felt every inch of the pressure and heat. And he wanted to feel more of it. The noise of the other customers moving around the tables, loading up their belongings distracted him only briefly. He didn't want to miss this chance to ask her out. "Emerson, would you like to have breakfast with me tomorrow?"

She tilted her head and narrowed her eyes. Her lips just barely creeping into a grin.

"That is," Nick paused, "if you don't already have another date planned."

Shaking her head, she said, "No, no more dates planned."

"Well, how about it?" His heartbeat thudded in his ears as he awaited her response. He felt like he was in high school again. But back then he never even spoke to her. He just fantasized about it.

"Okay, that sounds lovely." Her eyes sparkled a little with her grin. "Where would you like to meet?" she asked, sitting up straighter. Shifting her foot, he saw her cringe at the pain that action must have caused.

"Here."

She looked around, her brow furrowed in confusion. "Is the restaurant next door open for breakfast?"

"No. Thank goodness," he chuckled and rose to sit across from her on a neighboring picnic table bench. "I don't want to be another date you meet there." He patted her knee and winked.

That statement shot a laugh out of her, and she blessed him with her full-wattage smile. It about melted him. He felt its glow all the way to his gut, which had tightened already at her beautiful laugh. "I know this great breakfast spot just up the creek. We actually passed it on our trip."

Emerson's silky hair slid over her shoulder when she tilted her head in question. "We did?"

"Yep, it's tucked back in there. We'll have to get to it by water. Think you're up for another paddle? We can take a canoe this time, so you don't have to get your foot wet."

She paused long enough he wondered if she was going to change her mind. But then she helped him start breathing again when she flashed him her full-wattage smile and said, "Sounds adventurous, I'm in."

***

Callie helped her out of the front seat. Emerson put a little weight on her foot to see how it would respond. The skin pinched around the cut, and she nearly wanted to cry out. This was like a paper cut, but a million times worse. Picking her foot back up, she shook her head. "Nope. Not yet."

Callie wrapped her arm around Emerson's waist and helped her hobble to the front porch. "We'll let you put your feet up for a while and that'll help it."

"I think I need pain meds and a beer. That'll help it too."

"What happened to you?"

Emerson looked up to see her brother exiting the front door of the house. "I sliced the top of my foot on an oyster shell. The guide cleaned it out and wrapped it, but I'd appreciate you taking a look at it too."

Logan pulled a chair over to the edge of the porch for her to sit in. "Sure thing. I was just getting something out of the suburban. I'll grab my kit."

"Thanks." Emerson settled in the chair and leaned her head back. "All in all, Callie, it was a fun adventure and a lovely day on the water. Thank you for inviting me."

"You're welcome. I'm sorry you got injured." Callie patted Emerson's foot, avoiding the injury. "I will definitely be setting up a field trip for my students. Nick is so knowledgeable about the history of the area and that is exactly what they need to hear at the end of the semester. Plus, it'll be fun to get out of the classroom."

"You're an awesome teacher, Cal. I wish I'd had you when I was in eighth grade."

"Aww thanks. But Mr. Lassiter was fun too. Remember we thought he was so old that he must have experienced the history he taught us firsthand."

Logan plunked a large duffle bag onto the porch beside where Emerson and Callie sat. "Okay, let me see how bad it is." He worked quickly and carefully to remove the gauze wrap and then the protective pad over the cut. Blood was still seeping from the wound. The edges looked puffy and red.

"Yikes," Emerson said. "That looks worse than earlier."

"It's a rough cut. And with anything in the water there's an extra level of cleansing needed because of all the bacteria found there. Don't want a flesh-eating bacterium to take root here in your foot," Logan said almost gleefully.

Emerson looked aghast. "Yikes again!"

Logan set to work cleaning it with rubbing alcohol, thoroughly flushing it. Emerson winced with each dose, but she'd rather it be clean and not have to worry about her flesh dissolving because of bacteria in her wound. Logan applied an antibiotic cream then positioned a steri-strip across the widest part of the cut. "So, how did you manage to cut the top of your foot instead of the bottom? What were you girls up to this morning?"

"Callie dragged me along on a guided kayak tour up Blue Bottle Creek. I scuffed my foot on an oyster cluster when I was getting out of the kayak. Luckily, I had on my sandals, so I didn't cut the bottom of my foot. Just happened to kick it at the right angle, I guess."

"That part sucks, but the tour sounds like fun. The kids would love that." Logan's oldest was nearing double digits and he was as sporty as his dad. Sam was born to be on the water and loved to do anything that required balance. He was great at paddle boarding. In fact, he was likely out on the water now. The younger two, Sadie and Avery, loved to follow their big brother wherever he went.

Kinda sounded familiar to the way she and her sister Sidney idolized Logan, when he wasn't being a jerk to them.

Logan cleaned up his supplies and returned his kit to the vehicle before helping Emerson inside. She could hear the whoops and hollers of fun coming from the backyard. She knew her nieces and nephews were out there having a ball. Sidney and Dave were sitting down by the water's edge, a fishing pole in Dave's hands and baby Michelle in Sidney's arms. Eli and Sadie slid down the slide attached to the dock. Big splashes and loud laughter followed their entrance into the water. Sam was on the paddle board and Avery was doing cartwheels along the shoreline.

Emerson found her mother and aunt on the deck in the shade. She indicated to Logan and Callie that she'd like to join them. They helped her into the chair next to Carolyn's. Callie pulled up another chair and propped her foot on a pillow. "There ya go. I'll get you those meds and a beer that you requested." Callie bowed then left with a wink.

Carolyn turned in her seat, her expression concerned. "What happened to you, dear?"

"I cut the top of my foot on an oyster when we were kayaking this morning. Logan just cleaned it and bandaged it up for me. It's going to be fine."

"You'll want to watch it for infection."

"Yes, I was reminded of the flesh-eating bacteria that could inhabit my skin."

Carolyn chuckled. Aunt Deborah did too, then turned a serious look towards her sister. "Remember Jimmy Nixon who lived down the street from us? He lost his foot to one of those infections."

Emerson really needed that beer right about now.

***

By early evening all the kids were fed, changed and on the lawn for an outdoor movie. The grown-ups were gathered around the table on the deck, savoring the last of the dessert or finishing their beverages. Baby Michelle was happily being passed around, entertained by all her aunts, uncles, and gramma.

Emerson watched a great white egret stand on its stilted legs at the water's edge, searching for a snack. She raised her glass to her lips as she watched it dart its head into the water and return with the tail of a fish hanging out of its bill. Everyone was getting well-fed that night. She looked down at her empty plate and last spoonful of dessert.

"Well, dear family, I'm going to make my exit," Carolyn said. "I want to thank you all for being here this weekend." She turned her smile toward each person at the table. "I love having my kids and grandkids close. It warms my heart. But this old lady is tuckered out and needs her rest."

"Goodnight, Mom," Logan said. Others called out greetings as well. Aunt Deborah stood and helped Carolyn with her chair. Then she called out a goodnight and took her leave.

Emerson started to rise, anxious about how her foot was going to feel once she put weight on it again. She'd only gotten up one other time and had hobbled inside to the guest bathroom off the kitchen. She knew she'd looked like a waddling duck, but it was the best she could do.

Now she was dreading the stairs.

Suddenly, Sidney set Michelle in Emerson's arms and hopped up. "I'll help you get settled, Mom," Sidney offered. Emerson sighed and tucked Michelle in close to her chest, feeling only a little awkward since she didn't have much practice with holding babies. Michelle's eyes were so mesmerizing, staring up at her so trustingly, glowing in the candlelight. Her eyes were still a dark blue, but Emerson was hoping they would lighten up to the same shade as the family had. Sidney's son Eli's eyes matched his mother's. So there was hope.

Carolyn rubbed Emerson's shoulder as she walked by. "Goodnight, dear. That baby looks good in your arms," she whispered with a wink.

Emerson rolled her eyes as she swept her hand up to squeeze her mother's before she could get past. "Thanks, and goodnight, Mom. Sweet dreams." *Really smooth there, Mom. Not subtle at all.* How would she know what to do with a baby? Were babies even in her future? It wasn't a topic that she thought of, at all, really. Not even often, just literally not at all. There wasn't time in her work life to even imagine inputting something so tiny and so needy into the equation. Her last boyfriend, Evan, had been a workaholic like she was.

But holding Michelle, feeling the baby's subtle weight and body heat against her was sweet. Hearing her sighs and little happy sounds made Emerson's heart tweak a little. She didn't know the first thing about how to take care of a baby, but she did like holding and smiling at a happy and content one. Now, it would be a totally different ballgame if Michelle was having a fit and was inconsolable. She decided to take her small wins when they presented themselves and right now, Michelle was a happy camper.

Even so happy that she now had her eyes closed.

"That baby does look good in your arms," Callie said, nudging her thigh gently so as not to wake the sleeping babe. "I can see it. I could maybe even see a certain handsome brown-eyed, shaggy-haired man with the sweetest smile playing a role."

Emerson's insides twinged with a teensy bit of lust at the mention of Nick. She might have even blushed a little. Hopefully, the candlelight covered that telling sign. "Me and Nick with a baby?" Emerson tilted her head with one eyebrow raised in her cousin's direction. "How about we go on a date first? Then maybe we can schedule talks about the other stuff for the last quarter of the year."

"There's that businesswoman I know and love," Logan said then finished his last swallow of beer. "Now, who the hell is Nick?" Brenna elbowed him and shook her head. Emerson and Callie laughed.

It was almost like old times. Logan was a great big brother. Attentive, helpful, a teacher of many things, but he could also be annoying, manipulative and strategic. And he always pestered them about any guy they were even the slightest bit interested in dating. Then the protectiveness came pouring out of him.

Emerson was saved from explaining when Sidney emerged from the French doors. "Mom's all settled in. She's taken all her pills and looked quite comfortable when I left. Emerson, you've done an excellent job organizing and labeling all the medications. Thank you for that." Sidney hugged her shoulders before sitting back in her seat. "Want me to take her?"

Emerson smiled down at the sweet sleeping babe and shook her head. "No, she's fine. I'm enjoying this."

"Enjoy it now. She'll wake in about twenty minutes screaming for milk," Dave warned. "Then she's a bear until she gets what she wants. Kinda like her mom." Dave took the light smack Sidney laid on his arm, then pulled her close to his side.

"Speaking of a bear going after what she wants, so is Mom," Emerson began, anxious about starting this conversation but knowing that it was necessary with all of them there together. "She isn't thrilled about having any home health nurses in the house. But Mom is going to eventually need more help than I can give her. Plus, guys," she said glancing around the table, from Logan and Brenna to Callie, then over to Sidney and Dave. "I'm only here another three weeks."

Emerson saw the looks Logan and Sidney passed between them. "Please don't think that just because I'm the one who isn't married and has kids means that I can easily give up my job, my home, *my life* in another state and move here to help Mom 24/7." She shifted her gaze between her siblings. "That's not fair. I'm not a nurse. I don't have that kind of caregiving gene in my body. I love Mom and I will do what I can for her, but eventually she's going to need more."

Sidney closed her eyes and sighed. "You're right. I'm sorry. Having you move here and be with Mom was, in my mind, the easy answer. And I know that's not fair to you, sister, it's just what came to my mind first." Sidney took hold of Emerson's hand and squeezed reassuringly. She sent a knowing look to Logan and said, "So, now, we talk it out. We plan and we think of things that we can all do to help Mom."

"Or," Logan stated, "we sit down with her and ask her what she wants. Then we evolve that into what we think would be best."

"Evolve is such a pleasant way to say *manipulate*, Logan. Mom's mental faculties are still fully functional. She's not going to be railroaded into anything," Emerson reminded them. "I will be here with her for a few more weeks. But I'd like us to discuss the topic of home health nurses again and get her comfortable with it. If she accepts, then I'd like them to start before I go home so I can be here to make sure things run smoothly."

"That's a good idea," Sidney said. Then she obviously read her baby's signals and plucked her out of Emerson's arms just before any sound emerged from her bunched-up mouth. Sidney settled her in close and fed her baby, thwarting any of the screaming that Dave had mentioned earlier.

Emerson noticed the change in temperature on her chest and arms. She missed that warmth and sweet scent immediately. Stretching her arms and back, she shifted into a more comfortable position now that she wasn't frozen in fear of waking up the baby.

Emerson picked up her spoon and licked the last of the apple cobbler off. "Another thing I've been thinking about is getting Mom to switch bedrooms. She really needs to be on the first floor. And one more thing," she paused, taking a moment to look around the backyard and the deck. "What about this house? Should she really be living here all alone?"

"I can't picture her anywhere else," Sidney said immediately. She shook her head. "She'd never leave. Daddy's memory is alive in this house. We grew up here."

Logan nodded. "It is a big place for one person. But I agree, it would be better overall for her to live only on the first floor. The stairs are an accident waiting to happen," Logan grumbled. "I've attended many calls where elderly had fallen and were left bloody, bruised, or broken. It wasn't pretty."

"Okay, tomorrow then," Sidney said with an affirmative nod.

"I'll keep the kids busy," Brenna offered, looking at Dave for assistance.

"Sure thing. We can keep them occupied fishing and playing in the water," Dave agreed. "You guys can have plenty of time to talk after breakfast."

"It'll have to be around lunch time," Emerson said, sitting up. "I just remembered...I have a breakfast date tomorrow."

***

Emerson hobbled her way into her bedroom and crashed onto her bed. She'd grabbed an ice pack on the way through the kitchen and worked to position it just right on the top of her foot. She wrapped a tea towel around it and laid back on her pillows. What a night.

She was pleased with how the conversation had ended with her siblings. She knew that they'd been looking for her to take care of their mother because for them it was easier. They could go right on living their lives in their respective towns, with less than an hour's drive to visit, and know that their mother was settled and cared for by her youngest, who obviously could quit the job she loved and had been doing for the last eight years without any repercussions.

As if.

She was glad they realized their mistake in thinking that way. Hopefully, Carolyn would be more open to discussing having home health care come in each day to help her. With the right care and the right medication, she should be able to manage the current symptoms. But for how long? No one knew that answer. That question kept Emerson up at night. Worrying over how fast her mother's health would deteriorate.

But since she wasn't a fortune teller by trade she had to rely on the old go-with-the-flow method.

Knowing that and actually following through with it were two different things. She sighed and her heart felt heavy because she knew she couldn't be there for her mother. She had to get back to New York, eventually. Back to her job, her apartment, her life.

Right? She had to, didn't she?

Wasn't it funny how she hadn't even thought about those things lately?

She'd had to listen to her boss's instructions about turning off the phone and computer when on the third day home her repeated texts and emails went unanswered. She'd received just one response at the end of the day: *You're on leave. Spend time with your mother. Don't spend time worrying about work.*

She hadn't mindlessly checked her calendar, or the stock market numbers today.

She'd been so caught up in experiencing life here, with her family, going on dates, spending time in nature. All the things she didn't do in New York. All things she didn't have time for. Was that how she really wanted to live? Did she really want to go back to that hectic, fast-paced world that increased her hypertension and brought anxiety into her daily life?

Wasn't it amazing how, since she'd been here, she hadn't had any trouble with her blood pressure? It was like the instant she sat on her favorite swing and felt that south Alabama humidity wrap around her like a blanket, that she flipped a switch.

A calming switch.

The slower pace, the wide-open spaces, the centuries-old trees, the lapping shores, the humidity all made things here so much easier, so much calmer, so much more relaxed. This was something she never even noticed when she was a kid. Her mind had been hell-bent on living a different life that she didn't take time to smell the lilacs or listen to the bullfrogs or be soothed by the steady rhythm of the water washing onshore.

In the last seven days, Emerson had noticed all of that and more. She'd been breathing deeper, stretching her mind and her body more, and she'd been eating. Enjoying the taste of food even, not just consuming larger quantities. In New York she was always in a rush. Heading to work, to a meeting, to a class, or to another meeting right after the previous one. Food was an afterthought and was usually eaten on the fly or picked at while discussing stock market values and long-range goals.

This time she was here long enough to see those changes and take time to evaluate them. Any of her previous visits were short and sweet, mostly obligatory, then back to business. This time she was required to slow down and to think. To think about her mother and how she was changing, and how those changes were going to affect the family, in the short term as well as the long term. But also, to think about her future and what she really wanted.

Emerson hadn't actually done that in a long time.

What did she want? Right now, she wanted to quiet her mind so she could get some sleep.

She had a date tomorrow. Emerson slapped her hands over her quivering stomach. Just the thought of seeing Nick again caused that sensory reaction. His smile, the sound of his voice, good Lord, his deep, rumbling chuckle, all those things made her insides tingle.

She was intrigued by Nick Valentino, and she wanted to learn what made him tick. He excelled as a nature guide. It had surprised her how quickly she'd gotten sucked into the history lesson about the area. History had never been her favorite subject. It wasn't even in the top five. But it might have had to do with the sound of his voice rather than the subject matter that drew her attention.

Now she needed to stop thinking about her canoe-slash-breakfast date and all the possibilities that could come along. Which was quite impossible now that her mind was reviewing the trip this morning down the creek. He'd said they'd passed it. She hadn't seen any businesses along the route, just houses. She wondered where he was taking her the next day.

Emerson groaned then let out a calming sigh, hoping to relax her wound-up hormones and her busy mind. Now that her thoughts had changed from her crazy life to a sexy-as-sin man, she wasn't sure she was ever going to get to sleep.

# Chapter Seven

Nick couldn't think of too many things that would make him any happier right now.

He was on the water, paddling a canoe up Blue Bottle Creek with a gorgeous woman lounging in the front. Sun rays filtered through the trees, with beautiful birdsong echoing around them on this early spring day.

This was definitely his happy place.

"It is so beautiful out here," Emerson whispered. It warmed his heart to hear her in awe of her surroundings. She was "good people" in his book because she appreciated something that he didn't take for granted. He knew he lived in a jewel of a place and was one of the lucky ones to call this area home.

"This is one of the best times of year. Get too many more months down the line and it would already be hot and muggy at this hour, and we'd be covered in mosquitoes or no-see-ums."

"Ugh," she gasped, "those are the worst. I remember those little buggers. That is one thing that New York City has going for it. Not many bugs." She looked over her shoulder with a wry grin. "Now, it definitely has its own host of problems, but no-see-ums aren't one of them."

Nick paddled closer to the shore on the left after they'd been on the water for about fifteen minutes. A dock stuck out from the shoreline with several cleats on it where they could tie up.

"Is this it?" Emerson turned to take in the view. He grinned at her skepticism.

"It is," he confirmed and deftly sidled up to the dock and tied the stern line to the cleat. "I'm hopping out, so hold on." Then he shifted and stepped from the canoe onto the dock. Emerson reached for the rope tied to the bow and held it out to him. "Thank you." After he secured the canoe to the dock, he reached for her hands.

"I'm going to help you turn so you can sit on the dock first. Then we can pull you up to standing. Sound okay?"

Emerson tweaked an eyebrow at him and wrinkled her lips in a cute expression, once again revealing her skepticism. "If you say so."

Nick held her elbows tight as she turned and leaned back against the dock, then lifted herself up to sitting. "There, see. Easy peasy. Would you like me to carry you?" He was squatting beside her, getting an eye-to-eye view of her gorgeous ever-changing eyes.

"I can hobble my way," she stated then hesitated as her eyes took in the scene. "As long as we aren't walking up to that house, then I'd maybe change my mind."

"Nope, just to these chairs right here," he directed, pointing back at the Adirondack chairs set up around a large fire pit. An outdoor kitchen was located at the far edge of the concrete slab that held the chairs.

"Good," she said and rose to her feet. She dusted her hands off on her navy-blue shorts. She was going for a single-color palette today. Her shirt was also navy-blue, along with the sandals she wore on her feet. The top of her left foot had a fresh bandage on it. He hoped her brother had been able to put a steri-strip on her cut.

Nick watched her face as she took in her surroundings. "This is a beautiful place. Is it really a restaurant?"

"No," he laughed. "It's actually my house."

Emerson stopped mid-hobble and whipped her head around to look at him, her mesmerizing eyes huge in her gorgeous face. "What? This is your place?" She tossed her hair over her shoulder as she turned her head to look up at his house. "Nick, it's beautiful."

Nick took in the scene from a fresh perspective. The trees were lush and abundant on his property. His house could be seen from the water, but not the full view of it. The stone-lined path leading down from his back deck was winding and bordered with wildflowers. He'd tilled the ground a few years ago and dumped in all those cheap seed packets you get at the garden stores. He was impressed with what emerged each season.

But the kicker? It was the amazing outdoor kitchen down here by the dock. He loved cooking over a flame and had all the accoutrements to make that happen. He'd left all his wood staged and ready to light as soon as they arrived. Today, he was going to show Emerson how much he loved cooking outside.

Was he trying to impress her with his culinary skills? Absolutely.

"Thanks," he said belatedly. "Here, come sit down. I'll get you a drink. Would you like a mimosa to start?"

Emerson nodded and gingerly took a step towards the seating area. "That sounds lovely. Yes, please."

Nick's hands fisted at his sides. He let her hobble, even though he wanted very much to pick her up and carry her to the chair. Her independent streak was fierce, and he wasn't going to be pushy. Once she was settled, he moved a milkcrate into position with a pillow on top to support her foot.

"Thanks," she said softly, getting herself situated comfortably.

"You're welcome." He paused to light the sticks in the fire pit before he opened the mini fridge and popped the cork on the champagne he had chilling. He poured it into a tumbler and added orange juice. Remembering her previous drink orders, he went heavy on the OJ.

"Mm, that looks good." She sent him a sweet smile when she reached out for the drink. "Thank you." Her fingers grazed his and he lingered. The heat dancing up his arm quickened his pulse. He knew the heat he felt had to be radiating from his gaze.

Damn he loved that heat.

"Welcome." Nick cleared his throat and stepped back. "Now, what's your breakfast preference? Eggs, bacon, biscuits? Or would you prefer sweet, like, cinnamon rolls or pancakes?"

"I prefer salty over sweet," Emerson was quick to say.

"Salty, it is." Nick got to work setting out the carton of eggs, package of bacon and can of biscuits. "Scrambled or over easy?"

"Scrambled." Emerson took a sip and sighed. "Thank you so much for going to all this effort. This is an *amazing* spot," she said, her gaze focused out toward the creek. "I bet you do a lot of entertaining out here."

"My brother benefits the most from my entertaining. He lives on a sailboat, so he winds up over here or at my parents' place often for meals." Nick set the biscuits in the Dutch oven and placed it down in the embers. Nick paused and looked up at the tree overhead when a cacophony of chirps and squawks broke out between a couple pairs of cardinals.

Emerson had glanced up too to see what the squabble was about. "That sounds adventurous. Has he always lived on a sailboat?"

"Since he moved out of my parents' place after we graduated from high school. He worked hard our senior year to save up to buy one. The first one was small and not in the best of shape, but he's upgraded a couple times since then." Nick cracked several eggs into a bowl. He sprinkled in seasonings and added a dash of milk before whipping them into shape. He put a kettle of water on the grate over the fire to heat for coffee. "Speaking of high school," he paused and stirred the sticks to build up the fire. Glancing over he asked the question he'd been dying to know the answer to. "Have you remembered yet that we went to high school together?"

EMERSON HID THE deep breath she took behind her tumbler of mimosa. Nick's direct gaze turned her way and made her heart flutter. Geesh. *Now, I'm going to have to explain, no, actually, I have no memory of you from high school.*

"Nick, I have to apologize." Emerson thought it best to get that out of the way first. She paused and leaned forward in the Adirondack chair to set the tumbler down on the table next to her seat. "I was so focused that year, so ready to be gone from this small town that I didn't pay much attention to my surroundings."

Nick sent her a lop-sided grin and gave a hard shake of his head, shifting the hair on his forehead to partially cover his handsome eyes. "It's okay, no apology needed."

"I'm sorry I don't remember you." Her hands fluttered on her lap, and she sighed. "During my senior year, I had applied to several universities up north and once I received some acceptances my heart and mind were already there."

Nick turned from where he was opening the package of bacon, crouched in a squat beside the firepit and began laying the slices on the grate over the fire. "Where did you go to college?"

"Columbia."

"Nice," he said and nodded his approval as he stirred the eggs in the skillet. Reaching over the grill he used tongs to turn the bacon. Emerson tried to focus on his hands, but her eyes were drawn to how taut his shorts were over his very fine ass. She blinked and tried to tune back in. "Full ride?"

"Yes, thankfully. Otherwise, my mom probably wouldn't have let me go. I just needed to get out of this place." She paused and sighed. Her eyes took in the beauty of the nature around her. The creek had a bit of a current around a fallen log from the opposite bank to the left of his dock. A Great Blue Heron perched on the post at the end of Nick's dock. It turned its head toward the splash of a small fish as it leaped from the water. Emerson shook her head and shrugged. "I can't explain it. Being back now, I have no idea what I was thinking. I obviously took for granted where I lived and the absolute peacefulness and beauty of the area. New York City is completely on the opposite end of the spectrum from this place."

"Being from Jersey, I know what you mean." Nick shifted to standing and set the crispy bacon on the platter next to the scrambled eggs he'd prepared. "We moved here the summer before our senior year, and I was blown away. I fell in love with the water immediately. Obviously, my brother did too since he lives on a sailboat and races it every chance he gets." Using an oven mitt Nick pulled the lid off the Dutch oven to check the biscuits. "These are done too. Perfect timing."

"That is an amazing feat," she praised. "I can't ever get the timing right when attempting to pull together a multi-object meal." Emerson pulled in a breath of air. "It all smells delicious. Thank you so much for going to all this trouble."

"It's no trouble at all." The wink he flashed her way sent heat racing between her thighs. "I wouldn't have built all this out here if I didn't like using it," he explained as he set a plate on the small table beside her chair. "Now, tell me what condiments you'd like. Butter, ketchup, hot sauce?"

"A and B, but not C." Emerson adjusted her leg on the milkcrate and pillow, shifting it closer to better support the back of her knee. She flexed her foot, trying to keep it from going to sleep. Pain radiated out from the cut. When his back was turned, she took a couple deep breaths until the sting had passed.

Nick brought the items over along with the serving platter. Emerson scooped eggs onto her plate and picked two of the crispiest pieces of bacon before grabbing a steaming-hot biscuit.

"Coffee's ready," Nick announced, picking the kettle up from the grate. "Want some?"

"Absolutely," she said then cringed. "Oh, wait, do you have cream and sugar?"

"Absolutely," he echoed.

"Bless you," she sighed and picked up her plate. After adding the condiments, she waited until he had served himself and sat. Nick raised his coffee cup and his sandy-brown eyebrows. She hurriedly picked hers up and mirrored his pose.

"To our past adventures and those yet to come. Cheers." Nick tapped her mug, gave her a dazzling smile, and took a sip from his steaming cup. "Dig in before it gets cold."

Emerson did just that. "Mm, this is exactly how I like my bacon. Extra crispy."

"Me too." Nick turned one of his super-wattage smiles her way. She cleared her throat and had to force her throat muscles to work again to swallow the bite of bacon she'd just taken. Man, that smile.

They ate in silence, but her mind was awhirl with thoughts.

Wow, this was delicious. Every bite savory and so tasty. She hadn't realized until coming home that she hadn't actually been tasting her food while she'd been caught up living in her fast-paced world. It had been more of a perfunctory deal. Eat to live. Since being home her tastebuds had come back to life. And she was moving towards the "Live to eat" category.

This meal was a prime example. The salty bacon. The buttery biscuit. The seasonings he'd sprinkled onto the eggs. Her mouth was savoring each one.

He was a hundred times more skilled than her in the cooking department, and an excellent multi-tasker. And to think he made this beautiful and delicious breakfast in the time it had taken them to have a short conversation.

A few bites later Nick asked the question she'd been hoping to avoid.

"Are you just home for a visit?"

Emerson swallowed a sip of coffee and rested her nearly empty plate on her lap. Should she tell him the truth about her mother? She hadn't wanted to tell her dates, but Nick was different. This didn't have the same first-date feeling that those had. She didn't see any reason to lie to him. "My mom is ill. It was sudden and unexpected, and I came home last week on extended leave to help out."

Nick's eyes crinkled at the edges when he said, "I'm sorry to hear that. Is she feeling better?"

Emerson shook her head after she took another sip of coffee. "It's Parkinson's actually, so she won't be getting any better. We just hope the meds she's taking will help with the current symptoms and she can continue to function at the level she's at now. She was quite active before, and is an artist, so she doesn't like having any physical limitations put on her."

Nick set a hand on her propped-up leg. His touch was comforting. "Again, I'm sorry, Emerson."

"Thank you. Me too," she whispered into her mug. Her eyes focused on the Great Blue Heron, watching the tufts of feathers on his chest move with the breeze. Then she stated what was in her heart, realizing she hadn't spoken much of this out loud before now. "I hate that this is happening to her. She's always been the rock in our family, mentally, physically and emotionally so strong. The diagnosis has been really hard on her. Hard on all of us. My brother and sister are both married with kids and live nearby, in Pensacola and Dauphin Island. But since they couldn't get away for an extended period of time, it was up to me. My brother and his family, as well as my sister and her family, are here this weekend, so I've had more time to get away. She doesn't need full-time care yet, but it's coming."

Emerson stopped, realizing she was just rambling. Her zest for the delicious meal he'd cooked dissipating with talk of her mother's health complications, she placed her plate on the small table beside her. Cupping the coffee mug between her two hands, she continued to focus on the water gurgling a few feet away.

Saying all that out loud was making it more and more real in her mind. Decisions needed to be made soon. Even with daily home health nurses Carolyn was going to need family close by to be with her, check on her. Her sister Deborah lived a few blocks away and already came by often, but her husband was also ailing, and that kept her from her sister's side full time.

"Do you miss your job in New York?"

Nick's question whipped her out of her reverie, turning her gaze back to him, she blinked. Other than thinking about her job last night when she was trying to sleep, she hadn't given it much thought lately. Clearing her throat, she said softly, "Actually, I've recently realized—as in just a moment ago—that no, I don't miss it." Emerson paused as she let that sink in. The silence and stillness of the air around her helped her breathe through that statement.

His eyebrows disappeared in the hair covering his forehead. "Wow, you look like you're blown away by that revelation."

"I am." Emerson sighed and closed her eyes. "My job is everything to me. I have a senior position and am highly valued in the company. I know that sounds like I'm tooting my own horn, but it's just a statement," she stated with a shrug. "I live and breathe that job. I never, ever thought about going on vacation, let alone taking a leave of absence. I thought they'd never get by without me." She huffed out a laugh. "Again, that sounds pretty egotistical.

"The first few days I was home I couldn't put my phone down or close out of my laptop. Even at the dinner table with Callie at Keel & Rudder I was replying to clients. Callie had to take my phone away. I didn't know how to step away from the job I was so invested in." She paused for reflection, her eyes snagging on the Great Blue as he took flight. His garbled grunts when he flew off made her chuckle. Emerson blinked and brought herself back to the present. She turned to Nick and shrugged. "Things have been quiet the last couple days. So, I guess they can get by without me."

Nodding, he said, "That's good. Gives you more time to focus on why you're here." Nick settled back in his seat, stretching his long, toned legs out, crossing his boat shoes on the rim of the fire pit.

"Yes, and something else that I just figured out last night. Focusing on myself." Wow, this talk with Nick was really bringing things to light. It was like she was in a therapy session.

He stopped his coffee mug halfway to his mouth. "What do you mean?"

What did she mean? All these thoughts from last night were pinging around in her head. "In New York, with everything being so fast paced, there wasn't much time for thinking about life, about priorities, about whether I was happy in my job or not." Emerson took a sip of coffee. "Being home, I've had so much more time to think. The quiet at my mom's house was almost deafening at first. The noise level in New York City is unreal, but you get used to it."

"How long did it take you to hear the silence?"

"I sat outside in the backyard, hoping the wide-open space would help that dull roar of noise in my ears not be so loud. It lessened after an hour or so. Finally, I started recognizing the sound of ships' horns blasting, crickets singing in the grass, Jet Skis bouncing on the waves. It was amazing."

"Sounds like you need this break as much as your mom needs you. She's lucky to have you." Nick shifted in his seat and put his empty plate on the counter behind him. He took her plate and put it there as well. "More coffee?"

"Yes, please."

Nick rose to retrieve the pot. "So you said your mom is an artist?"

"Yes, she paints. Acrylics mostly, but some watercolor. We've been getting her ready for the festival later this week."

"Ah, that's great. That's a big event." Nick re-filled their mugs and doctored them up just right before handing Emerson's mug to her.

"My mom is one of the founders of it."

"An OG, then," he said with a chuckle.

Emerson laughed and nodded in response. Her laughter ended in a grimace when she shift-ed her leg. Having it up on the milkcrate had been nice, but now her leg was stiff as hell and her foot was just starting to tingle.

"What? What's wrong?" Nick reached out and touched the milkcrate, looking ready to move it. "How's your foot feeling? Is this uncomfort-able?"

"A little. I think my foot has gone to sleep and my leg is stiff. I just need to move it." Emerson started to pull her foot down, but Nick stopped her with his hand.

"Let me help." He moved his chair closer and gently pulled her leg across his knees. His large hands wrapped around her bare calf, and she about jumped out of her skin. Not wanting to spill her fresh, full mug, she reached to set it on the side table.

His touch was so hot and heavy against her leg.

A welcomed heat. A welcomed heaviness.

His hands felt amazing on her skin. "Let me help loosen your muscles a little. I'm sorry I didn't have better seating for you."

"No, don't be, this has been fine. I just sat still too long. I was enjoying myself and got caught up." Emerson's words came out a little fast and she had no idea how she'd been able to string all those words together coherently when his hands were moving on her body. His fingers were digging into the muscles behind her knee and gliding deeply down her calf. This was better than any massage she'd ever gotten. Emerson bit her lip in reaction. He must have taken her action to mean his ministrations hurt so he eased up on the pressure.

When, really, she'd bitten her lip to keep from moaning in pleasure.

Her thumping heart was sending blood racing through her body, practically making her light-headed. *Get it together, woman. Lock it in.*

"Is this better?"

Emerson gulped, keeping herself from blurting out that it felt heavenly and that she never wanted him to stop. Instead, she nodded and forced herself to say, "Yes, it is." Then she tried to gracefully extract her only-slightly-numb leg from atop of his and put some distance between them so her heartrate would slow back to a normal rhythm. Nick guided her foot back down to the ground in front of her. Always the gentle-man. "Thank you. That feels much better."

Emerson had to get out of there. She was getting too comfortable, too turned on by his touch. She started to stand up. "I need to be getting back. We're having a family meeting—"

"Wait." Nick jumped up from his chair, reaching for her. "Here, lean on me."

Oh, she very much wanted to do just that. That was another reason she needed to put some distance between herself and this handsome hunk who was turning out to be not only sinfully sexy but sweet. She wasn't sure her heart could take much more of that today. She needed to fortify her walls to be strong enough to withstand his sex appeal when she was in his presence again.

If, not when, she corrected herself.

No guarantee she'd see him again.

Knowing the spark she was about to feel when she reached out and touched his arms would be like a lightning bolt straight to her sex, she had to do it anyway. She couldn't brush off his help just because she wanted to keep her body from combusting.

Emerson ground her teeth into her bottom lip—holding back the groan that was sure to erupt if she didn't contain it—as his hands wrapped around her waist, helping her to her feet. Her only-slightly-numb leg was only slightly better. Her foot tingled when she set it on the ground. Putting weight on it was going to be uncomfortable. But not impossible. She could do this.Hopefully without hobbling.

Taking a step toward the canoe was her intention. But what actually happened was she nearly went down, her tingly foot not supporting her. At. All.

Nick's fast reflexes kept her from landing on the concrete patio. "Hey! I've got you."

He brought her up to standing and Emerson gripped his arm with one hand and swiped her hair off her face with the other.

"Oh my goodness. Guess I wasn't ready to walk just yet." *Wow, that was close! I can't believe I just about fell on my face. How embarrassing!* Emerson didn't want to look into his eyes, worried that he'd think she was a complete klutz, so she stared at his lips instead.

Mistake.

Big mistake.

Her whirling, swirling hormones weren't ready for that image.

His lips were too hot to be staring at from this distance. Heat from his fingertips soaked into her skin as they pressed into her arms. Heat from his gaze that she knew was directed on her face, possibly even on her lips, brought more tingles to her body.

Subconsciously, her tongue swept out to wet her suddenly dry lips. She heard his slight inhale, watched his chest expand and knew exactly where he was focused.

Nervously, her eyes rose from his lips to meet his gaze. Hot, molten honey shown back at her. Suddenly, hot, molten honey oozed through her bloodstream in preparation for the kiss that she knew was coming.

Everything about this moment...the stillness in the air. The proximity of their bodies. The heat radiating off both of them. All were the perfect ingredients for an amazing first kiss.

Emerson couldn't handle the wait. Nick looked ready and willing, but also seemed to be hesitating. Maybe he was waiting for her to make the first move or to give him a sign. She decided this was going to be the best sign to let him know she also was ready and willing.

Lifting up on her uninjured foot, she leaned into his warmth and pressed her lips to his.

Instant heat.

Instant zings of electricity radiating from her lips.

They seemed to lean into each other at the same time. Their breath escaping as their lips molded to one another's. Nick's hands cupped her elbows, then slid down her back as her arms rose to wrap around his shoulders. Her fingers found their way into his hair of their own accord and she caressed the silky, shaggy strands.

Nick's tongue slipped along her lower lip, seeking permission, making this first kiss hot enough to relight the flame in the fire pit. Emerson graciously accepted his request by parting her lips and licked his tongue with her own before nibbling a little on his bottom lip, taking the kiss to a whole other level.

The awful squawking of the Great Blue Heron wrenched them out of the passionate haze they'd fallen into. The bird's irritated call came just in time to warn them of approaching kayakers from the east.

Nick grabbed her elbows as Emerson stepped back out of his embrace, stumbling awkwardly on her injured foot. There were fewer tingles now, but the pain from the cut made putting weight on it hard. Emerson kept her hands off him, trying to right herself and move out of his touch without appearing abrupt.

*Wow, just wow.*

That kiss was spellbinding. She needed to get out of his force field before she found herself back in his arms with her lips firmly and happily pressed against his.

Nodding her head, she indicated she was good to stand on her own. "Thanks. I'm good." Though she was far from good. Her insides were sizzling, her pulse as shaky as her hands. She gripped those shaky fingers into loose fists at her sides and took a deep breath.

That kiss just changed the whole ballgame.

She had no idea his sexy lips, the warmth of his body, the weight of his hands on her skin would make her feel like that. What was she going to do now? Nick the bartender was much more than meets the eye.

He was an enigma that intrigued her.

Intrigued her enough to make sure that she saw this man again.

And then, maybe she could get him to repeat that kiss.

# Chapter Eight

"Well, look who the cat dragged in!"

Nick looked up from cleaning a glass at that roar. He saw a face identical to his own grinning at him, then shifting that gaze around the bar. Cheers immediately filled the room.

"Hear, hear, Captain!"

There were many salutes and calls for toasts from the crowd of regulars. Tony seemed to be soaking it in as he made his way around behind the bar. Nick set the glass and rag down, moving towards his brother with his right hand out. Tony grasped it in a firm shake, then drew his brother into him for a mighty hug. Full of backslaps and laughter.

"Congrats, man. Proud of you," Nick said before pulling back. After one last hearty slap, he stepped back to let Tony take the lead and get back behind his bar.

Tipping his head back, Tony closed his eyes and shouted, "This round's on me!" A raucous cheer went up. Then he ran down the length of the bar high-fiving the folks enthusiastically leaning over it to celebrate with him. Nick couldn't help shaking his head. The damn fool just won a huge money prize from placing third in the regatta and here he was spending it on his regulars at his bar.

Nick started filling orders so the toasts could begin. Tony was roasted rather well by the customers that knew him the best. He took it all in stride, laughing and drinking along with them.

Tony sidled up to Nick, clapped him on the shoulder. "See, told ya I was the more likable of the two of us!"

Nick rolled his eyes at Tony's wink. A common reaction he'd had towards his brother for most of this life. "Hah, in your dreams, T."

Tony stepped away from him down the bar and started stacking dirty glasses on the counter behind the bar. "Damn, it's good to be back."

"I'm glad you're back." Nick filled the sink with hot, soapy water and started washing those glasses. "Now I can get back to just my day job. Working days *and* nights has been kicking my ass," he added, leaning back against the sink, wiping his hands on a clean towel.

Tony walked towards him, hand outstretched. "I appreciate you filling in for me, Nicky."

Nick shook his brother's hand, and nodded, looking him dead in the eye. Messages passed between them with no words. None were needed. They knew they'd do anything for each other.

Always had. Always will.

"Since you're more than a little tipsy, guess I can't pass the bar off to you tonight." Nick pushed his brother toward the end of the bar. "Go. Celebrate. Enjoy it because you're not likely to feel this good in the morning. And life goes back to normal tomorrow, T. This is my last shift," he shouted as Tony didn't hesitate and rejoined the crowd.

Tony was welcomed on the other side of the bar with open arms, wild cheers and high-fives. Everyone couldn't wait to hear the details of the race.

*Maybe Tony was the more likable of the two of us.*

At least he was more outgoing in the people department. Nick tended to enjoy spending his time surrounded by nature moreover than people. He had his close crew, made up of family and his co-workers, but that was it. Give him a kayak, a sailboat, or a paddle board and a body of water and he was in heaven. Put him in a crowd, especially one this loud, like tonight, and he got a little antsy.

Thinking about loud crowds made him picture New York City and how crazy the streets were. He'd only gone once as a teenager with his family, and he'd been overwhelmed immediately. He couldn't imagine living there and being a part of that racket 24/7. He had no idea how

Emerson could stand it. Or why she chose to live there instead of here.

Her image popped into his mind and his blood began to heat. Remembering the kiss they'd shared twisted his gut. His mind was already planning on doing it again.

They'd left shortly after, loading up into the canoe for the return trip to Paddlers Paradise. There weren't any awkward, uncomfortable silences and for that he was grateful. They didn't talk nonstop or anything, just a few words here and there. Mostly they both seemed content to take in the sights and sounds around them.

He thought about sneaking another kiss when he helped her to her car, but he decided on a hug instead. More warmth spread through his body, heating his belly as he remembered her leaning into him, her breasts pressed against his chest, slowly wrapping her arms around his back, her fingers moving over his shirt, squeezing him.

It was a long, extended hug, that felt as intimate as a kiss.

"What are you daydreaming about?" Tony tossed a bar rag at Nick's face, snapping him out of the memory. Snatching the dirty, wet towel off his face, he turned his frown on his brother. "Get me another shot of whiskey, would ya, barkeep?"

"Sure thing, boss." Then with a wicked grin directed at his slightly arrogant brother, he shouted, "How 'bout another round on Tony?!"

Nick laughed at the look on Tony's face when the crowd let out another cheer.

✳✳✳

Callie handed Emerson the last dirty plate that had been stacked on the island. She rinsed off the chunks then placed it in the last free space in the dishwasher. It was going to be a pain to unload this in the morning. But when the whole family was here and lots of meals were eaten it added up.

Sidney's family and Logan's family had stayed for an early dinner then headed to their respective homes about thirty minutes ago. Carolyn was upstairs in the bath, relaxing after a very active weekend with the grandkids around.

Boy, they were a loud bunch.

Callie and Emerson were left to clean up the mess. They did it in synch, reverting back to their teenage years when it was their day to be responsible for the dishes. Callie was over so often that she got put on the revolving list.

Since Callie had been grading papers earlier today, she'd missed the beginning of the family meeting. Emerson was ready for her questions. "So how did your mom take the idea of home health nurses visiting regularly?"

After putting the soap in and starting the dishwasher, Emerson leaned back against the counter and wiped her hands on a dishtowel. "She reluctantly agreed. Sidney looked up a local business and read off to her the types of things these nurses could help Mom do or what they might check for each visit. She'd also qualify for physical therapy to work on her hands."

"I'm sure she would appreciate that. Then there could be more painting in her future," Callie added, tossing a chew treat to Goose who was sitting so patiently like a good boy beside her before hopping onto a bar stool at the island. She swirled the sweet tea in her glass, mixing the melted ice into the drink.

"That's what convinced her. Mom isn't ready to change her lifestyle or give up her passions." Emerson paused, hating to say or think the next part. "But she's going to have to. Eventually. At least she'll need to modify them to start with."

Callie picked her glass up and met Emerson's gaze. "What about changing rooms? Did you bring that up?"

Emerson almost choked on the last swallow of her tea. Recovering, she said, "She had a very sassy, southern, emphatic response." Laughing, she repeated the words in a voice very similar to her mother's, emphasizing each word. "I will not!"

Callie practically snorted sweet tea through her nostrils. Emerson probably should have waited until Callie had finished her sip, but she couldn't help herself. Callie coughed and wiped her lips with the back of her hand. "Well, that sounds very much like Aunt Carolyn."

"I will not!" Emerson repeated, because she thought it was very much her mother. Very stubborn, very strong-willed. They'd asked her to think about it and that was the response she gave. She'd looked each of her children in the eye after making that statement. They'd sat in silence after that. Until one of the older grand-kids came screeching through the room, break-ing the tension.

Meeting adjourned.

"We'll keep working on her about that. It makes sense to move to the first floor," Emerson added.

"But, I get why she doesn't want to," Callie whispered thoughtfully. "Too many memories to leave behind."

"Then we might have to think about putting in an elevator or a chair lift on the stairs. It's not safe for her to go up and down those stairs daily."

"Even you could use one right now, with your foot the way it is," Callie pointed out.

"Exactly. Good thing my bedroom is on the first floor. But, I've got to go up and check on Mom in a minute."

Callie hopped off the stool and pushed it un-der the counter. Goose jumped up from where he'd been snoring by her feet. "Okay, before I go, I can't leave without asking about your date this morning. Was it another guy from the dating site?"

Emerson stopped mid-step. She'd been taking the dishtowel to the laundry room off the kitchen. Instant heat oozed through her body at the mention of her date. She'd had a hard time putting her feelings aside the rest of the day and focusing on her family. When all she wanted to do was close her eyes and remember everything about that kiss.

Their first kiss.

Their smoking-hot first kiss.

Mmm, guess with her thinking so much about it being their first, she was thinking that there was going to be a second.

"You gotta tell me," Callie pleaded, her excited voice pulling Emerson out of her pondering. "Was it a second date? With the dentist?"

Emerson turned around, debating whether to tell Callie anything about her date. About her feelings. They were all so new. Her hesitancy and whatever look she was projecting caused Callie to make the jump to Nick.

"Was it with Nick the bartender?"

The look on Callie's face was priceless. Somewhere between astonishment and confusion. She could relate. That's how she felt about her date with Nick the bartender. Nick the kayaker. Nick the multitasker. Nick the massage therapist. Nick the excellent kisser.

Emerson grinned and finally nodded. Callie let out a very high-pitched squeal and launched herself at Emerson. She wrapped her arms around her dancing cousin, laughing at her enthusiasm. Goose joined in, tail wagging, happy yips coming from his open mouth.

"Em! I'm so happy for you. How did this happen? How was it? Where did you go? I have so many questions..." Callie trailed off then let out a slightly quieter squeal, her hands gripping Emerson's arms tightly.

Emerson took a deep breath and fought to keep a goofy grin off her face. "He asked me at the end of the kayak trip."

Callie's mouth dropped open. "And you didn't tell me!" Callie's hands pulled on Emerson, shaking her with each word she shouted. Emerson chuckled.

"No, I didn't. I was kinda shocked, so I kept quiet about it."

Callie seemed to realize she was gripping Emerson's arms. "Sorry." She dropped her hands to her sides and laughed. "Where did you go?"

"We canoed up Blue Bottle Creek to his house and ate by the water. Remember when we were kayaking there was that place with that outdoor kitchen setup that had the big stone fire pit? That's his place. It's amazing."

"I remember that. Wow, what a beautiful place to live."

Emerson agreed. "It was a very peaceful spot."

"So, how was it?" Callie waggled her eyebrows. "Got any details you wanna share?"

Emerson hesitated, then grabbed Callie's shoulders and turned her toward the side door. Callie started protesting right away. She knew her silence wouldn't sit well with her cousin. Callie was a demanding woman when it came to gossipy details. She did teach eighth graders, so it kinda went with the territory.

Callie screeched to a stop, her hands gripping the countertop she was passing, holding her position. "Wait! You can't leave me hanging like that."

Emerson stopped pushing and decided on revealing only this. "Well, he sure can cook. He put together a full meal, getting all the parts completed at the same time. It was like magic."

"Nice." Callie nodded. She had better culinary skills than Emerson did but could still relate to the specialness of getting all items for dinner prepared at the same time. "Did you plan another date?"

"No, we didn't. But I know I'll see him again. I enjoyed our time together too much for that to be it." Emerson grinned and started toward the door again. When Callie had taken a step out the side door, Goose leading the way, Emerson added, with her eyes closed and a slight sway to her head, "Plus, that man's kiss was as hot as the open flame he cooked our bacon on." She shot her eyes back open and zeroed in on Callie's. "There's no way I can have just one."

Emerson closed the door on Callie's squeal and laughed all the way to the back steps off the kitchen. *Yep, definitely no way I can have just one.* Just like a potato chip. She had every intention of getting back into that man's orbit, she just had to figure out how.

Did she need to buy a kayak paddle? Was she interested in paddle board lessons?

Hmm, that might be fun, she thought as she hobbled up the stairs. On second thought, maybe she needed to wait for lessons until after her foot healed. She'd have to come up with a different idea in the meantime.

Carolyn was sitting in her bathrobe at her dressing table combing her hair when Emerson poked her head in her mother's bedroom door. "Hi, dear. I so enjoy hearing your laughter. What had Callie squealing so?"

Emerson grinned but didn't reveal the truth. Instead, she said, "She was telling me about the latest date she'd been on. How are you feeling?" she asked to change the topic.

"A little tired. But otherwise, the warm bath was soothing. I love having all my family here. It warms my heart. But it also wears me out," she admitted grumpily. Carolyn pulled the comb through her hair one last time then paused to look at her hand. The troublesome appendage began to tremble, the comb loose in her fingers as they tried to keep their grasp but could no longer squeeze together. The comb fell silently to the tabletop. Carolyn grasped her right wrist with her left fingers and sighed deeply.

Emerson hurried over and joined her on the bench. She squeezed her shoulders, resting her head next to her mother's and hugged her. "I'm so sorry, Mom. I wish this wasn't happening to you."

Carolyn leaned her head against Emerson's and closed her eyes, releasing another sigh. "Me too, dear, me too."

They stayed like that for more than five minutes before Carolyn made a move to stand. Emerson thought she felt her mother's legs trembling while she was sitting there, so she figured she needed more time to let the trembles pass before rising. Emerson helped her to bed.

"Thank you, dear."

"You're welcome, Mom. I'm glad I am here with you." Emerson sat in the chair beside her mother's bed and sighed. "I'm sorry I haven't come home that often—"

"Honey, there is nothing to apologize for." Carolyn pulled the covers up to her chest. "You have a busy job and a busy life in New York. I don't fault you for having a strong work ethic. You got that from your father."

That made Emerson smile. She got that from both of her parents.

"I could have made more time." She could have. She'd just been too damn busy to notice."

Nonsense. Don't give it another thought," Carolyn declared, reaching her hand out to grasp Emerson's. Emerson leaned forward and wrapped her fingers around her mother's hand, loving the feeling of her soft skin. Wrinkles and sunspots marred her tanned skin, but Emerson felt like each one of them told a story. "I'm just thankful for video chats. Now listen," she added, then hesitated. Her eyes searching deeply into Emerson's in the low light cast from the lamp on the bedside table. "I don't need a babysitter. I'm very glad you're here, but you don't need to be home with me all the time.

"I want you to spend time with Callie," she continued, "and go on dates, see some of your old friends while you're here. Make the most of it."

Emerson started to protest. That was why she was there. To be there for her. To take care of her. She wanted to spend time with her. But she also knew that her mother was used to living alone and liked her routine. She didn't want to be babied. She didn't want to acknowledge that her body was going to start fighting her mind soon, and that even though her mind was amazingly strong and courageous, her body was going to win out.

Emerson just nodded. "I love you, Mom." Grateful for all these special moments with her mother, she wasn't going to take a single one for granted. "Get some sleep."

"You too, baby girl. I love you."

# Chapter Nine

"More to the left."

Emerson shifted the painting she was holding above her head, searching for the clip she'd attached yesterday to the wires along the side canvas of her mother's tent.

Carolyn stood near the opening of the tent, her head tilted with her hand above her eyes to block out most of the sun's bright rays as she glanced toward the make-shift wall. Emerson looked over her shoulder to see if she'd gotten it in the right position and sighed when she saw her mother's smile. "There it is. You've got it. Thanks, Emmie."

"You're welcome, Mom. I think it looks spectacular in here," she added bending over to pick up the remainder of the pillowcases and packaging that the paintings had been stored in. She rolled them up and placed them in a nearly full tub at the back of the tent.

"I agree."

"Me too," Sidney added, stepping over from her side of the tent. Her long, strawberry blonde hair wrapped up in a twist with colorful clips sparkling in the sun. She wrapped an arm around her mother's shoulders and gave her a gentle squeeze. "I'm so glad we get to do this together this year, Mom. I feel like I'm next to royalty."

"Hah." Carolyn let out a laugh at that. The smile on her face brought joy to Emerson's heart. It felt wonderful to see her mother so happy. And being in her art world definitely made her happy.

Sidney squeezed her shoulder again and emphasized, "No, it's true, Mom. You're a founding member of the festival. That's a big deal."

"She's right," Emerson added, stepping up to give her a hug also. Carolyn put her arms around her daughters. She'd been lucky so far to maintain her height as she'd aged, keeping all three Taylor woman even around mid five feet. "It is a big deal. We are so proud of you, your artwork and how you've helped others with their art over the years. You're a great contributor to this town and to this field."

"Thank you, honey. Those are kind words." Carolyn turned and moved over to her director's chair. Her daughters saw that she got settled then Sidney went back to supervise Dave hanging up her final two paintings with ten minutes to spare for the opening bell of the 35th Annual Art Festival.

Their shared booth was the third one in line on the entrance row, facing east. The morning sun shone in highlighting their brightly colored paintings hanging throughout. Sidney was practically beaming as bright as the sun. Her sister loved this event and Emerson was so glad that they were sharing a double booth this year.

She hadn't actually been involved with this for the last twelve years. Not since she'd left for college. Growing up, they were always there. Helping haul in, set up, then load out when it was over. She and her siblings would always run free throughout the multi-day festival, enjoying the sights, sounds and smells.

Taking in a deep breath now, she could detect the sweet scent of roasted cinnamon-sugared pecans on the light breeze. It was a scent that always brought up happy memories for her. She'd have to follow her nose over to that booth soon and get started on all the tasty treats that she remembered fondly.

Once her mother was settled, she'd set off and tour the other booths.

The weather was stunning today. April in south Alabama can be iffy. It can still be cold in the 50s, or it might have already hit a stretch of highs in the upper 70s. It just depended on the day. Luckily today was somewhere in the middle. Sunny, breezy and mid-60s. Perfect for getting outside and strolling through an art festival.

Emerson began to hear extra voices and realized that the gates had opened. She got to work playing assistant hostess as visitors began wandering in. Carolyn held court from her chair and only got up to visit with close friends. She sold a painting within the first hour. Sidney was getting lucky as well with several sales on her prints and her notecards.

There was so much talent oozing from both of them. Emerson was very proud. "Nice job, ladies," she praised when their booth was momentarily empty of guests after a few hours of a steady stream. Sidney hugged her and then their mother, happiness and joy radiating from her.

"Take a break, Emmie," Carolyn said, then sipped water from the bottle sitting beside her chair. "You don't have to hang around here the whole time. Go and see the other vendors. Enjoy some of those delicious roasted pecans."

"Oooh, please bring me back some," Sidney exclaimed with a grin, her dimples winking. "Those were always my favorite treat here."

"I'll bring those plus some lunch—"

Sidney shook her head. "No need, Dave can grab us something to eat. You just enjoy strolling around for a bit. No rush," Sidney pushed. "Go, sister. Take your time."

Emerson set off in search of the roasted pecans first. Luckily, that booth wasn't too far away. The man serving up the pecans recognized her and gave her an extra helping to give to her mother. "Yum, thank you. I've been smelling these for a few hours now and couldn't wait to break away to get my hands on some."

"Enjoy!"

Emerson popped a cluster in her mouth as soon as he put the bag of nuts in her hand. She tipped him extra and headed in the direction of the live music. A fiddle played alongside a guitar, and it sounded amazing. She stood and watched with a crowd of others as the two performed on a small stage. The age of the performers surprised her. They had to be in high school. She was surrounded by so much talent, it was incredible.

When the duo took a break, Emerson was drawn to the sound of windchimes tinkling in the light breeze. Heading in their direction, she admired the collection of sounds. The booth boasted wind chimes of all sizes. Resting atop the metal chimes were wooden sculptures of sea creatures and mermaids. A splash of color was added to each wooden piece, leaving most of the natural beauty of the wood to shine through.

"These are beautiful," she said to the woman in the booth. "Did you make all these?"

"Yes, ma'am. It was my daddy's business, but I started helping him when I was in high school and continued carving after he passed. I've been selling here at the festival for the last five years."

"You do beautiful work. I'm here helping my mother and sister in their booth, so I'll be here the whole time. I will definitely be back by," Emerson promised.

"Here's my card," the woman offered, holding out a business card. "In case you don't get a chance during the festival. I'm local and have a shop here in town. It's right next door to the pizza place on Bay Avenue."

Emerson accepted and pocketed the card before nibbling on another cluster of nuts. She happily crunched as she strolled along the booths on this side of the street, planning to double back and check out the other side. There were hand-painted metal signs with funny sayings that had her chuckling, watercolor paintings of beach scenes and animal life along the coast, as well as metal lawn ornaments, some standing at least eight feet tall.

She paused at a booth selling sea glass jewelry. The sun glinted off a sea-green pendant on a silver chain resting on a prop. Pretty.

"That color matches your eyes."

Emerson looked up at the speaker. A woman her mother's age stepped out from behind a table and pointed to the piece she'd been admiring. "That's a beautiful piece. I love walking the beaches each morning looking for bits of sea glass."

"Do you find a lot here?" Emerson touched a fingertip to the pendant, loving how slick it was. Sea glass was such a cool thing to find. It was just ordinary broken glass that had been tumbling over the rough sand for an extended period of time and became smooth. Thinking of sea glass made her think of the blue bottles Nick talked about on the kayak trip.

And a little heat rolled through her stomach when she pictured his handsome face.

"No," the woman said, interrupting her daydream, "not unless there's been a storm. Rough waves seem to wash up a lot of treasures. That piece was found on a Florida beach, but still the Gulf Coast."

"I'll take it." Emerson smiled, deciding on a whim. Looking at it brought her joy. Thinking about Nick when she first saw it might have played into her decision.

The brightness of the woman's smile matched hers. She started to reach for a box, then hesitated. "Would you like to wear it? If not, I can wrap it up for you."

"Wear it, definitely." She almost felt giddy inside. She couldn't remember the last thing that she'd bought for herself simply because it made her happy. In New York, she bought business suits and new slacks or skirts, definitely shoes, but that was all for work. Even her exercise clothes were just because. She went for basic colors and designs, not choosing a fun pattern or bright color because it was pleasing to the eye.

"It will look amazing on you. It's the perfect length with the shirt you're wearing."

Emerson set the bag of nuts down on the countertop, then accepted the necklace and opened the clasp. Using the oval mirror beside her, she placed the necklace on her chest and fastened the clasp behind her neck, thankful that she'd worn her hair up today, making it easy to connect the ends.

Straightening it, she pressed the sea glass against her skin and admitted the woman was correct. It looked good with her scoop-neck top. "Thank you so much. This is beautiful."

"Thank you," the woman insisted. She returned Emerson's bank card with her receipt and handed Emerson her business card. "In case you find you'd like another piece of my jewelry."

"I will absolutely keep you in mind." Emerson gathered her things and smiled again. "Enjoy your day."

She let her fingers slide over the glass as she stepped back out into the sun. There was a little spring to her step. It was silly sometimes how buying something as frivolous as a necklace can bring such joy to her heart. Her mind was still consumed with thoughts of how happy this simple necklace was making her that she didn't fully register the sound she heard right away.

After a few more steps and another crunch of sweet pecans, she heard it again. Stopping her in her tracks. Looking to her right, Emerson searched the area. Once the walkers passed by and cleared her view, she found the source of that little yelp.

A sweet, little puppy standing on its back legs, front paws leaning against a make-shift wire fence. Its ears bounced with each yelp it let out. Its pink tongue lobbed out sideways from its open mouth.

*Oh my heart.*

Emerson walked over to the pet adoption booth, drawn actually, by an invisible force. "Well, aren't you just the cutest little attention-grabber."

Laughter brought her eyes up and off the pup. A young woman stood beside the fence, chuckling. "I wish I could say I trained her to do that, but it was totally instinctual."

"Well, it worked, little one," she said squatting down to be on level with the pup. "You got my attention." She reached out and stroked those bouncing ears. Emerson's heart felt like it was thudding extra loud in her chest. Heat radiated from her heart up through her chest and neck, warming the new sea glass necklace. This pup was adorable.

"Here, I can hold that for you if you'd like to pick her up," the woman offered, holding her hand out.

Emerson couldn't help the side-eye that she sent the woman's way. Her smile only grew bigger, her hand still held out. "Oh, I really shouldn't, but I'm totally going to because I can't resist this cute little face. Sucker," she whispered to herself. Then Emerson let out a disgusted sigh—disgusted at herself for giving in to this little ball of fluff—and handed over her bag of pecans.

Emerson stood up and reached down, lifting the pup into the air. Her fur was so soft and fluffy. What an angel. Drawing her in close, Emerson was greeted with happy yelps and wet licks to her face, in her ear and down her neck as she cuddled the pup in close. The joyous giggles erupting from her couldn't be stopped. There was no way. Emerson just held on tight as the pup squirmed to get closer to her. "Oh, sweet pea, you are such a joy."

"He's already in love with you."

Emerson's laughter abruptly stopped, and she quickly looked to her left, startled out of her puppy haze by the sound of the man's voice who'd starred in her dreams last night.

Nick Valentino.

She turned her body toward him and took in his wide smile and dark sunglasses, her heart beating faster now for a completely different reason.

"Hi. You startled me. I was totally lost in the zone. It's a she actually," Emerson added, then had to clear her throat before continuing, "and the feeling is mutual." She pulled her gaze away from Nick's handsome face to focus on the squirming bundle of energy in her arms. "But I live in New York City." She shook her head. "In an apartment, and I work way too many long hours. There's just no way I could get a dog."

Emerson kissed the pup on the nose and accepted even more licks before settling her over one arm and traced her soft ears with her fingertips. Inside, her heart was melting at the deep, chocolate brown eyes looking lovingly up at hers. She laughed at the happy yelps that just kept coming. "I'm sure this sweet girl is going to find a loving home today, no doubt about it."

Nick held out his hands. "May I?"

"You? Are you in the market for a dog?" Emerson only hesitated a moment before shifting the wiggling puppy into his large hands. Gorgeous hands. Strong hands that had held her leg, massaging her sore muscles. Gentle hands that had wrapped around her, sliding across her back when they'd kissed.

"I could be—" His words were cut off by lightning-fast licks from the pup straight into his open lips. His words turned to laughter and Emerson felt that rich sound reverberate deep inside. The sight of his smile—bright white teeth against tanned skin, outlined by strong, masculine, rose-colored lips—coupled with his laugh just about did her in. She felt heat flush her skin, from head to toe.

She'd thought he was sexy before, but him smiling and laughing while holding the sweetest little fluffy Lab pup was just too much.

She wasn't sure her heart could take much more.

She watched with just the slightest bit of envy as his large, tanned fingers caressed the pup's head. The feel of his hands on her as they'd kissed had felt amazing. Emerson shook her head slightly, pulling herself out of that tantalizing memory, worried she might be drooling or something else foolish.

"I think she's in love with you too. Huh, how quickly she switched her allegiance." Emerson reached up and petted the pup's back, her fingers accidentally—but was it, really?—touching his. Emerson felt electricity zing up her arm. She liked it so much, she did it again. Touching his fingers with hers as she petted the puppy.

Emerson watched him pull in a deep breath and tilt his head, his gaze directed on her. Did he feel it too? She wished she could see his eyes behind those dark lenses. "I think she knows good people when she sees them."

Thankfully, Emerson was standing so close because the puppy decided right then to jump back into her arms. With a yelp of her own, Emerson quickly caught the fluffy little rocket. Nick still had one hand on the pup, so she wouldn't have fallen, but Emerson decided that was too close to disaster and kept a firm grip on the little fluff ball.

"Easy, girl," Nick crooned, stepping closer, his hand remaining on the pup's back, massaging her. "Easy."

What was he doing to her? Could his voice get any sexier? She could practically feel the heat radiating off his body, he was standing so close.

"So, you're in the market for a dog," Emerson said, bringing them back to the topic from a few minutes ago, pulling her mind off the sexy tone of his voice, definitely not picturing him speaking those words to her. Nope she wasn't. Well, maybe for half a second.

"I've been thinking about it."

"Your spot on the creek would be perfect for this water-loving baby." Emerson held up one of her paws. "Look at these big feet. She's gonna be a big girl. And probably a really good swimmer."

"My place would be perfect," he said slowly, as if just realizing how right this was. "She'd love playing in the creek."

Emerson could almost see the images in his mind that she was planting with her words. He was seriously thinking about it. This pup would be so lucky to have him as her dad. He'd be a really good dog dad.

"And you could take her kayaking," Emerson added, burying her nose into the pup's neck, loving the licks she received in turn.

"I bet she'd be a great kayaking dog." His smile was steady, and he was nodding ever so slightly. Yep, he was picturing it.

"Then this sounds like a perfect match. How serendipitous of you to run into us here today." Emerson leaned her head to the side, just now making the connection that he was here at the festival. "Are you just browsing the festival or are you working?"

"Working. Paddlers Paradise has a booth. We have gear for sale and guided trip packages and lessons, etc. You should come by and take a look."

"I think I will. What are you going to do about this little love bug?" She turned her attention back to the pup in question.

Nick looked over at the woman who was still holding Emerson's bag of pecans, her expression that of a person watching a romantic comedy. Emerson bit her lip to keep from laughing. Their encounter did seem like it would make a perfect meet-cute in a rom com.

"Can I take her now?" Nick asked.

The woman beamed. "Yes, sir. I just need you to fill out some paperwork. I'm so happy she's going to be with a loving family. And you say you live on a creek? Even better. You'll need to get her a life jacket," she warned. "She'll likely be fearless, especially after that death-defying leap she just made."

"Luckily, I own Paddlers Paradise and can get all the gear I need."

Emerson's breath caught in her lungs. What? He's the owner? Had she heard him correctly? *I thought he just worked there. Has he been lying to me all along?*

Nick must have read the questions in her expression because he immediately whipped his head back around and opened his mouth, then closed it again without speaking. A frown furrowed her brow as she thought about what that meant. He owned Paddlers Paradise. He wasn't just an employee. Was he really a bartender too? Why would he do both jobs if he owned a store? She was really confused, and it must have showed.

Thinking she might need to take a step back from where she'd been headed, she quickly handed the pup over to Nick and said, "I need to get back to my mother's booth. I'll have to stop by your booth another time, Nick." She couldn't resist petting the pup once more before physically stepping back from this enigma of a man.

Turning to the woman, she said, "Thank you for letting me pet her. She's adorable. And she's found a wonderful home with this guy here," she added with a smile. Backing up, she turned with a wave, but stopped when the woman called out.

"Miss, you forgot these." She held out the bag of pecans and Emerson quickly grabbed them, thanking her. She paused and looked at Nick directly in the sunglasses one more time before heading back.

# Chapter Ten

"I screwed up," Nick announced when he returned to his booth, the adorable, squirming pup held firmly in his hands. They'd given her a pink collar with white daisies on it and a thin leash, which he held loosely in his grip.

"What? How?" Amber jumped up and came around from behind their table. "What are you talking about? And who's this?" She reached out to pet the puppy and received many licks in return. "Hi, baby."

"This is my new dog. I just adopted her," he said, knowing he sounded distracted, but couldn't help it. His mind was consumed with the look on Emerson's face when she'd left.

"What? That's wonderful. Oh, she's adorable!" she exclaimed rubbing the puppy's ears.

Nick handed the puppy over to Amber and started pacing. He looked around, thankful the booth was empty for the moment.

"Remember when you told me that it wasn't good to start a relationship off with a lie?"

"I do recall that, yes," she said while dodging puppy licks to her mouth. "This is about the pretty redhead, isn't it?"

Nick nodded. Then ran his hands through his hair in frustration. He propped his sunglasses on top of his head and started pacing.

"What happened?"

Nick sighed. Frustrated with himself. "She was at the pet adoption booth when I spotted her. I was coming back from getting lunch and happened to see her getting mauled by this cute little thing. She looked so happy, so in love with it. So I stopped to talk to her."

Amber paused in petting the puppy. Her gaze bored into his. "Nick, you didn't get this puppy just because she was in love with it, did you?"

"What? No." Nick jerked his gaze away, shaking his head. "I've been thinking about getting a dog for a while now. I have the perfect life for it. And neither of us will be lonely," he added tapping the puppy on her nose.

"So what happened? How did she learn that you li—"

"Lied? Well, the woman was telling me I needed to get this dog a life jacket since I lived on the creek, and I said, well, it's a good thing I own Paddlers Paradise, I can get all the gear I need." He dragged his hands through his hair again and started back up pacing the small open area of their booth. He stepped past kayaks and around life jackets hanging from rods overhead. "She looked a little shocked. And maybe a little hurt. I didn't want her to hear it like that. I want-ed to tell her myself. I don't know why I haven't already. We went on a date Sunday. I had plenty of time to tell her that I'd misled her by letting her think I was a bartender and an employee here. I don't even know why I kept it from her in the first place," he groaned, scrubbing his hands down his face.

Amber stepped in front of him, to stop him in his tracks. "Okay, so it sounds like you're just going to need to explain to her that you omitted a couple of things, not that you outright lied."

"How am I supposed to do that?" His eyes went wide, pleading with her to give him the answer. "Just before, I'd asked her to come here to check out our booth. Maybe I would have told her then. But as soon as she found out, she quickly left, saying she had to get back to her mom's booth."

Nick stopped pacing and focused on Amber, who continued to cuddle the puppy. The puppy who was finally calming down, who looked so content she was actually falling asleep in Amber's arms.

"Must be this baby's nap time," Amber chuck-led, nuzzling the puppy's head with her nose. "Don't worry, Nick, you'll think of something. It's just an omission. It's not like you were out to trick her, right?" Amber asked, then smiled over at a visitor who'd just entered the booth.

Nick mentally shook himself. *I have to get my head back in the game. Return it to business mode and set aside all thoughts of Emerson right now.*

Nick focused on the man who was looking at the kayaks and greeted him. "How are you doing today, sir? Are you in the market for a new kayak or paddle board?"

The man shook Nick's hand and said, "A kayak, yes, but no, not a paddle board. I definitely don't have the balance for that," he added with a chuckle. "My wife and I just moved here from upstate and have kayaked a few times on the lakes up there. What do you suggest for an old, moderately adventurous couple like us?" He pointed across the lane and said, "There's my wife over there, talking to the artist about that giant metal blue crab she's hoping to put in our backyard."

Nick smiled and showed him the tandem they had in the booth. "I have this one here. If there's a particular color you're interested in, I also have plenty more back at the shop."

"A tandem's a good choice," the man agreed. "We tried kayaking separately once and it didn't turn out so good."

"This is a great kayak for paddling along the shore, up the creeks and out on the bay on flat, calm days. It's a sit-on-top, ocean-going kayak so you're likely to get wet, but they are sturdy and do well with a little extra tipping."

The man patted Nick on the shoulder and smiled up at him. "Thank you, son. I'm very interested. I'll get my wife over here to get her opinion on the color and we'll go from there." He started to turn away, then added, "We'll need life jackets and paddles too."

"We've got everything you ne—" Nick's eyes shifted off the man and snagged on Emerson leaning against the post of their booth, surprise cutting off his words. He pulled in a breath and continued, "Everything thing you need. Even guided group kayaking trips around the area."

How had he not seen her approach? Her eyes sparkled in the sunlight, bright and blue today, matching her teal blue top. Sunshine glinted off a gleaming piece of sea glass resting against her chest. Her gorgeous red hair, even though it was up in a ponytail, was still long enough to fall over her shoulder. As he continued to stare at her, she shifted on her sneaker-covered feet. His eyes moved back to hers and the light blush on her cheeks combined with the shifting feet made him think she was a little unsure of herself.

"I CAN ATTEST that he's a really excellent tour guide." Emerson wasn't sure she'd made the right move by seeking him out. She'd run off earlier—yep, run—she'd admit it to herself. Simply because she'd been caught off guard. After thinking it through for a few minutes, she realized she'd rather have answers than wonder for the rest of the night.

So here she was. Putting herself out there. Standing before him, hoping they could discuss what she'd just learned and see where that left them.

Was her heart beating overly loud? Yep.

Were her lungs working overtime to keep her breath nice and even, controlled? Yep.

Nick blinked. His lips curled up on one side before he turned his attention back to the man he'd been talking to. "Uh, yes, Emerson went with us on a kayak trip up Blue Bottle Creek just last week."

Emerson stepped forward into the booth, remembering the trip made her think about her foot. Luckily, the pain had subsided over the last few days, and she could walk without a hitch in her step. "Nick is very knowledgeable about the history of the area. And with identifying the local wildlife for the folks on the tour. And he's got pretty good first aid skills too," she added with a grin and a wink. "Just in case."

"Thank you, miss, for your testimonial," the man said with a smile. "We'll have to check that out."

A woman behind Nick, who was holding his sleeping pup, stepped forward into the conversation. "We have a list here of all our upcoming adventures if you're interested." She handed the pup off to Nick, and a piece of paper to the man.

Nick accepted the sleeping pup and curled her into his arm. Emerson watched the sleeve of his T-shirt pull tight as his muscles bunched when he shifted the pup into a good position. He looked so sexy holding that sweet baby. Emerson's heart expanded with lust.

He looked so damn sexy, even if he was only wearing a blue t-shirt bearing his company's name, khaki cargo shorts and dark blue sneakers. His work attire was the complete opposite of any other man she'd dated in New York. Custom-fit, sleek business suits were the norm. They were expected in her line of work.

Life was so much more casual here. And she realized she liked it. She didn't actually miss wearing power suits and heels each day. For the last week and a half, she'd only worn shorts, tops and either sports sandals, deck shoes or sneakers. Her friends in New York wouldn't even recognize her. Thankfully, the top of her foot was healing nicely, and she wasn't required to put on heels for another couple of weeks.

Once the man left, Nick turned to her and said, "Hi." His voice, usually deep and confident, sounded a little hesitant. Even his eyes looked uncertain, like he was worried about how she'd left things when she'd dashed away.

"Hi," she echoed, tucking her fingers into the back pockets of her shorts. She had to, in order to keep from reaching out to stroke the pup. And him.

"Wanna take a walk?" he asked.

"Sure." Emerson nodded and led the way toward the water.

"How's your mom doing? Is she feeling well today? Is she having good sales?" Nick fell into step beside her.

"That's sweet of you to ask." She bumped his arm with her shoulder. Then unable to resist for another second, she reached out to stroke the pup's incredibly soft ear. "She's doing well today. I think all the action might be distracting her from the pain, so she's not letting it show. But she's here, she's in her element and she's loving it. So many people have come by to see her. Past art students, current students, and many friends in the community. She's sold several paintings and it's only day one," Emerson added with a laugh.

"That's great. I'm glad she's feeling well and enjoying herself."

"Thank you."

They fell into a silence, not a strained one, but she could sense a change in his demeanor. Her being here, walking with him, talking with him was reassuring him. She needed to give him more reassurance through her words. But how was she supposed to ask him why he lied to her? Was she just supposed to come out and say it, point-blank?

When they reached the beach, they turned south and started walking along the shoreline. The tide was currently low, so the beachfront was wide. Driftwood, oyster shells and other debris had been left behind on the dry sand by the high tide. They walked along the wrack line.

Emerson's eyes wandered along the line, as they usually did, since that's where the best treasures could be found. Mermaid's purses, crab carapaces, catfish skulls, sand dollars. The possibilities were endless. As kids, she and her siblings would always compete to see who could find the coolest objects whenever they spent time on the beach.

"I'm sorry for leaving so abruptly," she started, thinking it best to just get that part out of the way. "Hearing what you said just caught me off guard."

"No, you don't have to apologize. I do. I'm sorry. I didn't mean to not tell you—"

"That you're a business owner?" She looked over at him, watching his reaction. He looked abashed. His cheeks turning red. Or that could be the sunlight and warmth brightening his cheeks.

"Yes, and not just an employee."

Emerson kicked a pinecone. "Why did you keep that from me? What was the point?"

"Actually, it started back when we first ran into each other at the Keel & Rudder. When you thought I was *just* a bartender." He bumped her shoulder with his arm and smiled down at her. "You kinda had this attitude that being a bartender was a little beneath you and you were blowing me off."

Emerson let out a sound but cut herself off. She started to say something, then shut her mouth. Looking down at the sand, she shook her head, mortified that he'd interpreted that from her previous behavior.

"By the way, here's another shocker," he taunted, laughter in his voice. "I'm not a bartender either."

She stopped short and looked up at him, eyes wide, mouth open wider. "What? Then just who the hell are you?"

Nick chuckled and held out his hand to her. "I'm Nick Valentino, the proud owner of Paddlers Paradise for the last eight years." His words warmed her heart and Emerson grinned at his introduction. Then she put her palm against his and squeezed his fingers. Rough calluses slid against her skin, causing a delicious friction.

"I'm a tried-and-true outdoorsman," he continued, "who is very attuned with nature and the history of the area that became my home back when I was seventeen years old. I love being on the water and I love exploring places around here that few have ventured to. I love pizza," he drawled with a wink, "grilling burgers on my deck, making gourmet breakfasts in my outdoor kitchen, drinking beer under the stars, and," he glanced down, "I think I love this little ball of fluff right here, snoozing in my arms."

Emerson sighed and grinned at the pup. "Well, Nick Valentino, it's nice to officially meet you." She gave his hand a squeeze, then raised and lowered her hand in a one-count shake. "So tell me more about you not being a bartender, because I specifically recall you behind a bar, tending it."

He chuckled. "It was my brother's bar. I was filling in for him." Nick shifted his hand, sliding his fingers around until they were laced with hers. Then he began walking again. His hand practically swallowed hers, but it felt nice. It felt right. "He's part owner of the Keel & Rudder. He just got back from a sailing regatta down in the Caribbean. For two weeks I was pulling double shifts. Working at the shop during the day and bartending at night. You just caught me during that time."

Wow. Now she understood why he had two jobs. "That had to be exhausting."

"It was. I'm not a night owl. I'm usually in bed before ten most days," he said sheepishly.

The puppy started to rouse on his arm. She lifted her head and let a squeaky yawn. Her little pink tongue arching out of her mouth. She blinked her eyes and shifted her gaze between them. Then, it was like she recognized them, and started yelping and jumping in his arm. He let go of Emerson's hand to get a secure hold on her. Since they'd already witnessed her death-defying leap, she thought that was a smart idea. He lowered the pup to the ground and let her go. "What do you think of this? It's sand. And that's the bay. You're gonna love the water, little pup."

The pup took off, nose to the ground, her ears flopping with each hop of her back legs.

She darted off, then raced back to them. Nick squatted down and ruffled her fur when she came close. Emerson joined him, wrapping her arms around her knees, laughing over the pup's joy at the new experience.

"You look so happy and carefree," he said.

That brought her up short. Looking over at him, her smile was slow to grow. Taking stock, she realized she felt happy and carefree. Here she was, in the middle of a workday, wearing cut-off shorts, hanging out on a beach with a deliciously handsome man, laughing at a sweet little puppy whose nose was covered in sand.

"Thank you. I feel that way."

"You sound shocked."

"A little. This—" she pointed to the beach and water "—isn't how I spend my typical workday. This isn't even how I'd say I vacation because I don't vacation. I'm a work-a-holic who doesn't take time to listen to the waves lap the shore, or watch a puppy experience the beach for the first time." She laughed. "I feel happy. In this moment, I feel ridiculously happy." Emerson reached a hand out and placed it on his forearm, squeezing the firm muscles beneath her fingers. "So thank you. Thank you for noticing. Thank you for mentioning it, so I would take the time to self-reflect and notice that about myself.

"Being home has changed me. I was so in tune with Lawson Financial, the stock market, my clients' needs nearly 24/7, that I completely neglected my own." Silence followed her words. Even the puppy was quiet, just sniffing the sand calmly. She glanced at Nick beneath her lashes, slightly embarrassed about sharing all that.

After a few minutes, he spoke. "When I first saw you at the restaurant with your cousin, you were a different person. I could tell that you were fresh out of New York City and still had that high-frequency mentality of the big city going on. You seemed anxious and were always glancing at your phone."

Emerson chuckled. "Until Callie snatched it from my hand. I needed that intervention though. In New York my phone is on 24/7 and attached to me. I'm 100 percent involved with what's going on with my company. Taking this leave of absence was extremely hard and painful at first. But as the days have passed, I'm finding it a lot easier. I haven't actually thought about my job since late last week."

She paused to take a deep breath and released it slowly. "I'm breathing easier. There's no tension in my neck and shoulders that I have lived with daily. It had become so common that I was starting not to even notice it anymore. Coming here where the pace is slower, there's less background noise—at least blaringly loud noises—here it's more like the sound of the waves, the cry of the gulls, the bark of a dog..." She turned her face toward him and rested her cheek on her knees. "I didn't even know how much I missed this place."

"It's a pretty great place," Nick agreed. "I'm glad your body is relaxing, letting you feel happiness in everyday things. And there's no way you wouldn't feel joy in the presence of this cutie."

Nick tickled the puppy's tummy when she flopped over onto her back, exposing her pink belly to him. Then she jumped up and launched herself at Emerson. She laughed and grabbed the puppy out of the air, hoping to avoid some of the sand on her paws, but hey, what did it really matter. The pup licked her face and neck, her little puppy teeth snagging on her earlobe.

"Yowch! Hah, she's got some little shark teeth. You better be ready for that." She stood up and cuddled the pup to her, placing kisses on the top of her head. "You're adorable. I'm so glad you got her today. Happy 'Gotcha Day,' baby girl!"

Nick rose and pulled his phone from his pocket and snapped a photo. Emerson posed, grinning at the camera, the puppy snuggled under her chin. She was pretty sure he even snagged an action shot of the pup's tongue swiping up across Emerson's nose. He laughed and put his phone back in his pocket.

"Here, want me to take a pic of you with her? She is your dog, after all."

Nick traded his phone for the pup. She looked so small in his arms. He cradled her like a baby on her back. She stretched up and scored a lick on his chin. Emerson captured that one. Then he smiled directly at her. Um, at the phone, but she felt that smile all the way to the middle of her bones. It caused heat to radiate from her core.

"What are you going to name her?" Emerson asked, to bring her mind back to the moment. She found a stick beside her and held it up. When Nick set the pup down on the sand, Emerson tossed it a few feet away from the puppy. She chased after it and pounced on it.

"That's a good question," Nick mused. "She's going to love her new life, being in the water at the house, here on the beach, going on kayak trips with me—"

"Oh, absolutely she will," Emerson agreed. "Should her name be water related? Maybe Kai or Creek? No, those sound like boy names," she added with a shake of her head.

"Sailor? Or Sandy?"

Emerson watched the pup follow the waves as the water rose and fell on the sand, then stop and bark at the water. Suddenly, she lost interest and returned to the stick Emerson had tossed to her. She flopped down and chewed on it for all of five seconds, before she hopped up once more and wrapped her little puppy teeth around the stick and started dragging it back to them.

Emerson laughed. "Living up to her namesake already. What a good retriever you are, little girl," she cooed and rubbed the puppy's head when she dropped the stick at Emerson's feet.

"What about Styx?"

Emerson frowned. "You mean, like the band? Or do you mean, like this?" she asked holding up the sandy, wet stick.

Nick shook his head. "Not the band. And only partially the stick, simply because of the spelling, but it would be implied. But Styx, as in the river."

"What river?" Emerson's frown deepened, a furrow forming between her brows.

"Didn't you go tubing on Styx River?" When she shook her head in response, his mouth fell open. "I thought it was a rite of passage for any high schooler in the area. You didn't go tubing with your friends or your family?"

"No. We lived on the bay. We floated on rafts out behind our house all the time."

"You were so lucky." His voice sounded dreamy. She watched as Nick lifted his phone from his pocket and opened it.

"What are you doing?"

"Starting a 'Gotta-Do List' for you. I'm putting 'Tube on Styx River' as the first item."

Her smile grew when she looked up from his phone. "I like that. What else should go on there?" Emerson tossed the stick again to the pup who'd been busy following a hermit crab. She quickly pounced on the stick and started gnawing on it.

"Have you been kayaking through the delta?"

Emerson only shook her head. "No."

"Have you camped on raised platforms in the delta?"

"Um, definitely, no. Too many alligators. Raised platforms or not."

He started typing again, presumably adding those to the list. Nick stopped typing when the puppy brought the stick to him this time, dropping it at his feet. "Styx. See it's a sign," he said grinning like a fool. "Hey, Styxy, how do you like that name?" He scratched her ear and grabbed the stick. She let out the cutest little growl and held on to the stick. "Hah, little one. You're a tough girl, I see. Styx, you're gonna love being a stick chaser and fetcher, I just know it."

"Styx, huh? What a fun and unusual name." Seeing him squatted down on the beach, tossing sticks to this incredibly small and lovable puppy made her heart so full. "But perfect for a retriever."

"It is," he agreed and looked up, their eyes meeting over the stick he held between them. "And I just realized I'm now a dog dad and I'm responsible for another living being. I have absolutely no idea what I'm doing."

Emerson let out a deep, belly laugh in response to his extremely honest statement. "I'm sorry," she forced out between laughs. "I'm not laughing at you—"

"No, you're laughing with me, right?" Then his laughter joined hers and the pup raced over and leapt up, dragging her sandy feet all over his chest and legs. Nick didn't even hesitate, he just picked her up and snuggled her sandy body to his chest, rubbing his cheek on the top of her head. "I deserve it. I'm thinking that laughing about this predicament is much better than crying woe-is-me. But I would like your help."

Emerson tweaked the pup's foot and said, "I'd be happy to help."

"Good. Wanna go to the pet store with me after we close up shop for the night? Styx is going to need food, bowls, a dog bed, treats, toys..." His voice faded off with his continuing list. His eyes seemed to lose focus as he stared off over her shoulder, probably calculating the multitude of items a puppy needed.

Emerson was thankful that her sister, brother-in-law and their kids were staying at their mother's house while the festival was going on. That gave her a little more flexibility with her time. She knew Carolyn was going to be exhausted after this big day and she'd likely be in bed an hour after getting home. Sidney could handle helping her get settled.

Emerson nodded. "I'd love to."

# Chapter Eleven

"This is your truck, Styx. You're gonna love hanging your head out the window letting the wind flap your ears." Nick handed his new puppy over to Emerson, who'd just settled herself into the passenger seat of his truck. She tucked the puppy in her lap, but Styx just jumped right up bracing her paws against the door. Nick started the truck and lowered the window. The puppy's nose started working right away as she leaned into the open space. "But only when you get a little older. You need to be taller to do that."

"Don't worry, I'll hold on tight. She's not gonna leap out. Isn't that right, girly?" Emerson laughed when Styx licked her nose in response then turned back to the window.

Nick shifted into drive and eased out of the parking lot. There were only a handful of cars left since the festival had closed down for the night about thirty minutes ago. After helping secure their respective booths, they met back at his booth since his truck was parked behind it.

"Luckily, there's a pet store downtown on Bay Avenue, so we don't have to go far." Then a thought came to him, and he experienced both excitement and trepidation in one single flash. "How do you feel about pizza?"

"I love it. New York Style pizza is hard to beat though."

"You might remember that my parents have a pizzeria downtown. It's just a few doors down from the pet store. Would you like to get some dinner there after my shopping spree?"

That way his parents could meet Styx and see just what he'd gotten himself into. And he wanted Emerson to meet his parents. His mother was going to flip her lid. Hopefully she can control herself around Emerson and not ask flat-out when the wedding was, or how many babies she'd like to have. Thoughts like that brought on the trepidation part and caused his heart to start thumping harder. He quickly began to rethink his offer.

"I went there often when it first opened."

Nick laughed and signaled to make a turn at the stoplight. "It hasn't changed a bit." He steered the truck into a parking spot in front of the pet store. There was a lot of activity for a Thursday evening. But the temps were in the 70s and that brought people out.

Especially to the downtown area. There were always events going on. Book signings at Turn the Page. Adoption nights at the pet store weekly. The wine bar had tastings on Wednesdays. And the pizzeria was always crowded. Nick could see that all but two tables outside the restaurant were filled. They would be lucky to get one of those when they finished in the pet store.

"Come on, Styx," Nick said and took hold of her leash. Back at their booth he'd snagged a leash off the rack. It was red with blue crabs all over it. He clipped it to her new collar in the same print and picked her up, tucking her under his arm like a football. "Let's go see what you need to get settled into your new home."

Emerson joined him by the door. He held it open for her to enter first. They were greeted right away by someone behind the checkout counter. She immediately came around the end and made a beeline for Styx. "Oh, what an adorable puppy. Did you adopt her today at the festival?"

"Yes, I did. Meet Styx. I'm going to teach you how to high-five people, Styxy, so you can greet them properly." He held her paw out to the girl and she pressed her hand against Styx's paw.

"Styx. That's cute." After another pet or two she stepped back and switched back into business mode. "What can I help you with?"

"Everything," he stated simply. "I have nothing at home for a dog. I'm starting from scratch."

"Well, you've come to the right place. Follow me," she said and led them to the far-right side of the store. "You got her a great leash and collar, so let's start with a harness to match, then a bed and next food and treats. Do you want a crate for her?"

Nick looked at Emerson who only smiled up at him and shrugged. He looked back at the clerk and asked, "Do I want a crate?"

She laughed and said, "Well, it would help with potty training. That way she can sleep in it at night and she's not wandering around your house peeing everywhere."

"Gotcha, yep, I definitely want a crate."

"Some dogs sleep in their crates every night for their whole lives, and other dogs just get acclimated as puppies then once they are potty trained can sleep elsewhere."

*Like in bed with me.*

He liked the idea of snuggling with a pup and wouldn't mind option B. Nick shook his head. He really had no idea what he was getting himself into. But he was game. He was willing to learn because he truly had always wanted a dog. When they were kids, his parents were always too busy at the restaurant to be bothered with a dog. Plus, they'd lived in the apartment above the place.

Once they'd moved here, the only thing that changed was they had moved into a house. But there still hadn't been any time for a pet. Then he'd gotten so busy building his business that it had slipped his mind. Seeing Emerson holding the puppy, smiling and laughing at her, had brought all those dreams from long ago flooding to the surface and he'd just acted spontaneously.

Realizing he'd zoned out for a minute when both women were staring at him, he cleared his throat and tuned back in. "Sorry about that."

The clerk laughed. "It's okay. It's a lot. Puppies can be quite a handful when they are little. They are just like babies and toddlers. They get into everything, bite, chew things up that they likely shouldn't, make messes, etc. But if they have good, consistent training they will turn out to be great companions."

*Good, consistent training.* He needed to get signed up for a class when she was old enough. He needed all the help he could get.

After Styx sampled some treats, they picked out her favorite and added that to the cart that was already overflowing with a dog bed, a bag of dog food, a crate, a harness, a life jacket, a lobster chew toy, a rubber squeaky pig, two tug ropes, two metal bowls and a tube of tennis balls. He thanked the clerk for all her help and accepted the flyer announcing their puppy training schedule.

They deposited all the gear inside his truck then Nick let Styx down so she could walk and sniff along the sidewalk as they made their way down and across the street to the pizzeria. Her little tail wagged so fast it was nearly a blur. She stuck her nose in between some flowers along the curb, and it came up covered in soil. Nick laughed and squatted to wipe her nose clean. "You sure are a nosy thing." Styx licked his chin in response and let out an adorable yip.

He pulled out a small treat he'd stashed in his pocket and broke off a piece for her. She appeared to swallow it whole and looked eager for more.

She was quickly distracted when they started walking again. Nick found his hand reaching for Emerson's and after a millisecond of hesitation, he decided to let it happen even if he'd thought twice about it. The instinct was there. To be close to her. To touch her.

Were they dating? Did he have the right to hold her hand? Well, he was about to find out. If she pulled away, then she just wasn't that into him. But, if she held on tight, then maybe there was a chance for them, after all.

His palm connected with hers, then slowly he laced their fingers.

Emerson looked over at him, one eye squinted shut against the light from the setting sun shining through the open street, a grin slowly growing on her gorgeous lips. She offered him a squeeze and shifted her fingers until they were just so. Yep, that was a good sign. Their hands felt good together, natural. Their arms hung comfortably at their sides. A perfect fit.

At the corner, he pressed the walk button and they waited for the light to turn green. "This place hasn't changed much," she said looking behind her down the street. "I loved going to

Turn the Page as a kid. Mom would take us there weekly for story time when we were young and for a new book when we got older. I wonder if Mrs. Crawford still owns it. She and Mom went to school together."

Nick tugged her hand when the walk sign lit up. He looked both ways to make sure it was clear before stepping off the curb, Styx strutting along at his side. "I'm not sure who owns it, but it's an active place with lots of weekly events."

Emerson nodded to the right. "The pizzeria looks busy. How are your parents doing?"

"They are doing great, same as always. They have their routine down and are still rolling out the best pizza in the state," he claimed with pride. The local paper put out awards for "The Best of" and the pizzeria had earned top prize every year that it had been open.

"Did you work here when you were a teenager?" she asked, stepping around Styx who'd stopped for a sniff around the man-hole cover.

"It was mandatory," he answered with a nod. "Same as back in Jersey. As soon as my brother and I were tall enough to reach the salad bar cart, we carried out the containers. When we were a little older, we helped stir the sauce." Nick paused to let a passerby pet Styx. He waved when they continued walking.

"Next, we got to chop the toppings and assemble the pizzas. My father didn't let us make the dough or roll it out until we were teenagers.

He didn't want us screwing it up." He laughed. "Even then he stood next to us and watched every move we made." Nick shook his head at the memories that flashed through his mind. "They don't like to give up control. They haven't ever taken a vacation. This place is their life. Tony has been trying for years to get them out on his sailboat, but they won't go."

"They don't take any time off?"

Nick shook his head and walked ahead of her to snag the only available table outside the restaurant. "Like I said, they have their routine down. There's not much time outside of this place to enjoy their surroundings. I'm hoping I can change that soon."

"Are you going to take on another job and work here so they can have breaks?"

Nick laughed. "No, not that exactly. Just hoping to help them make the decision to pull back a little bit." Nick dragged out the metal chair and offered it to Emerson. "Here, will you hold on to this rascal so I can go in and greet my parents? I can guarantee that my mother will be out to see you shortly. I'll place our order while I'm inside. How do you like your pizza?"

"With everything on it." Emerson sat in the chair and took Styx's leash. The pup immediately jumped up into her lap.

"Careful. In Italy that could mean anchovies or eggs or artichokes."

She cringed. "Yikes, thanks for the warning. How about more typical veggies like peppers, mushrooms, onions, and olives."

"A *Capricciosa*." At her quizzical look, he amended, "It means 'whim' or in this case a make-your-own pizza. Any meat or would you just like a veggie pizza?"

"I'm a pepperoni and sausage girl. But not too spicy. Is that okay?"

"Perfect." He grinned. "I like your style. What to drink?"

"Sweet tea if they have it."

"Yep, this is the south, after all."

Nick paused at the door to the restaurant and looked back at the table. Emerson's gorgeous red hair gleamed in the sunlight when she leaned over to hug Styx, wrapping her arms around the squirming puppy.

What a sweet picture they made.

He wasn't sure how his mother would react to the news of a new grand dog or the fact that the woman he'd lusted after for so many years was currently sitting outside waiting to eat pizza with him. They hadn't officially called it a date, but that's what this was. Were they already so comfortable with each other that he didn't have to make it a formal request?

"Nicky!"

Nick pulled out of his musings as he stepped through the front door and spotted his mother across the room. He made his way through the packed tables to wrap his arms around her. "Mamma!" He kissed her cheeks as she did his.

"How's my handsome boy?" She pulled back from his hug and patted his cheek. Her hand smelled of tomato sauce. A comforting scent. "What's brought you here tonight?"

"I have two surprises outside," he started, and laughed when she darted around him to get closer to the front windows. "One I get to call mine and the other I only wish I could...." he said when he caught up to her.

"Oh, my boy." She put her arm around his waist and squeezed him tight. "What a cute little dog. It's yours?"

"I adopted her today at the Art Festival."

"She's a cutie. I always wanted a dog." Her voice sounded wistful.

"What?" He looked down at her, his expression showing his disbelief. "How did I not know that? I always wanted one when we were growing up."

"Me too," she added with a nod, leaning her head against his arm. "I wanted that for you, but we just didn't have the right lifestyle for one. Now I get to enjoy one through you. She's my first *cagna nipote*, my first grand dog. What's her name?"

"Styx."

She looked up at him quizzically. "The band, the river or the tree branch?"

"The river, of course."

"I can't believe we raised such strong, handsome watermen." She squeezed his waist again. "Your father and I are proud of you and your brother."

"I know, Mamma. We are proud of both of you too. This place is still going strong. I'm seeing things through a fresh eye with Emerson back in town. She had no idea what she missed out on by leaving when she did."

"Are you going to show her the beauty of her hometown and all that it has to offer? Especially, a certain handsome, eligible bachelor?"

Nick didn't answer. He just leaned down and kissed the top of her head.

"I'm so happy to see Emerson Taylor here with you, Nicky. Did you take my advice?" She turned and looked up at him. There were those ever-present tears of joy in her eyes. "Are you giving her a reason to stay?"

# Chapter Twelve

Emerson sat back in the chair and took in the sights, sounds and smells of her hometown. A town she'd fled from the first opportunity she'd gotten. Not because anything bad had happened to her here. Just losing her father way too young. But there were mostly sweet memories of this place. She'd just had an itch from the time she was an early teen to see and do more than what was offered here.

The funny thing was Emerson had absolutely no idea what she could have experienced here. What she'd missed out on. Now as an adult she could see it was a thriving place with an abundance of art, flowers, architecture, and natural beauty galore.

She'd just been blind to it.

She'd had an ache to get to the big city and live a faster-paced life. To do bigger and greater things than she could in this small town. And she'd done that. She'd accomplished those goals.

Now, as she sat here on this lovely spring evening listening to bees buzzing in the potted flowers and songbirds in the trees bordering Bay Avenue, she realized she might have made the wrong decision as a teen.

Well, maybe it wasn't the wrong decision since she'd enjoyed going to Columbia, met some amazing people and earned her dream job working in the finance world. Plus, the decision was already made, no reason to think about it like that. What she could do something about was the now...and right now, she was in love with her hometown, and she was starting to have feelings for this extremely handsome, complex pillar of the community.

A man her heart had feelings for.

A man who brought a smile to her face just thinking about him.

A man she'd only kissed once.

She needed to rectify that. Immediately. Maybe tonight. Were they on a date? Maybe so. Then she'd definitely be getting a goodnight kiss. After they shared an amazingly delicious pizza.

Emerson knew Mrs. Valentino would be out here soon. She'd want to meet Styx. She wasn't sure if Nick's mother would remember her or not. As a teen, Emerson had been in here often enough, but sadly, as a teen sometimes does, she didn't really take the time to be observant and get to know the people who were behind the amazing pizza she enjoyed eating with her family and friends.

The door opened and she glanced over. A zing of nerves skittered through her stomach at the smile on Nick's face. It was like there was no one else there. Just the two of them, laser-focused on each other. Forcing herself to breathe, she struggled to make it not look like she was gasping for air.

Styx jumped off her lap and bolted for the door. The leash had just been sitting in her lap, so the puppy got away. Emerson leapt to her feet to follow, but luckily, Styx ran straight to her human. Nick laughed and scooped her up. He turned immediately to the woman behind him. The woman reached out and wrapped her hands lovingly around the puppy's face, drawing her in for a kiss on the nose. Styx licked her nose in return. The woman laughed. There were tears in her eyes. Eyes similar to Nick's. A rich, honey brown.

She accepted the pup when Styx jumped from his arms to hers. "Aww, *che dolce cucciolo!* What a sweet puppy. Hi, *cucciolo.*"

Emerson joined them by the door and stood close to Nick. She thought he might put his arm around her or take hold of her hand, but she watched him quickly tuck his hands in his back pockets. Like he was restraining himself from claiming her in front of his mother. Maybe she was the kind who'd immediately want to know what the wedding colors were going to be so she could knit them a baby blanket. Emerson tried not to cringe at how fast that would have them moving.

"Mamma, this is Emerson. Emerson, this is my mother, Sofia Valentino."

Emerson reached out her hand. After Sofia shuffled the pup to one side, she accepted her hand and shook it. She was the definition of the word petite, but she had strong hands. "It's a pleasure to officially meet you."

"Likewise, *cara mia*." Emerson didn't know what that meant. She'd taken Spanish in high school, not Italian. "I'm so glad you are here tonight. Are you staying for dinner?"

"Yes, ma'am. I loved your pizza when I was a teenager, and Nick has assured me that nothing has changed."

Nick took Styx and put her back on the ground. He held the leash out to Emerson and said, "I'll go put in the order and get our drinks. Mamma, do you want to sit and take a break? I can run orders for a few minutes."

"Don't be silly. You're on a date."

"Mamma, you work too hard. Sit with Emerson. Get to know your grand dog." He looked at Emerson and added, "I'll be back with our drinks."

Emerson felt a twinge of nervousness at being left alone with his mother, but she could handle small talk for a few minutes. Plus, it was sweet of him to want her to take a break. Nick was turning out to be quite a surprise.

Emerson waited for Mrs. Valentino to sit in the chair opposite her before returning to her seat. Styx followed Sofia and immediately put her paws on her knees, asking to be held. She picked her up with no hesitation to the amount of dog hair that would now cover her apron. Was that a health code violation? Hopefully, she had a number of aprons in the kitchen. But Mrs. Valentino didn't seem to care or notice as she brought the puppy up to her face and snuggled into her soft fur.

It was nearly impossible to resist puppy cuddles.

"Aww, Styx, *cara mia*, you are so pretty. And look at those big feet. You're going to be a big one."

Emerson loved hearing her gush over her grand dog. It was kind of the same way her mother spoke to her grandbabies. Nick appeared by her side with two glasses. She'd been caught up watching the display of love across the table that she hadn't heard him approach. The glasses were full of ice and dark liquid. Hers held sweet tea, but she wasn't sure what his favorite drink was.

"Thank you," she said when he set her glass down in front of her. After taking her first sip, she nearly snort-laughed when Nick spoke to her.

Whispering in her ear, his breath warm and fluttery against her neck, he said, "She hasn't asked you when the wedding is, has she?"

He chuckled at her obvious distress, her hand covering her mouth to keep her sweet tea inside. She swatted his arm as he headed back to the front door.

"How's your mother?" Mrs. Valentino's smile was all-knowing, like she was in on the secret they were keeping from her, from everyone. They'd only been on one date and Emerson already felt so close to him. "I haven't seen her at the market like I used to."

"She's doing well," was Emerson's automatic response. But then she realized Carolyn needed some friends in her corner, even if they were only acquaintances. "Not exactly well, but okay. She recently received some health news and that's why I'm here. She's going to need to make amendments to her active schedule, and my mother isn't too happy about that." Emerson wiped condensation from her glass. "She's a strong, independent woman who likes to make her own decisions. This diagnosis is trying to take that control out of her hands and she's struggling with it."

"I'm so sorry to hear about that, *cara mia*. I hope with medication she can continue to be active and independent for as long as possible."

"Thank you, Mrs. Valentino." Emerson's smile was genuine. She hoped for the same thing. "She's a fighter, so she'll find a way."

A few moments of silence passed, then Mrs. Valentino spoke. "You live in New York, is that right?" Her hands continued to stroke Styx from head to tail. The pup actually looked like she was content enough to fall asleep.

"Yes, ma'am, New York City. I work for a financial company and am on the clock nearly 24/7." She took a sip of her sweet tea and realized the impact of that statement.

"Being home must be a nice break for you then."

She nodded, realizing it actually had been. She was stunned once again to find that she hadn't thought about Lawson Financial or the stock market or her clients for many days now. What did that mean? Did she not want to return to NYC? Did she not want to continue the job that she'd worked so hard to score? A job where she was the only female to break through to a lead position in the company.

Emerson's breath seized in her lungs. *Maybe I don't.* Forcing herself to breathe past those words stuck in her throat, she tried to ease her racing heart.

Could she picture herself living here? Being back in this town again? With its slow pace, mild winters, hot, humid summers, and—

That's when Nick Valentino walked back out the restaurant door, a radiant grin on his handsome mug.

—and hunky, ruggedly handsome outdoorsy guys, this one in particular, that lit up her insides like the fireworks her family used to watch from the bayfront in her backyard on the fourth of July.

He pulled out a chair and sat down between the two women. Styx looked absolutely content sitting in her grandmother's lap, eyes on Nick, tongue lolling out the side of her mouth, happy as a clam. "You look happy," he said to his mother.

"I am. She's a sweetheart. Thank you for bringing her by so I could meet her. Did you tell your Papà?"

Nick nodded as he swallowed his drink. "I went back to the kitchen and visited with him. I told him you were out here loving all over a puppy. He just rolled his eyes," Nick added with a laugh. "He said he'd try to come out and say hello."

"He's probably thinking I won't be back in there tonight."

"You're welcome to sit here with us all night."

Emerson loved how easily he interacted with his mother, how much he cared for her and wanted her to rest. She could imagine how much work went into running this place, especially if the majority of the work fell on his parents' shoulders.

"I appreciate the offer, Nicky." Her hand took hold of his on the tabletop. "I've loved getting to visit with Emerson and this *che dolce cucciolo*. Now I need to shake off all this sweet little dog fluff and find a fresh apron, so I can get back in there and help your father. I'll bring your pizza out as soon as it's ready."

Nick leaned over and plucked Styx out of her lap and set her down on the sidewalk. He stood, putting his foot down on the leash so she couldn't run off, then wrapped his mother in a warm embrace, resting his head on top of hers. She barely came up to his shoulders. He practically swallowed her, his arms wrapping all the way around her.

"Pizza's ready!"

They looked over to see Nick's father holding their pizza over one shoulder and plates and rolled silverware in the other hand. He carried it over to the table, setting it all down smoothly. Then he turned to Emerson and held out his hand. His smile matched Nick's. One side of his mouth curved up when he greeted her. "It's a pleasure to meet you, Emerson." His accent was much stronger than Mrs. Valentino's.

"Likewise, thank you," Emerson said and shook his hand. He could have passed for petite also, except for the strength in the hand that held hers. Likely, it was the many years of working with dough, the kneading, the rolling, the shaping, that had made his hands and arms extremely strong.

"Papà, this is Styx." Nick proudly held his pup in his arms and faced his father.

Nick's father kept his hands on his hips, not reaching out to pet her even though she was practically vibrating with excitement. "She's cute. But she's going to be a handful. *Ti auguro buona fortuna, figlio.* Good luck, son." Before he turned away, he pressed one fingertip to the pup's nose. Styx with her ever-so-fast tongue got in a lick before he could pull away. He left them with a chuckle.

"That might not have looked like much, but that was my father's way of showing happiness. He was practically gushing." Nick laughed. His eyes nearly sparkled with happiness. "He's a pretty stoic guy. Very much old-school Italian."

"*Molto.* Very," his mother added, looking over at Emerson with a sweet smile. She hugged Nick again, then pushed him back toward his chair. "*È abbastanza!* That's enough. Get back to your date. Enjoy your hot, fresh pizza."

"*Grazie,* Mamma." Nick placed a kiss on each of her cheeks, then sat in his chair. Mrs. Valentino petted Styx's head once more before coming around the table. She surprised Emerson when she leaned down, placing a kiss on each of her cheeks. A blush swept across her cheeks, warming her skin. That felt overwhelmingly special.

Nick set Styx on the ground and put her leash under his shoe, keeping her in place. "Let's eat." Nick placed a steaming hot slice on a plate he set in front of her.

Emerson leaned forward, closing her eyes, and pulling in a deep breath. "That looks and smells amazing!"

"It's going to taste even better." Nick picked up his slice and took a big bite. She watched his jaws work as he chewed the cheesy dough loaded with vegetables, pepperoni and sausage.

Proudly keeping the groan in when his tongue darted out to catch an olive slice trying to escape his lips, she decided to focus on taking her own bite.

"You're right." Emerson opened one of the napkin-wrapped silverware sets and wiped the sauce from her lip. "Still as delicious as it was when I was here last. Do they have a secret ingredient they add to the dough or to the sauce that makes it so good?"

Nick smiled while he chewed his next bite. "I can't confirm nor deny."

Emerson laughed and ate another bite. She had to admit this might be better than New York style pizza. It was so rich and creamy, with the perfect blend of sauce, cheese and toppings that brought her taste buds popping to life. "So good," she mumbled around another mouthful.

"I have eaten pizza my entire life. I'll never grow tired of it. This is my favorite style. Loaded. My mother prefers the classic, a *Margherita* pizza, and I think that one is good as well. My father leans more toward the *Napoli* style, with capers and anchovies." She cringed at the mention of the oily fish. He shook his head and continued, "That one's not my favorite. Now my brother, on the other hand, likes his pizza with all the spice. His go-to is the *Diavola*, which means the devil."

Emerson shook her head. "That one would not be my favorite. I don't even want to know what's on it." Taking her last bite, she used the napkin again to wipe her lips. "So, I'm guessing that your parents were born in Italy. When did they move to the US? Did they move to New Jersey first?"

Nick pointed to another slice and asked her without words if she'd like to have it. Her first thought was no, it was too much, but after she let that ridiculous thought pass, she nodded, accepting another piece. This pizza was too good to only have one slice.

"Yes, they were both born and raised in a small town north of Naples. They moved after they got married, following my uncle and aunt to New Jersey. My uncle was going for a job and my father thought he could easily find work too. It took a while before they decided to go into business together."

"What does your uncle do now? Is he still in the pizza business?"

"Yes, back in Jersey. They still run the original pizzeria."

"What brought your parents down here? That's quite a jump from New Jersey to coastal Alabama." Emerson used her napkin to wipe her hands before taking another sip of her sweet tea.

"My brother and I were starting to get into trouble in school. Gangs were rampant in our neighborhood and my parents thought it was time to get us out of there." Nick paused to take another bite. "There was a customer that came nearly every day for lunch during the summer and early fall. He traveled down here during the late fall and winter, as soon as the temperatures dropped and before snow was in the forecast."

Emerson nodded her head and swallowed. "Aww, a snowbird."

"Yes, a snowbird. He and his wife have a place here on the bay and are regular customers here as well. Mr. Dillon would tell my parents about it, and they started planning for our move a year before it happened. My brother and I had no idea until the last day of school our junior year."

Emerson's eyes widened. "That must have been quite a shock."

"It was. We were born there and thought we'd never leave. And that's exactly why my parents got us out of there. We were good kids but there was trouble all around us. It wouldn't have been hard to find it and head down that rabbit hole. My parents wanted more for us and they found it."

"Did you live on the coast in Jersey?"

Nick shook his head and swallowed his last bite. "No. Smog-infused inner-city life. It was awful, but at the time it was all we knew. When we got down here it was like this was another world. The air was so clean, the pace was slower, the water was such an incredible sight and it was everywhere. My brother and I took to it right away. We befriended kids at school that had kayaks and boats, who went fishing and sailing. We got ourselves involved in any watersport or activity we could find."

"Did you go to a sailing camp, is that how your brother got so involved?"

"Yes, that first summer, as well as the one following graduation. It was like he was born to do it. He's a natural on a boat. How about you?" Nick huffed out a laugh and leaned back in his seat, his hands falling to rest on his stomach. "I feel like I've been talking for hours. Have you sailed?"

"I have. That's the one thing, other than paddling behind the house or swimming, that I did do on the water." She sat back in her chair and crossed her legs beneath the table, her shoe brushing against his calf. "My father owned a sailboat and took us out every weekend. I was pretty young when he died so I never learned how to do it."

Her smile dipped momentarily at the mention of her father, but she quickly tried to remain upbeat, sharing with him her favorite part of sailing. "My fondest memories are of lying on the deck under the jib, watching it shift back and forth in the wind. The feeling of my body rising and falling with the waves is forever etched into my brain."

Nick reached out and touched her hand resting on the table, cupping his fingers around hers. "I'm sorry about your father."

"Thank you. Me too. I miss him dearly. I was only six when he died suddenly of a heart attack at age thirty-seven."

Nick shook his head, his eyes solemn. "Way too young."

She nodded. "The last time I was on our sailboat I was five, maybe six, so I got to just sit back and enjoy the ride."

"Would you like to learn?" He pulled his phone out of his pocket and started typing.

"Are you adding that to my Gotta-Do list?" She chuckled when he just nodded.

Nick looked up from his phone, his eyes shiny with enthusiasm. "I can teach you. We can borrow my brother's sailboat and take a picnic dinner with us. It would be amazing to see a sunset out on the bay. What do you say?"

Emerson felt butterflies start to stir in her stomach at the idea. A sunset sail with Nick? Yes, please. "Borrow your brother's sailboat? Doesn't he live on it? Where's he going to go?"

"He'll be working at the Keel & Rudder anyway and he can always crash at my house."

"You sound really excited about this."

"I am. I love being on the water and want to share that with you."

Aww. That warmed her heart. "What about Styx?" She thought she ought to remind him that he was now a dog dad and needed to think about his puppy when making plans.

"Oh." He chuckled. "Thanks for the reminder. Um, well, she's got a life jacket and a leash. She can come along with us. You can be there for her first sail and help me with her since she's so little. Before long she'll be a pro." He smiled down at the sleeping pup at his feet. "Are you free this weekend? After the festival's over? I know it's calling for good winds this Saturday. I won't leave us stranded out in the middle of the bay, I promise."

She had faith in him as a waterman and had no doubt that they wouldn't end up stranded. But it wouldn't be a terrible idea to her way of thinking. She'd be fine with being stranded out in the bay on a sailboat, just the two of them, alone. She could only imagine the possibilities.

***

"This is where you grew up?"

His truck was parked in the house. Nick's jaw was slightly open, his eyes transfixed on her childhood home. She nodded as she looked out the front windshield and tried to see her family home through his eyes.

It was a two-story with bold, white columns and large windows across the front. Double doors sat centered on the porch. The yard held two massive Live Oak trees plus a Magnolia that her parents had planted when they got married and moved in. Flowers decorated beds in front of the porch and along the side of the driveway.

It was quite grand. The house had been in her father's family for a couple generations. Once he'd married, his parents had happily moved out and into something much smaller, handing the house over to him as his inheritance.

"It was an awesome house to grow up in. We didn't have to go far to have fun." She pointed to the view they could see around the side of the house of the bay waters.

"I wouldn't have ever left." His words had been wistful, but as soon as he said them, his eyes jerked to hers. He reached for her hand, the one resting on her lap. His fingers grazed her thigh and heat seeped into her skin. "I'm sorry, I didn't mean—"

Emerson cut him off with a shake of her head and squeezed his fingers, absorbing the heat radiating from his hand. "The longer I'm here now, the more I wish I hadn't."

Hadn't been in such a hurry to leave.

Hadn't been so oblivious to this man sitting beside her.

Hadn't spent so much time away.

That truth sat between them for a moment. Then she decided she wasn't going to waste any more time.

Leaning across the console, Emerson pressed her lips to his. After only a heartbeat passed, Nick reacted, deepening the kiss. His fingers caressed her jaw, stretching back into her hair, holding her mouth against his. Emerson breathed him in, his scent surrounding her. When his tongue touched her lower lip, she opened for him. Their tongues tangled as she shifted closer.

Nick broke the kiss and leaned his forehead against hers. Then he whispered, his voice gravelly, "For what it's worth, I'm glad you're here now."

If the console wasn't in the way, she knew she'd be in his lap right now.

Thinking that was actually a pretty good idea, she turned her lower body, bringing her knees up onto the seat. Nick reacted quickly to her move. He met her halfway, his strong arms grabbing her hips as she climbed over. After a few clumsy seconds, Emerson was settled across his lap, her knees straddling his thighs. Her fingers threaded through his surfer-boy hair, gripping the ends. From her higher position, she arched down to press her lips to his.

The feeling of his hands sliding up her outer thighs and gripping her ass through her shorts instantly made her panties wet. She leaned into his erection, drawn in by the heat, the pressure in her core building in intensity as she deepened the kiss. Nick released a groan and shifted his hands up her back, his thumbs just grazing the side of her breasts, caressing her through her shirt. A shirt she wished would vanish. She wanted his heat to touch her skin to skin.

Thoughts of ripping it over her head brought her up short. What was she doing?

Pulling back, her lips released his and she panted out a breath, then two. Sitting up only pressed her sex harder against him. She couldn't help the groan that escaped her lips.

His honey-brown eyes looked molten as he held her gaze. His chest rising and falling with his ragged breaths.

Catching her lower lip between her teeth, Emerson drew her thumb across his lower lip. Not yet ready to stop touching him. His tongue darted out and caressed her thumb. Damn this man. She wanted him. Couldn't get enough of him.

But they weren't in a bed, or on a couch.

They weren't even in private.

They were in his truck, in front of her mother's house.

His hand mimicked her move, caressing her face, his thumb trailing across her lower lip. Emerson leaned into his touch, her hips rocking forward. So good. Her body instinctively rocked again. It felt too good to stop. He felt too good. Thick and hard beneath her thighs. But she had to stop.

She couldn't have sex for the first time with him in his truck in front of her mother's house.

"Nick..." Emerson's voice was a whisper. Her tone implying the rest of what she should have said. She saw awareness in his eyes, dark desire, heat, lust, and maybe resignation too. He released a deep breath and pulled her to him as he leaned his head forward, his forehead coming to rest between her breasts. Heat from his deep exhale warmed her chest, causing her nipples to peak.

Emerson wrapped her arms around his head, holding him against her chest, her heart squeezing with the sweetness of it all. She'd nearly had sex with him in the cab of his truck. Wow, her hormones were on one helluva wild ride.

Blood flowed through her veins like molten lava, her sex still on fire, her panties soaked.

"So, Saturday, huh?" she asked against his hair, eyes still closed, soaking it all in.

A warm tongue stroked across her nose, causing her eyes to flash open. Puppy breath greeted her on her quick inhale. "Styx!" Emerson laughed and sat up, reaching out to the pup. "You finally woke up." She'd actually forgotten the puppy was in the truck with them.

Another good reason not to have gotten naked.

Nick accepted all Styx's happy kisses and stroked her head and ears, welcoming her into their embrace. The pup sat between them and couldn't decide who she wanted to lick more, so she divided her attention equally.

Laughing, Nick said, "Yes, Saturday. A sunset sail."

It sounded like an incredibly romantic evening. One where she hoped they'd pick up right where they left off.

# Chapter Thirteen

Emerson glanced at her phone one more time. The alert on the screen caused her heart rate to accelerate. Her palms to sweat. And a tightness to creep into her neck, sliding along her shoulders.

It jolted her out of the dreamworld she'd been coasting through the last two weeks and threw her back into reality. Her New-York-City-life-and-work reality.

The reminder was of an event that she'd had a part in planning. The planning had started a few months back and she'd been lead on organizing the details. Until she'd taken a leave of absence. Then all her duties were handed out amongst her two colleagues on par with her status.

She hadn't even given it another thought.

Hadn't actually thought about her job. About NYC. About her *real life* in more than a few days.

Emerson closed her eyes and pulled in a deep breath. She gripped the ropes on the swing and pushed her feet against the grass, propelling herself backwards. As soon as the reminder had popped up on her phone she'd stepped outside, needing air.

Needing a few minutes to take it all in.

Needing time to process what was going on inside her head and her heart.

*How could I have forgotten?*

Why had it been so easy to forget all about Lawson Financial, about her workload, about her clients, about her boss and colleagues? Even about Evan and the asshole she worked closely with, Don. Since she'd arrived here, her stress-load, her need to be on all the time, had lessened.

The second she glanced at her phone tonight, she could easily discern the tension crawling along her completely relaxed muscles. It had been so obvious. Like sensing a chill going down one's spine when watching a scary movie or reading a tension-filled book.

Being home, being here in this beautiful place, she'd been more relaxed than she had been in twelve years. The tension had gradually accumulated in her body over those years until it was her norm, her everyday state, and completely unnoticeable as she slugged through life, day by day, meeting one deadline after another, not giving herself time to just be. Any other time she'd been here for a visit, it'd been quick, and she hadn't let herself down off the high of living that life in New York City.

Emerson pumped her legs and climbed higher into the air letting the wind off the water cool her skin and help rid her of this immediate reaction to something work-related. Windchimes hanging from the branch behind her made a lovely sound helping to calm her accelerated heart rate.

Closing her eyes now left her feeling dizzy since she was going so fast, so she kept them open and scanned them along the bay as she swung back and forth. A few sailboats were out taking advantage of the wind and the beautiful weather. Pelicans and gulls were dive-bombing into the water right off their dock, partaking in a fishy dinner.

Their resident Great Blue Heron stood guard on the shallow end of their dock, his gaze intently searching the water for his own dinner. His plumy neck feathers shifted in the strong breeze.

*If my body reacts like this to a simple reminder of a work event on my phone, what the hell will it feel like to go home?*

To be in her apartment again—a place she certainly hadn't given a solitary thought to—or back in her office at Lawson Financial on the fifty-fourth floor? The view was impeccable and something hard-fought for, but taking in the scene before her now, she thought this view was pretty spectacular too.

"Emmie?"

The second she heard her cousin's voice she recognized the other sound she was hearing—heavy, thudding feet racing across the grass. Emerson turned in time to see Goose jumping off the back deck. Goose was on the loose. He tore off across the yard past her on the swing and bolted down the dock. The Great Blue Heron who'd been on the hunt for dinner didn't appreciate the interruption and squawked his displeasure as he took to the sky.

Emerson stopped her legs from swinging and slowed before calling out a greeting to her cousin. "Hey, Cal!" Seeing her favorite cousin helped flip her mood instantly, brightening the wattage of her smile. "What brings you out here tonight? No hot date?"

Callie shook her head, her blonde hair in a braid. She took a seat on the bench near the swing. "No, no hot date tonight. John and I have plans this weekend though. I hadn't seen you in a few days, so I thought I'd stop by and get in my cousin time."

"I'm glad you did." Emerson halted the swing and stood, trying her best to completely shake off her previous mood. She greeted Goose with a full head scratch when he bounded toward her on the beach. She joined Callie on the bench, putting her arm around her shoulders for a quick hug. "It's good to see you."

Callie squeezed her back. "You too. I heard that the festival's been a hit."

Emerson sat back and pulled a foot up on the bench, wrapping her arms around her leg just below the knee, her eyes drawn to the rough surf hitting the shoreline with extra speed and energy. "Yeah, Sid and Mom have both made great sales. Only one day left."

"They've had beautiful weather! Hopefully, it'll bring people out in droves tomorrow." Callie ducked her chin and tried to hide a smile when she said, "I hear you've got a hot date for tomorrow night."

Emerson rolled her eyes and shook her head. *Sidney.* That girl couldn't keep her mouth shut. She'd told Sidney about it the night Nick first asked for logistics reasons, hoping that she and her family would still be staying here Saturday night in case she was out late. She didn't expect her sister to spread it around like they were gossip girls in middle school.

Emerson watched Goose nose his way along the wrack line, chewing on driftwood as she thought about Nick's date proposal. How he'd added it to the growing list of things that he thought she needed to experience. When was she going to have time to go on those adventures? She only had a couple weeks of leave left.

Why had she agreed to another date with him? Why was she contemplating having sex with him? What was she thinking? She was leaving.

Emerson's foot dropped to the ground, and she fell forward, elbows on her knees. Head in her hands, she pressed her fingertips against her temples. The sound of the waves and shorebirds fading as blood rushed to her ears. "What am I doing?"

Callie jerked forward and put a hand on her back, stroking comforting circles. "Honey, what are you talking about?" Emerson felt Callie's cheek press against the back of her head. The soothing circles continued on her back. "You're having fun, enjoying life, taking time for yourself. Something you've needed to do for a long time. I'm so glad you're putting yourself out there, Em. Spending time with Nick has put a glow in your smile. He makes you happy. So, *what are you doing*? You're living, Em." Callie emphasized each word of her last sentence with a squeeze on her arm.

Emerson absorbed all of her cousin's words, just as she absorbed the comforting circles on her back, both doing wonders to help ease the constriction that was starting to take hold of her throat.

"But I'm going back to New York," she whispered through that constriction, head still held up by her hands, her eyes closed. *Aren't I?* She couldn't quite say it out loud. But she knew her cousin could practically read her mind.

"Are you?" Callie whispered.

Yep, they were on the same wavelength.

But those words set off her lungs with their suggestion. Lungs that immediately seized. Fighting with her throat to let air pass. White spots floated across her vision, even though her eyes were squeezed shut. Her blood thumped in her ears, racing through her body like it was on the last leg of a 5K.

"Emmie, sit up, take a deep breath." Callie's voice was sharp, cutting through the fog that had enveloped her head. "Come on," she coaxed, pulling on Emerson's shoulders. "Relax and let's talk this out. You're okay." Her words were reassuring. Was she okay? "Just breathe."

Callie waited patiently while Emerson drew herself back up to sitting, her back resting against the cushions on the bench, her hands gripping her thighs, her mouth rounded in an "O" as she sucked in a deep breath. Was she having a panic attack?

"There you go. Take another deep breath. Let it out slowly," Callie advised, taking a deep breath and slowly releasing it, modeling like she'd do for her eighth graders.

Emerson needed about three more of those deep, cleansing breaths before she felt control come back to her heart rate. Her breathing settled back to near a normal pace. With each deep breath, the photo reel in her mind continued to slow to a crawl, finally letting her focus in on her surroundings.

"Thanks, Callie," Emerson whispered. "Wow, I kinda think that was a panic attack. That's never happened before."

Callie held her hand with both of hers, her strength comforting, grounding her. Emerson continued to take deep breaths, working past that moment of panic, shifting into recovery mode.

"This is a pretty big deal," Callie assured her. "Even thinking about the possibility is a really big deal. You're allowed to have feelings, Em. To question them. To wonder what if."

Emerson's gaze shot to Callie's. The setting sun glinted off the ever-changing color that matched hers. "What if?" Her voice cracked with the question. She shrugged and said, "What? What if I quit my job and move back home?"

She bolted to her feet and paced to the water's edge, kicking an oyster shell in agitation. Goose ran to her, a catfish skull clutched in his teeth, wanting to show her his prize. But her mind was too conflicted. She spun back to Callie, her voice rising. "What if I give up the highly competitive position I've worked so hard for these last eight years and walk away?"

Callie appeared unruffled by Emerson's anger. Her comfortable pose and kind eyes brought Emerson up short. Some of her steam dissipated allowing her to focus on Callie's heartfelt words. "What if you move home and find joy and happiness here. I don't mean just because of Nick Valentino. But he could certainly help you with that," she added with a saucy wink.

The spinning photo reel in her mind came to rest on the image of Nick with his head nestled between her breasts, breath ragged, his exhale warming her skin. Yep, he could certainly help with that. Emerson scrubbed her hands down her face and released a deep exhale that ended with a groan.

"How do you feel now?" Callie rose from the bench and headed towards her.

Emerson's shoulders dropped and she stretched her neck from side to side. Her body was tingling, like her limbs had fallen asleep and they were just now coming back to life. How did she feel?

Exhausted.

Spent.

In need of a nap.

A total adrenaline crash was lurking just around the corner.

"Enlightened. But also exhausted."

Callie pressed her hands into Emerson's arms, rubbing up and down vigorously, bringing feeling back to them. "That's expected. Your body just went through something major. I would apologize for bringing it on, but I won't. You needed that, Em. You needed to process your thoughts. I'm just glad I was here to help you with that."

"I'm glad you were here too." When Callie's hands slid from her arms, Emerson gripped them tightly. After another ragged deep breath that came out choppy, Emerson stated, "Okay, let's do this. Let's talk it out."

Callie's smile was as bright as the sun. She met Emerson's gaze, then nodded once. "Okay, pros and cons of each." Callie dragged her back to the bench. Emerson gave her a wan smile, trying to get on board with Callie's enthusiasm, but she was drained. "Which do you want to start with? Which one will bring on the anxiety again?"

Emerson sat down roughly, thankful for the cushion to break her fall. That was a no-brainer. "Both. You pick."

"Alrighty then, pros and cons for staying here." Callie's grin glinted in the fading sunlight. "We get to see each other on the regular!" Callie threw her arms around Emerson and hugged her tightly. "That's definitely pro number one."

"That's a big incentive right there," Emerson agreed, wrapping her arms around her, squeezing with all the strength she could muster, and kissed her on the cheek. "Thank you. Thank you for this," she whispered into her hair.

"Anytime." The hug lasted for several more heartbeats, Emerson hoping with each one that Callie knew without a doubt that she appreciated her and was so thankful for having her in her life. "Pro number two—Nick Valentino." Callie pulled back, a gleam in her eyes. "So have you ever had sex on a sailboat?"

***

"Mamma told me you got a dog."

Nick looked up from the burger patties he was prepping in the kitchen when his brother walked in his front door. Tony's brow was wrinkled and his mouth set. It wasn't his typical look. Missing from his face was his ever-present smile, one that was a little lop-sided like his. A character trait passed on from their father. Tony kicked the door closed and glanced around the living room, presumably searching for Styx.

Styx had been asleep on her living room dog bed. When Tony shut the door, the pup popped awake and sat up. Realizing someone new was in the house, she leapt off her bed and ran to him, yelping with each tail wag. Nick couldn't help the smile that curved his lips. She was incredibly cute.

"That isn't a dog," Tony grumbled looking down at Styx, that furrow still in his brow. She jumped up on her hind legs, dancing a couple steps before tumbling down.

"What the hell else would she be?" Nick shook his head and carried the plate of burgers he'd made out the back door, and down the deck steps. He already had the wood burning in the fire pit by the creek. "Here, Styxy, come here, girl."

Seconds later, his dog bounded onto the deck. Nick paused at the bottom of the steps, waiting for her. She was pretty hesitant on the steps, taking them extra slowly. All four feet touched a step, then she whined and yelped, dancing a little before moving down to the next one.

Tony was right behind her at the top of the steps. "What's this?"

"She's not too sure of the steps yet," Nick answered. "Grab her, will ya?" He turned without waiting to see if his brother did as he asked and made his way down the path to the creek. Setting the plate of burgers down on the counter, he started shifting the wood, settling it so he could lower the grate over it.

Styx came running up to him. He turned on his knee and petted her. "Good girl, Styx." He stroked her ears and pushed her butt down gently. "Sit. Sit," he repeated. "Good sit, Styx."

Tony took a seat in one of the Adirondack chairs, a beer he must have snagged from the fridge in his hand. The last bit of sunlight glinted off his hair, making it appear much darker than Nick's. Their hair color was the same, but where Nick's was shaggier in nature, Tony kept his buzzed short. He said he didn't have time to fool with it since he lived on a sailboat. It made getting ready much easier.

"What do you know about training a puppy?" Tony asked.

Nick pulled a training treat from his pocket and gave it to Styx. "Google helps. And she's a good pup. Don't be a grump. You'll fall in love with her in no time." He dusted his hands off and set about getting the burgers on the fire.

Styx ran back over to Tony and sat near his feet and barked, her tail a blur of happiness. Tony leaned over and picked her up. He held her at arms' length, the pup's back legs running in the air, and stared into her eyes. She continued to squirm in his grip, trying to lick his face. "You," he said, a smile breaking through his grumpy façade, "are freaking adorable."

Nick laughed. He knew his brother had been pulling his leg. He'd always wanted a dog when they were growing up too.

"Styx, huh? Like the band?" Nick watched as Tony set the puppy in his lap and began petting her like the little puppy princess deserved. His hands kept her in place, effectively avoiding her tongue. For the moment anyway. Nick knew she'd get him before the night was over.

"No, the river," he corrected, then shrugged. "Plus, the tree branch." He flipped the burgers then opened the mini fridge getting out his own beer. He also grabbed all the condiments, the sharp cheddar cheese slices, lettuce, tomatoes and pickles he'd already prepped.

"Aww, such a fun place," Tony chuckled. "Remember that time during spring break our senior year? The time we camped over there and went tubing daily."

"That was the best time." Nick thought back to how much time they'd spent on the water and how little sleep they'd gotten that week hanging out with their buddies. "Yep, that's why I named her that. As an ode to one of my favorite places."

He looked out at the creek beyond the fire pit. Though it wasn't nearly as wide as Styx River, it reminded him of it. Just over four years ago, he had completely scored when this place had gone up for sale. The person who sold it to him was actually a frequent customer at the shop. The man knew that Nick was in the market and told him about it first.

"Plus, she's a retriever," Tony added, breaking into Nick's thoughts, "and will grow to love fetching sticks very much. Living right here on this creek will be the most fun for her. Has she gone swimming yet?"

"Not yet. But she's ventured down to the water a couple times."

"It won't be long," Tony said, then laughed when he was unable to avoid her fast-acting tongue. She happily licked every inch of his face.

"Damn, Tony, that's the most action you've gotten—"

"Bullshit. You weren't in the Caribbean with me, bro. I got plenty of action on my trip."

Tony had always been the more outgoing one. Living on a sailboat was sexy and it attracted a lot of attention. Tony sometimes accepted that attention. Nick wasn't wired that way. He needed to have a much deeper connection with a woman before having sex with her. He'd never been into the hook-up scene.

Nick flipped the burgers, then placed sharp cheddar cheese slices on top. He set the buns on the grate to toast for a couple minutes.

"Mamma also told me you've been seeing your old high school crush."

Nick couldn't help the smile that quirked his lips, or the heat that flashed in his belly. The reaction was both instant and intense. "Yep, Emerson Taylor. Do you remember her?"

"Vaguely." Tony had calmed Styx down, petting her into nearly a comatose state resting on his lap. He sipped his beer before continuing. "I knew of her because I knew what you were up to. But I was busy chasing after Amelia Denton. Remember her?"

Nick stacked the burgers and buns together and carried them over to the table between the chairs and set them down next to all the fixings. "I do. All-star cheerleader."

Nick sat and sighed, pressing into the cushioned back of the Adirondack chair. He was exhausted from being at the festival all day today. They'd sold several kayaks and he'd had to do a lot of heavy lifting since Terry was working at the shop today. This was really the first time he'd gotten to sit.

He was glad for the business, but his body was tired.

Now, he was ready to devour the burgers beside him. He loaded his with lettuce, tomato, pickles, and a homemade sauce made popular at the big M fast-food joint, then took a large, satisfying bite. "Damn that's good."

Nick closed his eyes and chewed, the tang of all the ingredients melding together on his tongue, zinging his taste buds left and right. There were certain foods that just lit them up and a perfectly cooked medium-rare angus beef burger with the right blend of condiments to veggies, and the cheese melted just so was one of them.

Tony set Styx down at his feet and wiped the hair from his lap and hands. Styx raced over to Nick's chair and sat dutifully, looking hopeful. "Sorry, girl, no scraps."

"How long's that gonna last?" Tony grumbled, setting about making his burger. After layering lettuce, tomatoes and pickles onto his burger, Nick knew what was coming next. He watched his brother pull a small bottle from the front pocket of his linen button-down shirt. He always had a bottle of hot sauce in this pocket.

Tony added it to everything.

After Tony swallowed his first bite, he said, "So, Emerson Taylor. What's she been doing since high school?"

Nick wiped his mouth with a napkin, removing the excess ketchup that had oozed out of the last bite of his completely demolished burger. His eyes trailed Styx as she started following her nose, leaving the concrete patio moving towards the water. "Went to college up in New York and has been working in finance on Wall

Street. She's home now for an extended visit because her mom is having health problems."

Tony sent him a look. "That sucks."

Nick nodded. "Yep. I ran into her when I was covering for you at the Keel. She was trying out online dating and was picking some real douches," Nick scoffed. His mind flashed on bumping into her in the hallway that first night. He'd been so damn stunned when he'd spotted her across the room, that he couldn't help himself. He'd had to talk to her. So just like in high school, he'd been loitering in the hallway, waiting for a chance to see her.

"So you thought you'd be the better pick?"

Nick could hear the teasing tone in his brother's voice. He got up to get them both another beer. "You shoulda seen these guys, T. I am definitely the better pick." He handed Tony's beer to him then sat back down. He whistled for Styx and had a treat ready for her when she ran back to his side. "Good girl."

A smile curved Tony's lips. "I'm only kidding, Nicky, don't sell yourself short. You are a great catch. Emerson would have to be blind not to see it. You're a successful businessman. You've got a solid home in a prime location. You're ridiculously handsome and now have an adorable puppy. What's not to love about you?"

Nick raised his beer in salute and lifted Styx onto his lap, giving her ears a good scratch. "I'm also an incredibly thoughtful brother and wanted to offer you a place to stay tomorrow night."

Tony looked over at Nick, his brow quirked. "And why would you do that?" he asked before taking a sip of his beer.

"Because I'm gonna need to borrow your sail-boat."

Tony nearly choked. He wiped his chin with the back of his hand. Tilting his head to the side, his eyebrows lowered, and he sputtered, "Come again?"

"I invited Emerson for a sunset picnic sail..." Nick's words trailed off, but the smile the image invoked could not be erased.

His brother's eyes went from squinty to wide open when he said, "What? It's not like a car. You can't just ask, hey, can I borrow your home to take a girl out on a date?"

"I'm a skilled sailor. You know I respect your home and will take excellent care of it," Nick reassured him.

"You're just looking to get laid."

Nick had to bite the inside of his cheek to keep from laughing out loud. "Not true."

"Bullshit." Tony laughed. He reached his deck shoe out and kicked Nick's runner where he had his legs stretched out, feet crossed. "There ain't no way you're taking her out on the water for a romantic evening and not even considering sex. Bullshit," he repeated with a chuckle.

Nick just stared him down, struggling to keep a straight face, but a grin slowly crawled across

his lips. "Damn right, man, but only if she's willing. Emerson is amazing and I won't fuck it up
by being stupid."

# Chapter Fourteen

The Art Festival was over. They were back at her mother's ready to rest and recuperate after the hectic few days. Both Carolyn and Sidney were successful, so that made all the energy and effort worth it.

Emerson had about twenty minutes to freshen up before Nick would be here to pick her up for their sailing date. She jumped in the shower and tried to control her anxious thoughts. After her panic attack last night, Emerson couldn't help thinking about all the topics she and Callie discussed. Was it possible for her to stay? Was it possible that she could live here, in this beautiful, thriving community that she'd been so eager to get away from twelve years ago?

She shaved her legs and soaped her hair at the same time, trying not to be too fast that she nicked her skin. And, yes, she was prepping just in case things escalated between them, picking up where they left off in the cab of his truck.

Rinsing her hair, Emerson tried to close her eyes against the steamy images of them wrapped in each other's arms. Their lips melding, their tongues caressing each other's. But those thoughts only made the hot water and soapy lather on her body more sensual. Emerson's eyes opened wide, and she blew out a breath. Turning off the water, she reached for a towel.

If things continued like they did the other night, then she'd likely be having sex with Nick Valentino tonight.

On a sailboat.

In the bay.

Emerson had never been very adventurous. Not with vacations. Not with food. Not with meeting new people. And she'd never ever been adventurous with her sex life. She'd only had a few partners over the years. Her last being Evan, and she'd gotten too busy with work that she'd practically forgotten he was there.

Just looking at Nick Valentino, she knew that he was out of her league when it came to sexual encounters. Having sex on a boat was likely not a new thing for him, but it was crazy talk to her.

She was also being presumptuous. The man had invited her for a sunset sail picnic. Yes, true, but then her mind flashed once again to how they'd ended the other evening.

Her rocking on the thick length tenting his shorts. His thumbs brushing the sides of her breasts. Her panties wet, heart melting.

Yeah, sex was definitely a possibility tonight.

Glancing at her watch, she let out a little shriek and pulled the towel off her hair. Running a brush through her wet strands on her way back into the bedroom, she tried not to overthink her underwear choices. Putting on a matching set was as sexy as it would get tonight.

She quickly donned her blouse and a pair of shorts, then slid her feet into her deck shoes. She threw a sweater into her bag for when the temperature dropped after sunset. Back in the bathroom, she swiped her favorite chapstick off the counter. Adding a layer of it to her lips, she tossed it into her bag and zipped it up on her way out of the bedroom.

Nick would be here any minute. Would he come to the door? Or would he honk from the driveway? Should she introduce him to her mother? Lordy, she felt like she was back in high school going on her first date again.

That had been a time that she'll never forget.

She'd been sixteen and her new boyfriend had asked her to go to a concert. He was picking her up early so they could go to dinner before the show. Right when he pulled in the driveway her brother had just happened to arrive home from college for the weekend. Logan made a big deal out of it and embarrassed the crap out of her. She hadn't really forgiven him for that.

Tonight, would definitely go smoother.

She placed her bag on the bench by the front door and headed toward the noise in the kitchen. Nerves started to skitter around in her stomach in anticipation. A blush slowly crept over her cheeks.

"What's got you so red?" Sidney asked the second she entered the room. Her sister was pacing across the kitchen with baby Michelle on her shoulder. A half-asleep baby.

"Must have gotten some sun today," Emerson answered, not wanting to share the real reason. She glanced at Carolyn who was sitting at the kitchen table drinking a glass of well-deserved wine. She had been a big seller at the festival this weekend, having sold twenty-five paintings and numerous prints. Sidney had a successful weekend as well, though her sales were fewer. She wasn't as popular as their mother, yet, but she was very talented.

Events like these festivals can be hit or miss. You never know if you're going to sell anything. The weather had been perfect, and it brought out the crowds. Crowds eager to shop.

"I'm so happy for you both. What a successful festival you had this year." Emerson patted her hand where it rested on the table, happy to feel no shaking currently. As soon as they'd gotten home, she'd taken her next dose of medication, and it was keeping the symptoms at bay for now.

"Thank you, dear. I couldn't have done it without all of your help." She smiled up at Emerson, the line of their mouths so similar. Her mother's eyes began to twinkle. "I hear you're going on a date tonight. On a sailboat."

Emerson quirked an eyebrow at Sidney who huffed out a laugh and paced the opposite direction, Michelle now sound asleep on her mama's shoulder.

"Yes, I am." Emerson willed the blush to stay away for at least another five minutes. "I'll be home late—"

"Or not at all," Sidney mumbled under her breath, though loud enough to be heard across the room.

"—so don't wait up." This time she scowled at her sister. It didn't matter that they were in their early thirties and Sidney was married with kids, talking about staying out all night with a man just wasn't discussed in front of their mother.

Carolyn was biting her lip now, obviously having heard Sidney's comment. "You have fun, dear, don't worry about me and my beauty sleep," she said with a wink.

Emerson practically ran to the front door when she heard the doorbell. She knew she'd have to bring him to the kitchen to formally meet her mother and sister, but damn if she didn't wish they were already on the boat.

With her hand on the doorknob, she took a deep breath and let it out slowly in an attempt to calm her nerves before she opened the door. Nick Valentino stood on the front porch looking like sex on a stick. She had no idea what that phrase actually meant, but it had popped into her mind the second she saw him standing completely at ease in well-worn gray shorts and a tight navy-blue tee that stretched across his chest and shoulders. On his feet were boat shoes similar to hers. His hair must still be wet from his shower, the strands darker than usual, and curling at the ends. She wanted to run her fingers through those curls, but she kept them tucked by her sides. The heat from his smile raised her body temperature by a few degrees. Damn he was sexy.

"Hi."

"Hey."

Yep, almost like that first date when she was sixteen.

"Come in. I want you to meet my mother and sister before we go."

"Absolutely." He followed her inside and placed a hand on her lower back as she led him to the kitchen. The heat from his hand sent lightning bolts zinging across her skin. There was no way a blush wasn't flashing on her cheeks right now. She decided she'd have to power through it and get them out of there as fast as she could.

They entered the kitchen and Emerson quickly tossed out introductions. "Nick, this is my sister Sidney and her sleeping baby, Michelle." Nick stepped forward and shook her sister's outstretched hand and whispered a hello. "And this is my mother, Carolyn." Nick quickly moved over to her when she attempted to stand.

"No need to get up. It's a pleasure to meet you," he said and shook her hand gently.

"Same here, Nick. How are your parents doing?"

"They're doing well. Thank you for asking about them. Emerson got to meet them officially the other night when we stopped by for a pizza dinner."

"Oh, pizza! That's what we need to have for dinner," Carolyn said, gazing over at Sidney. "Would Dave go pick it up if I ordered it?"

Sidney nodded as she continued to pace. "Of course, he will." She turned to look at Nick. "We love your parents' pizza. We get it every time we are over here on this side of the bay." Michelle started to squirm since Sidney had stopped moving. She preferred to be moving when she first went to sleep. If Sidney stopped too early, she'd wake right up.

"I'll let them know that." Nick smiled and nodded, then turned his head toward Emerson. She tipped her head toward the door, and he quickly said, "Well, goodnight, it was nice meeting y'all. Enjoy your pizza."

Emerson tugged on his hand and asked on the way to the front door, "What are we having for dinner?"

Nick held the door open for her to pass through first after she grabbed her bag. She paused in the doorway when he didn't answer right away, looking back at him. Her eyes met his, then drifted down to his glowing smile. It had his characteristic lop-sided look, his left side pulling up higher than the right. He shrugged sheepishly and winked. "Pizza, of course."

HE COULDN'T BELIEVE he was finally picking Emerson Taylor up for a date. It was over twelve years later than he'd expected, but he wasn't going to complain. He was just so happy that she'd said yes to a sunset sail with him. He'd stopped by the pizzeria on his way to her house to get a piping hot pizza pie with all the fixings that she liked and two bottles of wine.

Styx was currently sitting in her lap, the wind from the open windows whipping her ears about. She was so stoked to be going for a ride in the truck, her tongue lolling with happiness. She had no idea what was in store for her tonight.

"The winds are holding steady from today's heat. It should make for a very smooth ride." Nick signaled as he pulled into the marina and navigated the parking lot.

"Was it easy to talk your brother into letting you borrow his boat?"

"Hah! Nothing's ever easy with Tony." He couldn't help the grin that crept over his lips, smiling over the fact his brother had immediately called him on wanting to have sex with his date. Remembering his response was important. *Damn right, man, but only if she's willing. Emerson is amazing and I won't fuck it up by being stupid.* He wasn't going to do anything to screw up his chance with Emerson.

Nick cleared his throat when he realized he'd zoned out.

He pulled the truck into his brother's space and put it in park. Turning in his seat to face her, he shrugged. "He had a lot of questions, but in the end, he knew I was going to take good care of his baby. So he was cool with it. He's working until close, so he plans to just crash at my place tonight."

Emerson's gaze shifted out to the sailboats docked in the marina, but he thought he'd seen a blush rise on her cheeks before she turned away. Was she thinking about them spending the night on the boat? Was she as anxious as he was?

"Well, we better head out before we end up seeing the sunset still tied up at the dock." He powered up the windows and turned off the truck. "If you'll be in charge of Styx, I'll carry our gear."

Emerson jumped down from the truck with Styx under one arm and her bag over the opposite shoulder. Styx's tail wagged non-stop. She yelped a couple times when she saw gulls flying closely overhead. Emerson laughed. "Easy, girl. Those gulls would eat you for lunch. You'll have to work up to getting to chase them."

Nick hauled out his backpack with a folded-up wire crate attached to it, an honest-to-God wicker picnic basket his mother had packed for them, and a small cooler from the rear of the truck. With his arms full he used his knee to lift the tailgate and his hip and elbow to shut it.

The sun still shone brightly in the low western sky, and he was glad for the sunglasses covering his eyes. He guided them through the parking lot and down the ramp to Tony's slip. He couldn't wait to get out on the water.

The breeze caused the rigging to clank against the masts. It was like a musical symphony, and he loved the sound. The tinkling sound was quickly drowned out when the gulls raised a raucous as a fishing boat entered the marina. The fishermen were cleaning the decks and the birds started dive-bombing the water searching for scraps that were washed overboard.

"Here we are." Nick stopped beside dock number 24. Tony's 38-footer was named 3 *Sheets to the Wind*. Appropriate for a bar owner. He waited for Emerson to catch up. She'd set Styx down on the boards and the puppy was using her nose to guide her. Here and there and everywhere. He was pleased when he saw her squat to pee on the last patch of grass before the dock stretched out over the water. Nick whistled and it made him happy when Styx looked up and zeroed in on him, then pulled at her leash to get to him. "Good girl, Styxy."

The first thing he did when they stopped in front of him was to pull her life jacket from his backpack. Slipping it on her, he immediately felt the knot in his stomach ease a little. He'd been nervous thinking about bringing his puppy out here for the first time. Thankfully, Emerson was here to help keep an eye on her.

"I'll go first." Nick stepped onto the boat with his backpack and cooler. Setting those down, he reached back to lift the picnic basket and set it behind him on the deck. Finally, he turned back, hands outstretched. Emerson handed him Styx and he lowered her to her feet on the deck, looping his hand through the end of her leash.

"Now, it's your turn." Emerson looked down at him, the sun glinting off her bright smile. Her beautiful sea glass necklace glowing against her chest. She held her hand out and he grasped it, loving the feel of her skin against his. His fingers curled around hers and he helped her down, pulling her into his arms. "Welcome aboard."

"Thank you," she whispered, her gaze shifting from his to his lips. Did she want to kiss him? Because he sure as hell wanted to kiss her. Leaning forward, Nick placed his lips against hers, pressing, molding them with his. The zing he felt instantly on contact shot from his lips along a direct line to his dick. He deepened the kiss, losing himself in her softness, her eagerness, only breaking apart when the leash around his wrist tugged hard enough to snap the buckle on her life jacket. "Easy, Styx," he grumbled, his eyes focused on Emerson's, pleased to see hers were as glazed as his felt.

Styx, excited to explore this new place, pulled at her leash, her feet scampering over the smooth deck. Nick cleared his throat to focus his mind back on the task at hand and transferred the leash to Emerson's waiting hand.

Nick set about readying the boat. After unlocking the cabin and storing the backpack, picnic basket and cooler inside, he checked all fluid levels and thankfully, the engine started with a purr. He left it to warm up while he readied the lines to release them from the dock.

"Where should we sit?"

"Anywhere you like."

He paused in pulling off the bow line, his gaze stuck on how the wind teased her long locks, blowing them across her cheek. Her blue eyes glowed in the lowering light as she followed his every move. This was another happy place for him. He loved being on his brother's sailboat. But really it was the water for him. He could be on a paddle board, and he'd be just as happy.

Once he'd untied them from the dock, he motored out of the slip and headed for the bay. He felt so at ease at the helm. He wanted to impress Emerson tonight and by the looks she was sending him under her lashes while trying to appear interested in her surroundings, he figured he'd succeeded.

"Just remember the most dangerous place to be on a sailboat is within range of the boom when we are under sail," Nick explained, resting his hand on the stationary boom.

"Understood," she said with a nod, "thank you for the reminder." Her eyes returned to focus on all the boats that they passed. She looked happy to be here. He had hoped that being on a sailboat again wouldn't bring too many sad memories to her about her father. He planned to help her create new memories tonight.

Pulling his mind off those thoughts, he reeled back in and focused on the water in front of him. When Styx barked, a smile curved his lips. She stood with her back paws on Emerson's legs, and her front paws leaning against the top of the bench, nose into the wind. It twitched, sniffed and snorted. Her ears flapped when she turned her head, looking over at him, with a look of such pure joy on her face.

She was going to have the best life with him. He was so happy to have stumbled across her. Thanks to Emerson.

He was beyond happy to have both of these girls in his life.

After they cleared the jetty on the outside of the marina, Nick turned the boat into the wind and powered down the motor. "Are you ready?"

"Yes!" She actually clapped with excitement. He was so glad he'd asked her to come out here. He hadn't forgotten her story about her dad and her favorite spot to sit on the boat. He'd make sure she had time to relive those memories. "What can I do to help?"

"First, let's clip Styx's leash here," he said pointing to a carabiner near him, "so she's securely out of the way."

Emerson clipped Styx's leash then got to her feet, avoiding the boom that was shifting as the boat rocked. Emerson stepped agilely up onto the deck. He unzipped the cover on the mainsail and watched as she ran her fingers through her gorgeous hair, which was sparkling gold in the sunlight, pulling it back and up into some kind of ponytail, but more like a bun. He didn't know the technical terms for women's hairstyles.

It was up and out of her face for now, at least until the wind loosened a few of those strands. Or his fingers did. He couldn't wait to help loosen her hair for her later on tonight. If he could be so lucky.

# Chapter Fifteen

Emerson closed her eyes, letting the wind whip against her face, breathing in just a hint of salt in the air. Because Mobile Bay was an estuary, it held a mixture of freshwater and saltwater. And since they were near the north end closer to the delta, there wasn't much of a briny breeze here.

See, she had been paying attention in school.

Emerson felt a calmness spread throughout her body starting at her hair follicles and oozing all the way to the pads of her toes inside her deck shoes. A calm brought on by the wind on her face, the water lapping at the bow of the boat as it started cutting through the waves, and the sunlight warming her from the outside and penetrating deep within her soul. Something was happening here. Emerson just wasn't sure what it was.

But one thing she did know.

Happiness was taking root deep in her soul.

She turned back to look at the man who was the reason behind that happiness. He looked so confident and competent hoisting the mainsail. His biceps stretched the hem of his t-shirt sleeves, making her drool a little. Sweat beaded on his brow, but the smile on his handsome face told her that he was in his happy place. That he loved what he was doing.

Seeing him in that moment her mind flashed to a memory she had of her father in much the same position. The wind in his hair, the sun on his face, his hands confidently trimming the sails to keep them moving over the water at a fast clip. She'd enjoyed their weekly sailboat rides. After her father died, she'd often wandered down to the dock and sat on the sailboat and cried. She'd been heartbroken when her mother had sold the sailboat. It had been a link between her and her father and when it was gone, she'd been devastated all over again.

"You ready to unfurl the jib?"

Nick's voice broke into her memories, pulling her out at the right instant, right before she became teary. Snapping out of it, she realized the mainsail was already up and secure. She'd been daydreaming for a while then. "Ready, Skipper."

Nick's usual lop-sided grin stretched into a full-blown, blazing smile. Chuckling, he pointed to the mast. "Okay, first mate, I want you to come over here and grab the furling line and the jib sheet. You're going to ease up on the furling and wrap the jib sheet around the wench and use it to unfurl the sail."

Emerson sat down on the deck where he indicated. She took hold of both lines. "There you go, ease this one out. Now start tugging on the jib sheet." She watched as the jib unwound from the wire coming down from the mast to the bow. The boat terms were starting to come back to her now. She'd heard them as a child but hadn't spoken the words in twenty-five years. The clanging of the rigging against the metal mast was music to her ears as the jib opened up.

"Now use the cleat to lock it in place. We'll have to trim the sails as we go to keep them taught for any wind changes, but that's how we get started."

Nick used the mainsail halyard to trim the sail and the wind pushed the boat through the water. Styx barked with joy and Emerson grabbed onto the railing to steady herself. Looking ahead, she was surprised to see only two other sailboats on the water today. The weather seemed absolutely ideal. Sunny, warm and with a strong wind just right for keeping the sails popped open.

"It's time."

Emerson looked over at him, holding the flyaway hairs off her face with one hand. "For what?"

"Lying in your favorite spot." He nodded his head toward the bow. It warmed her heart that he remembered. She unclipped Styx and took the pup with her, wanting to share this memory with her and make new ones in the process. The pup's feet scampered over the decking, her nose pointing into the wind.

Emerson sat down and crossed her legs. Styx jumped into her lap and licked her neck. She stroked the pup's soft fur and took another minute to stare at the view before her. The view of Nick, sunglasses on, face awash in the fading light, hands on his hips, feet spread for stability, looking a thousand times more handsome than should be allowed.

She took a deep breath and laid back, her head resting against the deck, the top of her head pointed towards the bow. The white sail flapped in the wind above her as Nick corrected the sailboat to go with the slight dip in the wind. The sail billowed out propelling them through the smooth water. Emerson's eyes closed and she held tightly to Styx while she relaxed into the rhythm of the boat, her upper body rising and falling slightly with the waves.

Happiness blossomed from her soul, a place where memories of her childhood were stored. Memories of her father and the fun they had together as a family out on the bay. Memories of him teaching her how to hold a slimy worm and pull the hook through it before casting her line into the water. Memories of him holding the back of her bike encouraging her to keep her balance and to pedal as hard as she could. Memories of him reading to her. She loved reading books in his lap.

Tears leaked from her closed lids. They were inevitable. Being on a sailboat reminded her of him. He'd been gone for twenty-four years but stepping onto this boat brought him to life again, like he was here beside her, and she needed to thank Nick for that.

Emerson felt Styx start to wiggle, her tail flopping back and forth across her arm, so she figured Nick must be nearby. She was prepared when his thumb brushed lightly across her cheek, wiping away her tears. Blinking her eyes open, her lips curled into a soft smile. "Thank you."

"For what?" His brow arched as he wiped the tears off her other cheek. He tucked the loose strands of hair the wind had grabbed ahold of behind her ear, his hand lingering on her cheek. The heat from it soaked into her skin, grounding her back in the present.

"For this." Her hand pressed into the deck below her. "For the invite, for the chance to be on a sailboat again. For a chance to relive some of the sweetest times of my life. So thank you," she whispered, tears unabashedly slipping from the sides of her eyes as she turned her head towards him, following his moves as he went from squatting next to her, to lying on his back beside her. His fingers clasped around hers and they held Styx's leash between them.

The pup immediately took his position as an invitation for kisses and jumped onto his chest, licking his neck and ear when he tried to duck her affection.

Emerson laughed and leaned towards him, pressing her lips to his, getting an extra kiss from Styx. Nick secured the pup with his other hand and kissed her back. It was the oddest sensation to have her body rising and falling with the waves and kissing him at the same time, since it alone caused her to feel lightheaded.

"You're welcome." Nick pulled back, resting his forehead against hers. They laid together like that for a few minutes before she started to worry that they might run into something and sat up. "It's okay," he reassured her, reading her mind, "we're clear for miles." Nick sat up and put his arm around her shoulders and tucked her into his body. "Selfie time?"

She chuckled and ducked her head. "Absolutely. Nothing like 'sailing hair, don't care'!" Emerson pressed her cheek against his and smiled at his phone. Styx also found her way into the picture, so he took a few more with all three of them.

"You're beautiful. Wild hair or calm." Nick kissed her lips but pulled back before she was ready. He probably needed to get back to manning the boat anyway. "Hungry?"

She paused. His deep, sensual tone could just be the aftereffects from kissing. He could simply be asking if she was ready for the pizza he'd promised her. Or, he could be asking if she was ready for the other tasty morsels on the menu that his lips and eyes were promising her. Hmm, she was really hoping for the latter.

Biting her bottom lip so she wouldn't giggle out loud, she said clearly, "Yes." And left it up to him to decide what their first course would be.


NICK COULDN'T READ her expression. He wished she'd elaborate, because when he'd asked the question, he'd innocently meant dinner, but from the reaction in her eyes and the heat on her cheeks, he realized she might have thought he meant sex. Well, he was hungry for that too. Like, ready to strip her naked and feast on her body right here and now.

But either way, he should probably stabilize the sailboat. He needed to take the sails down and drop anchor. "Okay," he stated, not alluding to either dinner option at the moment. He'd just have to see how things played out. "But, we have to work for it."

He got to his feet and turned back to her, hands stretched out to help her up. He pulled her to standing, then straight into his arms. Wrapping his arms tightly around her back, he buried his nose in her neck and shoulder, knowing that if he kissed her now, he'd lose track and he really needed to keep an eye on the water. Placing a soft kiss on her neck, he pulled back.

"Time to lower the sails."

He stepped away from her and maneuvered his way back to the cockpit, adjusting the mainsail to direct the sailboat where he needed it to go. Emerson followed him, stepping easily along the decking back to the cockpit. She clipped Styx back into the carabiner then said, "I'm ready to help, Skipper."

He couldn't help chuckling at the title. "Grab the jib sheet and the furling line." He watched her sit and grab hold of the lines, tugging as the sail rolled back up on the wire. "Great job, now for the mainsail."

Emerson worked with him to grab hold of the whipping sail, then bunch and secure it to the boom. The water lapped harder at its hull as the sailboat slowed. Emerson was a good sailor. They worked well together. He could picture them out here again on the water, even making it a routine event.

But then his brain rudely decided to remind him that she didn't live there.

That she was only visiting temporarily.

After his heart skipped a couple beats at the thought, his brain kindly reminded him of what his mother had said to him. "*Then,* mio caro, *maybe you should give her a reason to stay.*"

That jumpstarted his heart. He pulled himself out of his thoughts and stepped down into the cockpit. He ruffled Styx's ears on the way. "Hey, Styxy, are you loving this, girl?"

She let out the sweetest bark in response.

Nick turned over the motor and directed them into a shallow cove. The depth finder read twelve feet deep here. Knowing this area to be free of any seagrasses or oyster beds, it was safe to anchor in the sandy bottom. Luckily, the wind seemed to be dying down as the heat of the day faded, and they'd be protected here.

He turned the sailboat so that the bow was facing into the wind and killed the engine. Hopping onto the deck, he hurried to the bow to start paying out the chain on the anchor. "Okay, now we get to do some math. Ready? It's twelve feet deep here, plus there's about five feet from here to the water line. So now we're dealing with seventeen feet. We need to multiply that by the scope. Since it's a chain anchor we use the number five to multiply by to get the length of chain we need to pay out. Let's go, finance lady. Are you a human calculat—"

"Eighty-five," she interrupted with a smile.

Color him impressed. "Alrighty then, eighty-five feet of chain." He would have needed a calculator if he'd been alone. He released the brake on the windless and let the chain out, slowly, so it wouldn't pile up on top of the anchor. The wind caused the sailboat to drift backward, pulling on the anchor. Once the amount of chain he wanted was out, he set the brake on the windless. Taking a short piece of line, he tied it to the chain and transferred the load to a nearby cleat.

Moving back to the cockpit he started the motor again and put the engine in reverse to back down on the windless, setting the anchor into the seabed.

Once he was confident they were secure, he powered down the motor, flipped the switches for all the proper lights for anchoring, then took a moment to breathe in the silence that followed. "Ahh, listen to that. Beautiful, isn't it?"

"Well done, Skipper. Yes, the silence is lovely after the popping of the sails and the rush of the wind."

Styx yipped, standing on her hind legs.

"You did great, Styx! What an excellent co-skipper you are." Nick unclipped her leash from the carabiner and picked her up. He kissed her snout and accepted all of her kisses in return. "Now, it's time to eat."

"What can I help with?"

"Will you monitor Styx while I set up her crate? She can eat her dinner in there."

"Of course, I'm always happy to love on this sweetie for a bit."

"We can set out our dinner after we get her secured. She's too interested in people food, so I'm hoping to keep her away from it for as long as I can."

Emerson accepted the leash from Nick, and she stepped up onto the deck with her. Styx led Emerson for a "walk" around the decking, her nose leading the way. Nick watched them for a minute before heading into the cabin. He unclipped the crate from his backpack and quickly assembled it. He tossed her blanket into the bottom of it and set up food and water for her inside. Grabbing the picnic basket, he carried it back onto the deck.

The sun was getting lower in the sky, and he wanted to toast to the two of them before it went down.

"Oh, Nick!"

His head whipped around at her call, scared that Styx had fallen over or jumped. But when he saw both woman and dog, he started breathing again.

"She peed on the deck."

Nick hung his head, glad there wasn't anything big to worry about, and let out a ragged breath. "No problem. I'm glad she took care of that before going in her crate. We can throw some water on it to wash it off."

"I'm sorry, I didn't mean to scare you. It just surprised me, that's all."

"I thought she'd fallen in or something. I'm glad that it was only peeing on the deck. I'll have to tell Tony that Styx christened his boat. He'll love it."

Emerson's grin turned to a cringe. "I'm thinking he might not love it."

Nick laughed. "Well, we could just not tell him then."

"Maybe we should go with that," she agreed.

Nick grabbed a jug of water from the cabin and brought it to the spot, pouring it on the area, washing the pee over the side of the boat. "There, all gone."

Nick held his hand out for the leash and led Styx back to the cockpit. She took the big leap and jumped to the bench then to the lower decking. He carried her down the ladder into the cabin and when she saw her food and water bowls, she eagerly pushed against him to get down. He lowered her to her feet and took her life jacket off her first before she ran inside her crate. "Happy eating, sweet pup." He rubbed her ears while she lapped at the water, then he closed the crate door and grabbed the cooler before heading back up top.

Emerson was standing on the bow looking out at the setting sun. She turned when he approached and the smile she flashed his way warmed him more than the sun. He didn't know how he'd gotten so lucky to be here in this moment with her, but he was thankful. Even if they only had this one night, he was going to make the most of it. He could hope for more but would have to be satisfied with what he could get since her home was in New York City.

Nick knelt and opened the picnic basket. On top was a red and white checkered tablecloth. He chuckled when he spread it out. Only his mother would pack that for a picnic on a boat. The pizza box was inside a warming bag. He was surprised to find the box was still warm. Deciding against the plates she'd added, he set the box on the tablecloth. They could hold their slices over the box. He knew Emerson could handle that. Next, he pulled out a bottle of wine from the picnic basket. From his cooler he took out two stainless steel wine cups that had been chilling, and a bottle opener.

Emerson had taken a seat across from the pizza box and held the cups while he poured the wine. After securing the bottle he raised his glass and felt his lips curve just from looking at her beautiful smile. The sun rested just above the horizon, and the waning light caused Emerson's eyes to glow as her gaze held his. She held her cup up. He had so much he wanted to say, but all the words that were flowing so smoothly in his brain got jumbled up on the way to his mouth. The one thing that did come out was a line from a post he'd seen about sunsets. He figured it was perfect for this situation.

"Color-soaked skies and you at my side. Paradise."

Emerson blushed and her smile widened. "I'm no good at poetry, so I will just agree with that statement. This *is* paradise. I love being here with you. So thank you." She tapped her cup to his and they both took a sip. "Thank you for speaking to me at Keel & Rudder. Thank you for asking me out on a date. Thank you for making this such a special night."

"Cheers." Nick thought it was indeed a special night. "And you're welcome for all of the above. Thank you for accepting." He poured more wine into both of their cups. "Now to test how good the pizza tastes after it was baked almost two hours ago." He opened the box and pulled a few slices apart. Emerson reached down and grabbed one. She brought it to her lips and took a big bite.

"Delicious," she said around the mouthful, one hand coming up to cover her mouth. Her eyes twinkled and she took another bite. "So good."

Nick thought so too. He was pleasantly surprised how good the pizza tasted. The sauce was still warm and tangy. The cheese was still stretchy when he took his first bite. After he enjoyed his slice, he picked up another. Out of the cooler he grabbed a bowl of cold grapes and strawberries and set them by the box.

"Ooh, yummy fruit. This is the best picnic I've ever had, Nick," Emerson said, then popped a grape in her mouth. He couldn't help but watch her lips curve as she chewed. He wanted to taste those lips, and the rest of her, but first, the sunset.

# Chapter Sixteen

Emerson finished her slice. She couldn't eat anymore because her stomach was currently knotting up. She was anxious. Nervous. Ready, but not. She wanted to be in his arms, so she shifted around the tablecloth and sat beside him, their bodies facing west. The sun was just starting to dip below the horizon. Nick put his arm around her and pulled her snug against his side, their thighs molded together. The heat from his body was incredible. It slowly oozed into hers, making her skin tingle. Leaning her head against his shoulder she watched the sun sink below the water line.

"Have you ever seen the green flash?" she asked, trying not to blink, hoping to catch a glimpse of the phenomenon.

"I've been lucky to a couple of times. Have you?"

"Yes. Ah! There it was. Did you see it?"

He laughed. "I did. Spectacular. It was just for us," he added smiling down at her. Emerson met his gaze. His eyes were much darker in the post-sunset glow. More smoldery. More intense.

"Just for us," she repeated and tilted her head back, using his arm as a pillow. "It's time for you to kiss me, Skipper."

Nick's lips curved into his adorable lop-sided smile, and he leaned down to meet hers. She opened for him, and their lips molded, their tongues teased. She tasted the wine on his lips and felt drunk from all the sensations rushing through her body. His arms shifted around her, bringing her body to straddle his.

"This seems familiar," she whispered against his lips. "Though not as cramped." No steering wheel jabbing her in the back. But he was just as hot, just as aroused as he was in the cab of his truck. She wrapped her arms around his neck and shoulders and leaned all the way in, enjoying the rumble that radiated through his body when he chuckled in response.

The sensation of Nick's hands sliding up her body, from her hips to her shoulders then back down made her instantly wet. Heat flared where his fingertips slid along her skin under her shirt, gliding up her ribs to rest beside her breasts. His thumbs teased the sensitive skin below her bra cups, sliding back and forth before lightly caressing her peaked nipples through the lace.

Emerson sighed as his mouth left hers to kiss a path down her neck to her shoulder. A shiver

coursed through her body when his teeth barely grazed her skin. Oh my God, she was already
so wet, and her body felt so incredibly hot and
flushed, and they were only kissing. She knew
they were going to combust when they finally
got naked.

"I want to taste you. All of you."

His words sounded as delicious as they felt
against her overheated skin. She wanted that.
She did. But she wasn't too keen on all that out
here on deck. They were totally in the spotlight
from the beacon light overhead, now that the
night sky was darkening to a beautiful blue purple.

"Can we go below?" Her words were whispered but he pulled back and paused in sliding
her shirt up.

He met her gaze and nodded. "Of course. That
light is kinda bright. Not an exhibitionist, I'm
guessing."

She shrugged sheepishly. "No. I'm not into
that."

Nick's warm gaze moved over her face, settling on her lips. "What are you into, Emerson?"

Her immediate response. "You."

Nick's eyes flashed back to hers. Their gazes
held, and Emerson tried to see deep into his
soul. Then he kissed her, a deep, drugging kiss.
Her hands framed his face. The feel of the
prickly stubble tickled her skin. What would it
feel like on more sensitive skin, like, her inner
thighs, her stomach, her breasts?

She couldn't wait to find out.

Pulling back, she put her hands on his shoulders to push off him and stand up. His strong hands on her hips supported her, which she needed, since her legs were a little wobbly. Most of her blood had pooled elsewhere, so her extremities were tingly. He rose and led the way, his hand wrapped securely around hers. Emerson admired the strength in his forearm muscles and biceps stretching his shirtsleeve hem while she focused on putting one foot in front of the other so she wouldn't trip and embarrass herself.

Nick helped her down into the cockpit and went first into the cabin. He turned and looked up at her. His finger pressed to his lips as he pointed to the crate. Styx was sleeping. Aww, sweet pup. She crept down the ladder and walked softly past the crate to catch up to him at the bow. She didn't want to think too much about this being his brother's bed, and who he might have done this very same thing with, so she quickly muted those thoughts.

"I changed the sheets." He smiled at her. "I know what you're thinking."

She laughed and looked around. The two narrow windows alongside the room, plus the skylight above the bed let in the white beacon light so she could see the details of the space. It was similar to what they'd had on their sailboat. She'd loved it when they'd all crowded into the cabin with their parents on the rare occasion they sailed far enough away to spend the night on the water.

"Come here," he whispered, tugging her hand. She fell toward him and landed in his arms. His eyes were clear and focused on hers. She knew his next words were going to be serious. Sincere. "Are you sure about this? I don't want to rush you."

That was sweet of him to ask, but she was more than ready. The knot in her stomach had loosened and turned to spaghetti noodles the second he'd started kissing her above.

Her body was hot, wet and ready for him.

"I'm ready. I'm sure. I want to be with you Nick." She moved her hands up and down his arms, wrapping around his biceps. "I want to touch all these glorious muscles, feel all your heat against my skin—"

He cut off her words with his lips. "No more chit-chat," he laughed against her throat. Picking her up, he tossed her onto the V-shaped bed and crawled in with her, his body pressing her down into the surprisingly soft mattress.

Oh, lordy, his weight against her body was the best thing she'd ever felt. He was like her very own heated, weighted blanket.

Nick's hands framed her face, his thumbs caressing her cheeks, trailing down to move across her lips. One hand slipped behind her head, threading through her hair. She tilted her head to give him access to her ponytail, hoping that he was doing what she was thinking. Letting her hair loose. His fingers deftly removed the band and tossed it aside. Then those same fingers threaded through her hair once again, fanning it out across the pillow. "*Sei bellissima.* You are beautiful."

Oh my God, to hear those words in that deep rumble, and to feel the vibration against her chest, was just about too much. Her breath quickened. Stroking her hair more, he added, "I love your hair. The color, the texture, the length. It's so silky. I can't wait to feel it sliding across my skin." Then he devoured her lips again.

Emerson slid her fingers beneath his shirt, drawing it up to his shoulders. He broke the kiss to pull it over his head, then his lips found hers again. She traced all the muscles along his spine and shoulders, caressing his fiery skin with her palms.

So many muscles.

So much time to explore.

Then he rolled them. Sitting up, she pulled her blouse over her head and watched his eyes heat. His hands reached up to stroke the bare skin of her stomach and sides. His palms rose and his thumbs once again caressed the skin beneath her bra cups, then up over the silk to tease her nipples. Lightning bolts of sensation shot from her nipples to her toes, curling them into the sheets.

His hands moved behind her back to unhook her bra. She slid the straps down her arms, and he tossed it aside. His melty honey-colored eyes turned even darker as he took in her naked breasts and her flushed nipples. Looking down she saw that she was spotlighted from the skylight above. Damn his hands were big and so sexy. And surprisingly gentle. His hands cupped her sensitive flesh, letting their weight rest in his palms. He rolled her nipples between his thumb and finger. Synchronized delicious torture. Emerson let her head fall forward, her hair covering his hands, teasing her skin, making the sensations even stronger.

Nick rose up on one elbow, his mouth exploring one breast while his other hand continued squeezing her nipple. His tongue darted against the rigid peak before taking most of her breast inside. The wet heat and tug of his lips almost made her come. Her fingers raked through his hair, holding his head in place, asking for more.

He fell back against the bed, pulling her with him, switching to her other breast. Emerson's hips began to move, to press into his erection. Their clothes needed to be gone. She needed to see him, to feel him, to touch him. Reaching down between them she rubbed his hard length through his shorts, sliding up and down. Mimicking the instinctive movement her hips were making.

Nick took the hint and reached for the button on her shorts. Lowering the zipper, he hooked her underwear with her shorts and tugged them down over her hips. She shimmied to get them off, then tossed them aside. Reaching for his button, his hand stopped her. "Not yet."

She looked at him quizzically, her brow furrowed.

"If my pants come off, then so will I." He laced his fingers through the hand he stopped, bringing it up to his lips. "I don't want to come yet. I want you to come first. And second. And third, before I do. I want to make you feel so good, to be so wet and ready for me."

"Yes, please." She chuckled and molded her hands to his pecs. "But I have to tell you. I'm already wet. But why don't you find out for yourself." Emerson didn't know what was happening to her. She'd never been this bold in bed. Never been this chatty. Or felt this free.

"Yes, please," he repeated her words, and rolled them again. Emerson laughed at the speed at which he had her in position and how fast he moved down the bed, folded over on his knees with his feet hanging off the mattress. "I want to taste all of you, Emerson."

Emerson fanned her hair out behind her head and smiled as he watched her hair move. Then she placed her hands on her hips. Nick's hands covered hers, shifting them to her core. "Show me what you like."

Emerson's heart triple timed. She'd never touched herself in front of a man before. This was a whole new ballgame. At first, his words made her feel panicky. But the sincere look in his gorgeous gaze changed that panic to confidence. She pressed the sides of her thumbs into the skin above her pelvis, rubbing. Oh, the friction felt so good. And the second his thumbs joined hers, she almost came.

Biting her lower lip to keep from falling over the edge too soon, she continued rubbing her thumbs across her heated core to the inside of her thighs. Nick's fingers following her every move. His eyes bouncing back and forth from hers to their joined hands. Then her fingers caressed up her seam, spreading her. God, she was so hot. She felt like she was about to ignite. She had no idea foreplay could feel like this.

Closing her eyes to the sensations, she dipped her finger inside and spread the wetness up to her clit. When Emerson heard a rough growl and felt his hot exhale against her clit, she knew Nick had had enough of a tutorial. The second his tongue touched her, she emitted her own growl.

Oh my God.

Her hands dropped to her sides, and she fisted the sheets as his tongue stroked over her bundle of nerves. When he dipped his tongue inside her entrance, touching her soul, flashing lights pulsed against the backs of her eyelids like a disco show.

"Damn, you're so wet, baby."

His lips were touching her skin when he spoke and his words rumbled over her sensitive flesh, bringing her nearly to the peak. Her muscles strained to get there. He must have recognized she was close because he put pressure on her clit again, and dipped his finger inside her heat, stroking. When he pushed another finger in and slid them in and out rhythmically, she came. Her whole body bowed up, her toes curling into the back of his thighs, her hands pulling on the sheets, her mouth releasing a deep, satiated sigh.

Emerson was slow to come down from her high. But when she opened her eyes, Nick was looking at her from between her legs. The smile on his face was the brightest she'd ever seen. She'd never forget that image. It would be emblazoned on the backs of her eyelids, along with the disco light show, forever.

She tugged on his arms, wanting, needing him closer so she could kiss him. Thank him for the most amazing orgasm she'd ever experienced. He crawled up her body, dragging his nose along her skin. The prickly stubble on his cheeks scraped seductively across her overheated, ultra-sensitive skin raising goosebumps all over her body. He kissed each breast in passing before sliding his wet lips across hers. Wet from her. That turned her on even more. She stroked her fingers through his hair and held his head against hers, deepening the kiss, tangling her tongue with his.

She could feel his rapid heartbeat thumping against her breasts. It was running in time with hers. Her legs wrapped around the backs of his, pulling his erection closer to her seam. She needed those shorts gone. Sliding her hands down his back, her fingers inched under the waistband and squeezed his firm ass.

Nick shifted to the side, just enough that one of her hands could remain inside his shorts, gripping his ass. His leg rose so his knee rested between her thighs, pressing against her heat. She couldn't keep her hips from rising against it. Turning to her side, she curled her leg over his, squeezing, grinding, practically riding his knee.

Emerson closed her eyes when his lips left hers to blaze a trail down her neck, across her collarbone, brushing against the sea glass pendant before nuzzling her breast. More of those lightning bolts zinged when he suckled her nipple into his mouth, nipping it gently with his teeth. Nick stretched his hand around her back, smoothing across her ass and sliding between her legs. His fingers stroked her inner thighs and found her heat. Fingering her seam, he sliced her open, tweaking her clit before dipping deep into her entrance.

The pressure of his knee against her pelvic bone, his hot mouth devouring her breast, his hand caressing her from behind was an erotic assault on all her senses. She exploded on another powerful orgasm, this one topping the last. Stars twinkled in her vision.

Nick pressed his knee hard against her. She rode it as the waves of orgasm flashed through her body. She was so ready to have him inside her. "Now, Nick." Her voice was breathy. She'd never heard that tone from her before. But she'd never experienced anything like this before. So there was no comparison. These sensations and feelings were all new to her. And she was in heaven. "I need you in me. Those were the most beautiful, most incredible orgasms I've ever had. Now it's your turn."

Nick kissed her lips once more before rolling back to remove his shorts and boxer briefs. He pulled something from his pocket before kicking his clothes to the side. When he ripped the foil packet open, she sat up. Distracted by the strong length of him bobbing towards her, she paused in her reach for the condom and put her hand on him instead.

His skin was practically sizzling. She wrapped her fingers around him, and he groaned. Squeezing him, she slid her hand up and down his length. His hips rose with her actions. She knew he was ready. He'd been so patient giving her all the feels this whole time.

But she couldn't resist just one lick. Her tongue darted out and tasted him. His hand instantly gripped her hair. She wasn't sure if he wanted to hold her there or to pull her away. But he didn't move, like he was frozen, waiting to see what she'd do next.

What she'd do was give him pleasure. He'd given her so much, she wanted to return the favor. Licking him again, she pressed her lips against his head. Opening them, she took him into her mouth.

That was as far as she got.

"Too good, baby. Too good. I'd never last." Nick slid the condom on and pulled her over the top of him. She straddled his hips, sitting up on her knees. "*Sono pazzo di te.* I'm crazy for you." Her heart melted at those beautiful words. She'd never had a man speak another language to her, especially, not one so sensual and seductive. *Be still my heart.* Nick took hold of her hands and drew her arms out to her side so he could see all of her. "You're gorgeous."

She felt gorgeous. Her hair wild and hanging down to her breasts, teasing her sensitive skin. His heated gaze blazing a trail wherever he looked at her.

She felt the need to touch herself again. Who was she? Who was he turning her into?

He made her feel so powerful, so in tune with her body.

She released his hands and cupped her breasts, squeezing them. His heated stare penetrating her hands gave her the courage to do more. She rolled her nipples between her fingers and watched him lick his lips.

"I loved it when you nipped me right here," she said, rolling her nipples again. "I'd never felt that much pleasure before. I can't wait for you to do it again."

Her hands slid lower across her jittery stomach. Jittery from sexual tension building up, but also from her boldness. Her thumbs stroked across her pelvis, her fingers streaking down her thighs. She placed her fingers over the backs of his hands and moved them to where she needed him most. His thumbs brushed over her curls, barely touching the skin beneath. That feeling of anticipation had her dripping wet.

She let go of his hands, letting him explore, while she did the same. She grabbed his length with both hands and stroked him. Shifting her knees and coming forward, one hand resting on his pec, the soft hairs on his chest tickling her palm, she guided him inside. Letting him go once he slid in deep, her hands gripped his shoulders as he filled her. Her mouth dropped open at the intense pressure and pleasure she felt in her sex. He was so big, so hard, and felt so right. He touched her soul and her heart flared. This man was incredible. She leaned down, her hair curtaining him and kissed his lips.

His hands pulled at her hips, helping her to rise and fall on him, bringing them both the most immense pleasure. She'd truly never felt like this before. No other man had ever made her feel this deep connection with her soul.

Nick Valentino made every single inch of her come alive.

Emerson rose up, arching her back, her hands twining in her hair as she rode him. The beacon light shone through the skylight above her, spotlighting her. Never before had she ever wanted to be on display, but tonight she did.

Tonight, she felt sexy.

She felt happy.

She felt alive.

Nick's hands caressed her breasts as he pushed up inside her. One hand trailed down her stomach to press against her clit. Could she have another orgasm? Three would be a record for her. But in this moment, she thought she could. This man was on fire, and he was turning her on even more with every touch of his body to hers.

Emerson concentrated on the sensation of his fingers, now sliding against the sides of her clit. Every muscle was in tune with his touch. Even her heartbeat tapped in rhythm with his fingers and his thrusts. When those fingers pinched her clit, her orgasm skyrocketed out from her on a hearty moan. Shocked, she covered her mouth with her hands and laughed.

NICK PULLED HER down to him and rolled over so she was tucked underneath his body. Her breathing was erratic. And her pulse thumped in her throat. "Nick..." She didn't say more, she couldn't seem to catch her breath.

"That was the most beautiful fucking thing I've ever seen." So he said it for her.

It was. He loved watching her explode. She seemed so shocked by her orgasmic moan of pleasure that she laughed. Most. Beautiful. Fucking. Thing. Ever.

"Em..." He ached so badly. He needed to move. But he wanted to give her a minute to come back down to earth. "Are you ready?"

Emerson nodded, pulling at his body, so he'd line up with her. Nick didn't need help this time, his dick knew where to go. To heaven. He slid inside her so easily because she was so fucking wet. He pulled out nearly to the tip and slid home again, faster and faster, building up the friction he needed.

Emerson's hands roved over his back, down to his ass, gripping his slick skin. Her legs wrapped around his hips, helping to lock him in place. His lips took hers, his tongue moving in rhythm with the rest of his body. Her hot breath pulsed against his ear when his lips trailed down her neck to her collarbone. He needed her nipple in his mouth. She said she couldn't wait for him to take another nip, so he certainly wouldn't leave the woman hanging. He twisted so he could still be balls deep inside her, his hips pistoning for all he was worth. Once his lips closed around her nipple he heard her sigh. Her fingers threaded through his hair, scraping against his scalp.

His tongue rolled over her nipple, lathing it, loving it. Then his teeth surrounded it, scraping against the pebbled skin. When he felt he couldn't hold on another moment, his balls drew in tight and his toes curled so much he thought he'd lose the ability to walk, he bit down on her nipple. She cried out, and so did he, as the orgasm rushed through him like a freight train. The sensation seemed to pulse forever. He lathed her nipple again, trying to heal any hurt he might have caused in his moment of bliss.

Pressing his head against her chest, he listened to her heart thunder under his cheek. The beacon light above illuminated the sea glass pendant making it glow as bright as her eyes.

He never wanted to move.

He could live like this forever.

They could get pizza delivered.

They could survive on pizza, wine and each other.

When his breathing had come down to a reasonable level, he looked up at her. The light from above shone on him, but her face was lit enough to see that beautiful post-sex glow in her eyes. The glow he was proud to know he was responsible for. What'd she say? *Those were the most beautiful, most incredible orgasms I've ever had.* Well, damn, that just made him hard again thinking about that. *Easy. No need to rush things.* They both needed time to recover from the best sex he'd ever had.

Nick slid out of her and off the bed to dispose of the condom in the head. Returning, he paused in the doorway, leaning his arms against the frame, taking in the sight before him. She hadn't moved to cover herself up and she was on full display. Damn, she was gorgeous. And he didn't mean just her outward beauty, or her sexy body. But her, who she was. He had a feeling tonight had been different for her. It sure as hell had been for him.

"Can I get you anything? Water? Wine? Pizza?"

She chuckled and shook her head. "No, just you." She held her hand out and he crawled up the bed to her, lying back, pulling her into his body. Emerson wrapped her leg across both of his, and her arm across his stomach, settling her head on his shoulder. Having her there, lying against him was heaven. He kissed her forehead and closed his eyes, soaking in all the sounds around him. The water lapping softly against the hull was music to his ears.

Sighing deeply, he said, "That was beautiful. Not very poetic, I guess, but fact. My body is still humming."

"Mine too." Her breath blew across his nipple when she spoke, and he felt himself stir.

# Chapter Seventeen

A soft whining woke Emerson. It took a few minutes to come to consciousness. Her limbs felt like cooked noodles, limp and heavy as they lay pressed against a hot, hard surface. Her face rested against a similar hot, hard surface, her nose feeling tickled intermittently as that hot, hard surface rose and fell.

Her eyes flashed open with recognition.

Last night, after another glorious set of orgasms her body had been spent. They'd both flopped back on the bed and lay there panting. Holding his hand she'd fallen into a deep sleep. Somehow, she'd wound up curled around and over him in her sleep. She'd probably been seeking out his warmth since they'd never pulled any covers over themselves.

Her nose twitched again, tickled by the silky hair covering his pecs. She shifted back, easing the kink in her neck. She heard the whine again and realized it was Styx. Poor pup probably had to pee. She leaned back slowly, trying not to wake him, but his arms banded around her and held her against him. Her lips curved in response.

"Good morning, *bellissima*."

She felt the deep rumble of his words from inside his chest. Feeling them as well as hearing them made her heart squeeze. "Good morning, Skipper."

His chuckle shook his chest and made her laugh. She kissed his pec, his neck and stretched up to find his lips. His were warm and soft against hers. "Your puppy has to pee."

"I know," he whispered, "I just don't want to move."

She concurred. This was the best way to wake up. Magical even. She could feel the boat swaying in the water and wondered if the wind was going to be up again today. She'd love to spend more time sailing with him. But she didn't know his plans for the day. And she probably needed to get back to her mother's. Sidney and family will be heading home today. She'd like to see them before they leave.

She squeezed his pec before bracing herself on it and sat up. Her hair fell around her shoulder, and she wondered how frightful her bedhead looked. His hand reached up to gently run through it, curling the ends around his fingers. His eyes focused on her hair, watching it slide through them. It felt amazing. She'd always loved having someone play with her hair. Sidney, Emerson and Callie used to play beauty shop and they'd style each other's hair. She just enjoyed someone running a brush through hers, or like Nick was doing now, letting it slide through their fingers.

"Your pup's not the only one who has to pee. As much as I love how that feels, I gotta get up." His hand moved up to cup her cheek and she kissed the heel of his hand.

"Okay, you take care of you. I'll take care of Styx."

With that, Emerson tried to gracefully get herself off the bed and out the narrow doorway without mooning Nick too much. He chuckled at her wobbly attempt to cover her ass. She turned and threw a pillow at him, hitting him in the chest. His laughter followed her to the head. Once inside, she closed the pocket door and braced herself before looking in the mirror.

Damn. She'd never seen that glow on her face before. Her eyes were actually sparkling. Her lips were so flushed and a beautiful, deep rose color. It was like she had makeup on but didn't.

And her hair.

She'd expected tangled knots, but it hung loosely against her bare shoulders. Leaning forward she wondered if that red mark on her collarbone was a hickey.

She quickly covered her mouth trying to suppress the giggle that escaped. She'd just heard Nick walk past the door and hoped he hadn't heard her in here laughing. He'd think she was nuts.

Emerson froze. Her eyes bored into her reflection in the mirror. Could she be falling for Nick? As in, falling in love with him? As in, happily ever after, two point two kids, a dog and a house on the creek?

Her hands moved from her mouth to her forehead, pushing back her hair. A loud rushing sound filled her ears, and she drew in a few deep breaths, releasing them slowly until the rush receded and she could once again hear the call of the gulls and Nick's voice talking so sweetly to Styx up top.

Whew, she'd warded off that panic attack successfully. It was good she was recognizing the signs.

Okay. She could handle this. She just had to think this through.

Love?

Really?

She'd never felt like this with Evan. But he wasn't the best example. She didn't think she'd ever actually loved him. She'd just loved the idea of dating someone. At first. Then because she hadn't loved him, she'd found it easy to pull away from him and focus on work instead of their relationship.

Nope. She'd never felt this heart-pounding, fire-in-the-pit-of-her-belly feeling before.

She needed Callie. She needed her cousin to talk some sense into her. Love? Yes, she'd just had the most incredible sex—twice—and she loved the way he made her feel. She loved how much he cared for his parents and how he asked about her mother. She loved how excited he got about adding to her Gotta-Do list. And she wanted to experience all of those items with him. Tubing and camping. She hadn't realized how outdoorsy she'd actually wanted to be.

She needed more time—and space, she couldn't pace in this tiny bathroom—to think about this. She needed Callie to talk this out with her. And right now, she needed to pee, freshen up and head out there to look the man she was falling in love with in his smooth-as-whiskey-colored eyes and not let these newfound feelings for him ooze out of hers.

NICK THOUGHT HE heard Emerson laughing in the head when he passed by. What was that about? Though he couldn't blame her. He felt so good this morning that he too felt like laughing. He smiled down at Styx, who was trying to stand up on her hind legs and paw at the sides of her crate. Her yelping sounded so sweet.

"Good morning, Styxy! Calm down, baby, or you're going to pee in your crate. Here, let's get you outside." He popped the lock on the door and swooped her up. Holding her under his arm like a football, he dashed up the ladder and onto the deck just in the nick of time.

"Good girl, Styx. You did good holding your pee all night. I'm proud of you." Styx finished squatting and looked ready to take a walk-about. But he hadn't grabbed her leash or her life jacket in his quick dash up the ladder. "Not yet, girlie, we have to put your jacket on."

When he turned with her securely in his arms, his breath caught in his throat. Emerson stood at the top of the ladder dressed in the shirt he'd worn yesterday. She looked doubly gorgeous this morning in the pale light of dawn. The sun wasn't even up yet, the sky only lightening to a whiter shade of blue in the east. Stars still shone above, but the beacon made it easy for him to see her. All of her. Most especially the glowing smile on her lips. Then he noticed Styx's life jacket and leash in her hand.

"Thanks." He reached out and took it from her, slipping it over his pup's head. He set her on her feet on the bench and finished clipping it securely in place. He wrapped the leash around his wrist and followed where Styx led. "Join us for a stroll?"

Emerson chuckled and climbed out of the cockpit, taking hold of his hand. Lacing his fingers with hers he tugged her into him and placed a kiss on her forehead, breathing in her scent. He'd smelled it all night. A hint of lime. Must be her shampoo.

Styx sniffed happily while Nick and Emerson remained silent on their stroll, leaning into each other, walking slowly. He longed to pull her into his arms and kiss the breath out of her, but he held back, wanting to take things slowly.

Nick decided he would forget ever having a crush on teenage Emerson, because what he felt then was weak compared to what he felt now. That was puppy love, infatuation based only on her looks. Now what he felt was deep, strong, emotional love that was based on who she was as a person, not just her physical attributes. She was stunning to look at, but her mental beauty was so much more.

He didn't know what exactly caused him to fall over the edge of like to love, but he was there, and he wasn't going anywhere. His mind tried to pull what it had last night and remind him she was only here temporarily, but his mother's words spoke loudly over his. *Give her a reason to stay.* He was paraphrasing, but those were the important words. The ones that stood out. The ones that meant the most.

Would knowing that he loved her be enough to have her want to stay? He was afraid to ask. Afraid to be wrong. Afraid to not be enough. So he decided to keep this newfound discovery to himself for a bit. See where this thing between them would go.

He was startled out of his thoughts when a loud squawking rent the air. A Great Blue Heron had been resting on the bow. He let them know that their interruption displeased him.

Emerson stopped immediately at the sound, her hand flying to her chest. "Oh my God, that scared me."

Nick laughed. "Me too. Guess he wasn't too happy to be woken up." Styx pulled at her leash, trying to get to the spot where the bird flew off. She didn't bark, just yelped a little. Nick let her get closer to the spot, her nose working along the deck and up the railing.

"Well, that jolted me awake," Emerson whispered. "Got any coffee on this boat?"

"Absolutely."

Styx led them back around the port side and stopped at her pee spot. She added a little more to the puddle then Nick carried her back into the cabin. He'd wash that spot off later when they went back up top. Once he helped Emerson down the ladder, he closed the hatch so he could take Styx's leash off. She ran straight to her crate and lapped at the water left in her bowl. Next, she sat by her empty food bowl and waited.

"Aww, she's so cute," Emerson gushed. "What a good girl, Styx. So patient. That's exactly how I'm being too while waiting on my coffee."

Nick laughed as he scooped grounds into the drip coffee maker. He added water and pushed the on button before getting Styx's food. Priorities, right? Coffee before dog food. "Have a seat. I'll bring it to you." He placed a scoop of puppy food into Styx's bowl and watched her immediately start crunching.

Emerson looked around the galley, perusing the bookshelf along the back of the couch. "I like your brother's selection."

"You read thrillers? I'd peg you more as a rom-com reader."

Her head turned his way, her right brow lifted. "What if I'm both?"

"That surprises me. But I like it." Nick leaned back against the counter, crossing his arms over his chest as the coffee percolated in the background. When she leaned over to read more titles, his eyes dropped to the hem of his shirt rising up the back of her thighs.

"What's your favorite genre?"

Nick blinked, bringing the conversation back into focus. "Nonfiction. I'm more of a sports guy, maybe some military hero stuff."

Emerson turned to face him, pursed her lips and nodded. "Interesting."

"I don't find much time to read." He shrugged. "I'd rather be outside doing something. I don't like to sit still too long." His head tilted as he realized that wasn't true. "Unless I'm down by the creek, kicked back in my chair, my feet propped on the fire pit with a cold beer in my hand. Then I can sit for a stretch and listen to the water flow by."

Emerson sat on the bench seating with an extra-thick cushion that doubled as a couch. She drew her legs up, crossing her feet, her hands pressing down the hem of his shirt so she wouldn't flash him. "That's a perfect spot for sitting and watching nature go by. I enjoyed sitting there with you, having our first date."

"I did too." Nick smiled as he got two mugs off the shelf above the coffee maker. Opening the mini fridge, he pulled out the creamer and added some to both of their mugs. He scooped a small amount of sugar into hers. Nick brought both mugs over and joined her on the couch. He handed hers over and said, "Now, there are plenty more places around here for doing just that. We could go camping at Blakeley." Nick sipped his coffee and stretched his arm along the back of the couch. "They have a beautiful boardwalk along the river where we can sit and watch the wildlife, or the boat traffic go by. We could kayak in the delta—"

Her eyes widened. "What about the alligators?"

"Or we could go for a boat ride in the delta. That would give you more protection from the alligators." Her shoulders relaxed at that idea.

"I like that idea better." She looked thoughtful for a moment then blew on the surface of her mug. Nick had no idea how much time she had left here on her leave of absence. Was she thinking about that right now too?

"Well, you just have to decide what you'd like to do next on your Gotta-Do list." He hesitated with his next question, not sure he really wanted to know the answer. Especially if the answer was next week.

"Do you have a scheduled return date?"

Emerson looked down at the mug in her hands and seemed to hesitate before saying, "In two weeks. My month is half over."

Those words hung in the quiet space between them. Two weeks? Here he was thinking about forever and all he had was two weeks to *give her a reason to stay*.

# Chapter Eighteen

Emerson breathed in the sweet strawberry scent of her niece's baby shampoo as she hugged Michelle closely. She blew puffs of air into her hair drawing out the loudest giggles. This felt different than it did two weeks ago when she'd held her at the family cookout. A lot had changed in that time. For the better. She was more in tune with her surroundings. Slowing down to take time to see the people around her and interact with them on a cellular level.

She kissed her niece's head one last time before passing her off to her mom. Her nephew Eli tried to dash around her legs, but she quickly turned and wrapped her arms around his middle, lifting him off the ground. His feet wiggled wildly, and his giggles resembled the octave of his sister's.

"Eli, don't kick your Auntie Em," Dave said with a snicker as he strode past carrying three suitcases.

"Yeah, bud, I've got to get in all my tickles before you can get in the van." She dropped him back to the ground gently and gave chase when he ran off. He circled the van, and she kept pace behind him, making goofy sounds that only amplified his laughter. Her hands made contact with his ribs from time to time, and that only made him run faster.

Emerson heard Sidney ask Dave when she ran by, "*What's gotten into her?*"

*Sister, it would take too long to unpack all that.*

Emerson wasn't sure she had the words to explain it all anyway. Most of what had changed inside her had to do with feelings and ideas, and those were always so difficult to describe with words anyway.

She placed kisses on Eli's cheeks after she loaded him into the van. "Bye, my sweet nephew. Bye, my sweet niece. I love you." She blew them kisses. Eli returned a ton of them with both hands. Michelle's attempt was adorable. Her hand smacked against her mouth and that was it. But she'd take it.

Emerson's heart swelled with love for these two cuties. She couldn't believe how much she'd been missing out on by being so far away. So distant. And she didn't just mean not being in the same state, but emotionally distant. Not being involved. Not taking an interest in her sister's kids, or her brother's kids for that matter.

Emerson decided now wasn't the best time for self-condemnation.

Suddenly Sidney was there, arms open wide for a hug. The expression on her sister's face was pure joy. Her blue green eyes sparkling, her smile wide, showing a flash of dimples. She was the only Taylor kid who had them. They were passed down from a great-great-something on their mother's side of the family.

Emerson had always been a little jealous of her dimples, spending time as a kid looking in the mirror, pushing pencil erasers deep into her cheeks hoping the dents would stay and look like Sidney's. Thinking about it now, her plan was pretty ridiculous, but she'd wanted to be just like her sister.

Being only two years younger, they shared friends or sibling friends growing up and were always in school together. After graduation, Sidney had gone to a local university, so they'd still been close. But as Emerson approached her graduation date, her feet had gotten antsy, and she knew where she was headed. Once her sights were locked on New York, everything and everyone sort of faded into the shadows.

She couldn't believe how much life she'd missed out on these last twelve years.

Emerson walked into her sister's arms and wrapped hers tightly around Sidney's back. "Thank you for all your help with Mom this weekend."

"No, Em, thank you. You're doing an amazing job," Sidney said against her ear. Squeezing two extra times before pulling away, Sidney gripped

Emerson's shoulders and looked her in the eyes. "Thank you so much for taking time away from your life to come here and be here for her, for us. I know it was a lot to ask."

"I'm glad I'm here." And she was. She just wished it was for different reasons, of course.

"I can see that you are." Sidney pulled her head back, angling her jaw up and with a raised brow said, "But, you didn't feel that way when you first got here."

Emerson slowly shook her head, looking down at the grass under her deck shoes. "I've changed, Sid. Coming here, coming home, to this place," she nodded at their childhood home, "to this town, spending time in the quiet and moving at this slower pace, has changed me. It's hard to explain," she ended with a huff, pulling away to pace.

"I think you're explaining it just fine, Emmie. I've never understood how you could enjoy living in New York. Visit, yes. I've loved visiting you there. But to live at that speed, in that level of noise pollution, with that many people is astounding to me. Yet you've thrived there. You're an extremely successful businesswoman in a high-level position at Lawson Financial and they are lucky to have you." She paused, following after Emerson, stepping away from the van with the loud, fussy kids. "But are you happy?"

Emerson's heart thudded heavily in her chest. Wasn't that the million-dollar question? Breathing in deeply, she took a minute to respond.

Well, more than a minute, because she didn't know what to say. Or how to explain all the emotions swirling around in her head right then.

Sidney put her hands on Emerson's shoulders again and squeezed, massaging, comforting. "It's okay. Don't answer. I can see the answer for myself. I think you can too. There's a lot to think about, little sister, so I hope you take some time to reflect. Plus, I haven't even gotten to mention Nick Valentino," she threw out with a chuckle.

Emerson immediately blushed, her lips curling just from hearing his name.

"Exactly. Even more to think about. Maybe it's time for a change. It'd be good to have you close. I've missed you. Besides, Eli and Michelle need someone around who can help them with their math homework. I'm an artist, I don't math," Sidney announced, then hugged her sister once more before getting into the passenger seat of the van.

Emerson laughed and waved goodbye as Dave beeped the horn twice while backing out of the driveway. *I've missed you too, Sid.* Life was different now that they were in their early thirties, but she did miss being around her sister. Reminiscing, talking, laughing.

Argh, she hated having to think about change.

Taking the path around the side of the house, she went through the garden gate and entered the backyard. The flowers were starting to bud with a few overachievers already open and ready for business. Pinks, yellows and purples dominated the fence line. Her favorite, Shasta daisies, sprouted intermittently throughout the garden. She liked the splash of bright white amidst the sea of color.

Making her way across the thick, green grass to the water line, Emerson forced her mind to focus on what Sidney had just said. *Maybe it's time for a change.* Squatting on the sandy beach, she picked through the shells at the wrack line, turning over the broken moon snail shells and open butterfly clams. The water lapped gently near her feet.

The wind hadn't actually picked up today like it had yesterday, cutting their morning of sailing short. She'd been disappointed over not getting more sailing in, plus all that extra time with Nick, but also grateful since she'd needed to get home to say goodbye to the family.

And bonus, it gave her more alone time to think.

To think about their amazing night together.

To think about her feelings for him.

Was she falling for him?

And now, on top of that, Sidney gave her something else to focus on. Change. Emerson got to her feet. All these thoughts made her feel the need to move. Stepping onto the dock, she strolled slowly to the end, gazing at the sun sparkling on the water's surface. Her eyes searched the water like they always did, hoping to spy a blue crab swimming at the surface or a mullet jumping out.

*Change.* What would it be like if she made that big of a leap? Quitting her job, moving home? She couldn't live here, with her mother, even though there was plenty of space, and her mother would welcome her. That's just not what she'd want to do.

So she'd have to get a place, get a job. What the hell would she do for work? Emerson sat down at the end of the dock. Holding her hands above her eyes to block the glare from the sun, she stared out at the water, shaking her head.

This was crazy to even think about. Yes, her heart, mind and body had changed just from being here for two weeks, but that happened on really good vacations too. People paid really good money to make that happen in their lives.

What if it didn't last? What if she started to regret the decision to leave NYC, to leave the job she'd sweat, bled and cried for, to move back home, to a place she hadn't lived in for over twelve years? What then?

She'd never be able to get her job back if she changed her mind.

They wouldn't even blink an eyelid if she turned in her notice. As much as she thought that she did for Lawson Financial and how important she was in the day-to-day workings of the company, they could obviously get by without her since it'd been two weeks, and they weren't knocking on her door begging her to come back.

Emerson's eyes caught on a dark fin cresting the surface of the water about twenty feet out from the end of the dock. Not blinking, she waited. There it was again. And that dolphin had a buddy. She saw two dorsal fins pop up at once, then slice back down through the water. She'd always loved dolphins. They were interesting creatures and so playful. A laugh burst from her when one of the dolphins she'd been watching leapt from the water.

Okay, that was a nice distraction.

Now back to the next important topic at hand. Love.

Her mind snapped back to that neon sign flashing in the background. Was she really in love? She felt happiness, joy, desire. She adored his laugh, his kind heart. She was infatuated with his lop-sided smile, his sexy abs, his strong hands holding hers.

Did all that put together equal love? Emerson smoothed her fingers over an empty moon snail shell she held in her hand as these thoughts raced through her mind.

What happened if she made the big leap, quit her job, moved back here, and started a relationship with Nick...and it didn't work out? What then? Then she'd be stuck in this small town with the man she thought she'd fallen in love with and made all these big changes to be with. Maybe since this thing with Nick was so new she shouldn't use him as her only reason for even contemplating a move this big. She had to focus on all the other positives that were in play here.

Her health—her body definitely felt more at peace.

Her happiness—she certainly hadn't smiled or laughed this much in years.

Her heart—being around her family made her realize how much she'd missed them.

And right now, she needed to get back inside and check on her mother. If she wasn't up from her nap yet, maybe Emerson could close her eyes for a few minutes. Having not gotten much sleep last night, she was exhausted. Now, if only she could actually rest and not just relive all those magical moments from last night the instant she closed her eyes.

***

Nick pushed open the back door of the pizzeria, leading into the kitchen. He wasn't at all surprised to see Tony seated at the worktable chopping vegetables. Tony sent him a head-nod greeting when he noticed Nick entering the room.

Setting the picnic basket down by the office door, he stopped to wash his hands before joining his family.

"Nicky!" His mother grabbed his face, pulling him down so she could kiss his cheeks. "So, how did it go last night?" Her eyebrow rose with her last word.

"Is he in the same clothes from yesterday?" Tony asked, tossing the chopped mushrooms into a container.

Nick kissed his mother's cheeks and smiled in answer. Nothing Tony said could make him agitated today. He was on cloud nine. Picking up a knife he started slicing a green pepper.

"Thank you, Mamma for the picnic basket. It was perfect. And Papà, the pizza was still warm and delicious about two hours later when we anchored up for dinner."

His father groaned, and punched the dough harder, rolling it and stretching it into shape.

Waiting to eat a freshly made pizza pie for two hours was sacrilege.

"Was it a beautiful sunset?" She obviously wanted more details. "It was windy."

"Yes, perfect for sailing, Mamma." He turned and watched her eyes when he said, "And the sunset was almost as pretty as Emerson." He'd added that for her benefit, but also because it was true.

His mother squealed and a rosy blush bloomed on her cheeks. She started stacking the containers for the salad bar and nodded her head toward the dining room. "Come with me, Nicky. Bring the lettuce, will you?"

Nick picked up the large bowl of salad greens and followed her through the swinging door into the dining room that was as familiar to him as his own. Although, he had nothing in his house that was red, possibly because of the overabundance of it here in the pizzeria.

Setting the large bowl down in the center of the chilled cart, he reached for the containers she had stacked on her arms. Placing them in their slots, he turned and leaned back against a chair nearby. And waited. He knew she was just chomping at the bit to interrogate him.

"Are you just getting back from your date?"

Nick nodded, his lop-sided grin in place.

She bit her lip to hold back her squeal of joy this time. Tears filled her eyes. He wasn't alarmed, she always cried when she was happy.

"Oh, Nicky, I'm so happy for you. She is lovely. I'm so glad you came by the other night so I could meet her formerly. And meet your sweet pup." Her brow furrowed and she looked around the room. "Where's Styx?"

"She's in the truck. I know she can't come in the restaurant. I don't want y'all to get any violations."

His mother wiped a tear from her cheek. "Thank you for understanding."

"Of course." He crossed his arms over his chest. "She's fine. The windows are down, and her leash is clipped to the seat so she can't jump out. I'll go check on her in a minute."

"How did she do on the sailboat?"

Nick's lips curved. "She was an excellent sailor. We aren't going to tell Tony she christened his boat twice," Nick said in a stage whisper. She laughed and hugged him again.

"I'm so, so happy for you, *caro mio bambino*," she whispered against his chest.

"Thanks, Mamma." He pulled back, holding onto her elbows. "But she's only got two weeks left of her leave of absence from work."

"Two weeks left to make her want to stay," she added emphatically, poking him in the chest.

"How am I gonna do that, Mamma? She's got a career in New York, a life, a home."

"She could have all of that here too. And," she drew out the word, "she could have love. If you show her what's in your heart, Nicky, she will choose you."

He frowned. "How can you be so confident?"

"Because that's how I chose your father. He showed me what was in his heart, and since I felt the same, it was perfect."

"That's beautiful, Mamma, but that was a different time, in a different country. You were much younger than we are. Emerson has a career, not just a job."

"So do you. But would you give it up for love? If it was something you could do somewhere else, wouldn't you rather be with someone that makes your heart happy?" She pressed her palm against his chest right over his heart.

"Sì, Mamma. Yes, I would." And his heart was happier with Emerson in his life. And now Styx.

If he could have them both, and live in his home on the creek, and work in his shop, and be near his family, then there wouldn't be much more he could ask for.

# Chapter Nineteen

"Mrs. Taylor, it's a pleasure to meet you."

Stacy, the home health nurse took a seat in the chair beside Carolyn's. Emerson sat on the edge of the couch, antsy about this visit for some reason. Maybe it was because her mother prided herself on her stubbornness and it would be just like her to refuse this woman's time. Carolyn Taylor did not want to admit that she was in need of assistance in her own home.

But Emerson wouldn't be here forever to help her with things, like opening her medication bottles, getting the laundry done, making meals. Stacy was here to interview for the job.

"Nice to meet you too." Carolyn was a southern woman, so she had impeccable manners. She just chose when to use them. Today, so far, she was playing nicely.

Stacy opened a notebook and started on a list of questions about her mother's health and her needs, writing down all her responses. Emerson listened to her answer each one fully. She could hear the slightest amount of frustration at the inconvenience of it all in her voice, but she didn't think it was coming across to Stacy.

Emerson's phone vibrated and she pulled it from her pocket. Thankfully, she'd silenced it before Stacy arrived so it wouldn't interrupt this meeting. Seeing who was calling caused her heart to leap into her throat and her skin to flash with an instant chill.

It was her boss.

A lightheaded feeling passed over her, forcing her to blink her eyes rapidly while taking a deep breath.

She needed to step out of the room. She needed to take this call.

She didn't look over at her mother and Stacy, didn't offer any reason for leaving the room abruptly. Stepping into the kitchen, she was drawn to the sunny deck beyond. Moving through the French door she took another deep breath before swiping her finger across the screen. Holding the phone to her ear, she said, "Hello, Mr. Samuelson."

The pause that came next spoke volumes. This wasn't a welfare check. He wasn't checking in to see how her mother was doing. She stepped into the shade of the covered deck on the far end of the porch.

"Emerson." His voice seemed gruff, holding no positive emotion whatsoever. "I'm sorry to call you like this. I know you have more time off left, but we have a developing situation here."

Her throat squeezed. A developing situation? What the hell did that mean?

"Well, there's no other way to say this than to just say it," he grumbled. She could picture him taking off his glasses and rubbing his eyes. Emerson blinked to stay focused on his words. "Don was fired this morning for misconduct. He's in the process of being arrested at his home as we speak."

"What?" she choked out. "Why?" She couldn't get any other words out. Her mind raced with possibilities. Misconduct? He'd always been an entitled asshole, but had he sexually harassed someone? Or did it have to do with a client? Fraudulent accounts or money laundering?

"I can't discuss the details." Of course, not, but that was frustrating. "Since he was managing some of your clients while you've been away, we need you back immediately to handle your affairs, plus help with his. This is a mess, Emerson. A total shit-show, if you will. Again, I'm sorry to do this to you, but we need you back here tomorrow."

Emerson's heartrate hadn't slowed down since she'd seen his name on her caller ID, so it didn't accelerate at his last statement. It stuttered. Missed at least two beats before trying to catch back up with the correct rhythm.

*Tomorrow?*

***

After setting a daily schedule for Stacy to come every weekday, Emerson saw the nurse out and took a deep breath before returning to the living room.

"What's wrong, dear? Didn't you like her?" Carolyn shifted back in her chair, looking more relaxed now that the nurse was gone.

"Yes, Mom. Stacy is very nice and she's going to be so helpful for you." Emerson hesitated. She was still reeling from the phone call. Her boss's words had left her speechless and she hadn't actually confirmed that she'd be back in New York tomorrow. But her boss hadn't really been listening anyway. She'd heard someone enter his office with a raised voice, so she knew Mr. Samuelson was too distracted with the developing situation to bother with getting a response from her.

He just expected her to do it.

Expected her to be back in New York tomorrow.

"I got a phone call earlier." Emerson sat down on the couch and slumped back, closing her eyes and rubbing her forehead. "It was my boss."

"What did he want?" She could hear the question in Carolyn's voice, but also a hint of worry.

"He wants me back tomorrow." Emerson kept rubbing her forehead, physically aware as the tension started to creep back in, to tighten her muscles along her neck and shoulders. It was slow, but it was so obvious to her now that her body had completely relaxed over the last two weeks.

Having multiple orgasms would do that to a person.

"He can't have you back tomorrow," she said, sitting forward in her seat, her temper flashing. "You're still on leave for two more weeks."

"There's been a situation. A developing situation is the way he described it." Emerson dropped her hands in her lap, her fingers instantly fisting. She was not okay. Her body was overflowing with cortisol, her stress hormone, and she needed to get out of here soon. "He couldn't tell me the details but a colleague of mine has been fired. He was handling some of my clients, so I'm needed back to manage those plus help with his."

"Don't you have other colleagues that can handle your clients?" Now Carolyn was wringing her hands.

"Only two that were on par with me. And one of them just got fired. That leaves Jack and he'll be in manic mode because of this event. I have to go back." She sat up, but her head hung down. As if her neck muscles were so weak from instantly tightening that they couldn't do their job and hold her head up. Damn this hurt. The tension, but also the thought of getting on a plane tomorrow and returning to the hustle and bustle of New York City.

And she didn't even want to think about the stress levels inside Lawson Financial right now and what it would feel like to be standing smack dab in the middle of it all.

"I'm sorry, honey." She shook her head, soft gray hair shifting around her face with the move. "I knew you'd have to eventually. I just wasn't expecting it so soon."

"Me, either." Emerson stood and took hold of her mother's hand. "I need to go see Nick. Will you be okay here for a while—"

"Go! I'm not an invalid," she grumbled. "Go see your man."

Emerson shook her head slowly, her hair sliding over her shoulders. "He's not my man, Mom."

"Are you sure about that?" Carolyn's fingers were strong around hers. Thankfully, she didn't feel any shakes. "I bet he would be if you asked him to be."

Emerson slanted her head down and a frown stretched her lips. "This isn't the Sadie Hawkins Day dance."

"No, it isn't. But it is your life, Emmie, and your happiness." Emerson shifted, her ears hearing the words, her heart starting to realize the truth in them. "You didn't have the spark of joy I saw in your eyes this morning when you came here two weeks ago. I think the life you've been living in New York is hard and stressful. And that's not good for your body. Just because it's your career job doesn't mean you have to keep doing it." Carolyn shook her hand, squeezing her fingers, emphasizing her words. "You can change careers. You can change locations. You can change your mind about what matters to you. And I know Nick matters to you."

Her heart constricted at those words. "Yes, he does. But what if it's fleeting?"

"There are unknowns in this life, honey, and you just have to take a chance once in a while and chase that happiness." Emerson felt her mother's hand start to tremble a little. Her grip loosening. She turned her hand over and soothed her muscles with her fingers. "Think about this," she continued. "How did you feel when you saw your boss's name on your phone?" Carolyn placed her other hand on top of theirs to get Emerson's eyes to focus on hers. "Were you elated? Or were you scared? Now, think of the same situation, but it's Nick calling you. Would you be elated? Or would you be scared?"

"I get what you're saying, Mom, I do. I just can't make—"

"Honey, people have made crazier decisions for love. Follow your heart and do what makes you happy. If going back tomorrow, and continuing to live in New York makes you happy, then do it. But if you hate the idea of going back. If your heart feels anxiety instead of joy, then maybe you should think about making a change." There was that *change* word again. It was so easy for other people to toss around, but much harder for one to actually do. "Don't go back just because of obligation. You've given them enough of your expertise. Now you can give them your two weeks' notice."

Inside she screamed. *Two weeks' notice?*

Her mother thought she should quit? Lordy, she was feeling overwhelmed. She could feel heat starting to rise on her skin, starting at her core and working its way out. She needed some fresh air. And she needed to think.

Dammit. She was getting tired of thinking.

"I'll be back in an hour."

"Take your time, dear. And think about what I said. If there's no joy in going back, just stay."

"If it were only that simple, Mom." Emerson leaned down and hugged her.

Once in the car, she found herself driving around reminiscing about high school, passing childhood homes of her friends, and ending up at their favorite pizza joint. She had no idea then what it would mean to her now.

Parking along the curb she looked up at the shop in front of her and suddenly remembered the girl at the art festival who was selling wind chimes. Exiting the car, she found herself walking towards the friendly shop. Barrels of bright flowers framed the entrance, and the soft mellow sounds of wooden wind chimes greeted her from the overhang above the bright yellow door.

The girl from the art festival sat behind the counter and offered her a warm welcome. Emerson smiled in return and let her eyes flow through the store. There were so many beautiful chimes on display, an assortment of both metal and wooden. From the smallest set that was maybe only a foot long to an enormous set that had to reach closer to three feet in length. She bet those sounds were deep and loud. Hand-carved shapes of blue crabs, pelicans and dolphins on top held just a splash of color, letting the grain of the wood show through.

Emerson trailed her fingers along the tubes and set them swinging. She felt like a kid getting away with something. But the melodious sounds made her heart happy.

She stopped in front of one with a sailboat carved in the rounded-edged rectangular-ish piece of wood adorning the top of a set of wooden wind chimes. Of course, it wasn't meant to be just like Tony's boat, but it sure looked like it to her. Picking it up from the hook, she knew she had to buy this one. It was too meaningful.

The chimes couldn't be for her though. She didn't have a balcony in New York. No outside place to display them that would allow the wind to make pretty music. But Nick did. He had a beautiful deck on the back of his house.

If she was leaving tomorrow, she wanted him to know that their night on the sailboat meant something to her. It meant everything, actually.

Emerson exited the store with her purchase, a smile on her lips. Her head whipped up when she heard her name called. Looking to the left she saw Nick's mother next door in front of the pizzeria.

"Hi, Mrs. Valentino!" Emerson lifted her hand to wave, then saw that she was trying to lift chairs over the side rail of a rolling cart. It looked like she was just starting to set up the tables and chairs on the patio outside the restaurant. "Oh, here, let me help you," she called out, jogging over to set her package on the closest table. Then she helped her lift the stack of two chairs, setting them down before lifting out another set. Carrying chairs over to the table farthest away, she pushed them under the tabletop and moved back to get another stack.

"*Grazie, cara mia.*"

The *grazie* part was easy. She still had no idea what *cara mia* meant. "You're welcome. I'm happy to help." In a few minutes all the tables and chairs were set up for the day.

There were only a few people out on Bay Avenue today. A few walkers and window-shoppers. Mrs. Valentino greeted the two women that walked by on the sidewalk.

"I appreciate your assistance," she said, pushing one last chair in place, and turned to face her. "How is your mother doing today?"

Emerson thought it was sweet that she asked. "She's doing well. Recovering from her busy week and weekend at the art festival."

Mrs. Valentino's eyes lit up. "Did she have success?"

Nodding, Emerson answered, "Yes, she sold several paintings. She was very pleased."

"Wonderful for her. Are you out shopping today?" Focusing on Emerson's shopping bag on the table, she nodded her head toward the shop next door. "I love that place. We have several of her wind chimes at our house."

"Yes, they are beautiful. She does amazing work." Emerson shrugged sheepishly. "I actually bought one for Nick."

"Oh, he'll love that," she crooned. Emerson noticed Mrs. Valentino's eyes appeared wet. Was she tearing up? She was just the sweetest woman. So thoughtful to ask about her mother. So loving towards her son. "That is sweet of you, *cara mia*."

Should she? Yes, she would. She had to. "I have to ask—what does *cara mia* mean?"

"My dear," she explained, her lips curving into a generous smile.

Aww, that made her feel special.

"Well, I'll let you get back to getting ready to open." Emerson picked up her shopping bag and turned toward the direction of Nick's shop.

"You were so sweet to help me set up. You come in soon for pizza." Mrs. Valentino opened the front door to the pizzeria. "*Offre la casa.* It's on the house. You and Nicky should come back here for lunch."

She wasn't sure they'd be having lunch together after she told him she had to be back in

New York tomorrow, but she nodded anyway. "Thank you. I'll suggest that to him."

"And say hi to Nicky for me," she added with a wink.

"I will." Emerson set off in the direction of Paddlers Paradise. She couldn't believe that she'd be back in New York this time tomorrow. Walking down Bay Avenue was completely tame compared to Wall Street. The buildings were mostly one-story and small. The sidewalk was narrow, and the street had angled parking spaces on each side. She only passed five people on the way to the other end of the block. In New York she'd likely have passed five hundred by now.

There were muted sounds around her. A loud laughing gull cry from down by the water. A garbage truck beeping as it backed up from behind the building she was walking in front of. Someone sweeping the sidewalk in front of their shop.

She could hear her own thoughts here. She could think. She'd been doing nothing but thinking the last few days. In New York City, the hum of activity on the streets came in at a dull roar most days. She'd learned to tune most of it out, but it took concentration. And it was taxing.

Stopping at the crosswalk, she pushed the button for the light to change. She waited by herself. In New York City, there'd be a horde of people waiting behind her, pushing forward, eager to get on with their day, to fulfill their busy schedule. Here in the peace and quiet she was able to take in the beauty of the flowers draped over the sides of the hanging baskets on the corner light post, and those beautiful blooms crowding the barrels lining the streets.

She crossed the street when the light turned and opened the front door to Paddlers Paradise. She came up short when she nearly collided with a woman on her way out the door.

"Oh, sorry," she said, stepping back quickly.

"Hi, Emerson," the woman said, "I'm so glad you're here." Shaking her head, the woman passed her in the doorway. "Nick's in his office and he needs you," she called out as she rushed down the sidewalk.

Was that Amber?

Emerson frowned after the woman but shook it off and entered the store. Where was his office? She heard grumbling coming from behind the main checkout counter, so she headed that way. "Nick?" She didn't want to just walk in on him. Peeking her head in the door, she dragged her teeth across her bottom lip, not wanting to let out the chuckle that wanted to burst from her lips.

Nick sat behind a desk, elbows on the surface, head in hands, fingers splayed through his hair, causing it to stand up in riotous fury. His eyes were closed, and he looked adorably frumpled.

Styx was on a dog bed in the corner, chewing on a squeaky toy. As soon as she noticed her, the pup popped up and ran to her, letting out adorable yips.

"Hi, sweet girl," Emerson crooned, bending down to pet the happy, dancing pup.

At her voice, she watched Nick's head shoot back, and he sat up straight, his eyes unfocused, a little wild even. "Emerson?"

"I'm here." She stood up, holding the puppy in her arms, and his eyes zeroed in on her. "Are you okay?" Now she was worried that something could be wrong and regretted her earlier laughter. "What's wrong?"

Emerson entered his office and rounded the desk. He turned to face her, spinning in his office chair, and slumped back in his seat, bouncing a little with the force of his sigh.

"Amber just left. She has finals to take. Payroll is today." Words came out in chunks. With extreme effort. Emerson had an "a-ha" moment while he was speaking. Remembering back to the kayak trip, he'd told her on the beach after doctoring up her foot that Amber was graduating and moving away. She was his payroll person.

She also remembered his words, which made a whole lot more sense now, "the boss isn't happy" and "numbers are not his game."

"O-kay," Emerson drew the word out, hoping a soothing voice would calm him. "How can I help?"

His glazed eyes snapped to hers. He blinked and they became crystal clear. "You can help me?" Then it seemed to dawn on him. He sat up straight in his swivel chair and said with much more confidence, "You can help me."

She allowed her laughter out this time. Nodding her head, she said, "Yes, I can try. How hard can it be? Now move it." She pointed to his computer and made a shooing motion with her hand. Nick hopped out of his seat and accepted Styx when she passed her over to him. She swiveled to face the computer and put her hands on the keyboard and mouse. "Okay, what program do you use?"

When he didn't answer right away, she looked up at him and received his blank stare. Letting out a sigh, she nodded her head and said, "So, I take it Amber does it all." She used the mouse to click through the history on his browser and found the payroll website they used.

"Yep," he said, sitting on the edge of the desk, stroking Styx's ears. "I'm not a math guy or a computer guy, for that matter. Amber graduates soon." He sounded so depressed, his voice just a bit grumbled.

Sneaking a peek at him under her lashes, she felt bad for him. "You mentioned that she was helping you set up a job announcement. Have you interviewed anyone yet?"

His head bounced up and down. "Yes, two people."

"That's great." Emerson smiled up at him. She thought he looked sad. She wasn't sure he was so happy about change either. "Will either one of them be a good fit?"

Nick rolled his shoulders and grimaced. Definitely not good with change. So she wasn't the only one. Numbers and computers weren't everyone's game, certainly not Nick's, but luckily, she excelled at both. It wasn't Wall Street, but maybe if she did choose to stay, she could find work easily. To her, numbers were easy, and she was happy when she was manipulating them.

Payroll wasn't playing the stock market, but it was still using her brain and her math skills, and she could even branch out. Do this for more businesses, or something else even. She could find something fulfilling here, right?

"Well, having people interested in the job is a good start. I can help you with this problem now, but Amber is leaving soon."

"No need to remind me." He scrubbed his free hand down his face. She could hear his palm scrape against his stubble. Styx helped ease his pain by licking his cheeks. His lips pulled up into their lop-sided smile as he held the puppy close.

Once Emerson was in the site she asked Nick several more questions about his employees, their hours and pay scale. She found most of that information already logged in but wanted to verify everything before issuing checks. Luckily, he only had a few employees.

"Done," she announced and pushed back from the desk, the chair rolling easily on the tile floor. Styx barked her confirmation and Emerson laughed.

"Done?" He stood up, looking bewildered. "Already? That was only like, twenty minutes." His eyes were huge as they stared into hers, disbelief and admiration swirling in the dark depths. Emerson's lips curved.

Damn he was handsome. Even in his bewildered state with his disheveled hair, the dark stubble covering his chin and the tightness around his eyes, her insides turned gooey just looking at him.

She realized this was the first time she'd seen him since he'd dropped her off at her mother's house yesterday.

After they'd had a mini-make-out session in the truck.

This time at a dead-end road near her house. Definitely not near her mother's house since her sister's family was still there.

"Hiya, handsome." She leaned back in the office chair and tilted her head, her eyes roaming over his face, pausing on his soft, kissable lips. Her tongue darted out to moisten her lower lip as she watched his part under her heated gaze.

Suddenly, Nick leaned down and dropped Styx into her lap, threading his fingers through her hair, and pressed his lips to hers. She wrapped her hands around the ecstatic pup to hold her in place and breathed him in, deepening the kiss. When he pulled back, she licked her lips and wished for more of that. Yes, please.

"Hiya, back, *bellissima*. Thank you for helping me. Thank you for rescuing me." He hung his head, once again leaning back against the corner of his desk.

"It was easy. Amber had everything ready to go. You're gonna miss her."

*Are you going to miss me?*

Emerson knew she needed to say what had to be said. She lowered Styx to the floor and stood. Moving between his thighs, she pressed herself into his lower body, wrapping her arms around his neck. His hands came to rest on her hips, rhythmically squeezing his fingers into her flesh. Oh, how she wished for her clothes to disappear with just the snap of her fingers.

Nick chuckled. "If that gig in New York doesn't work out, I've got a job opening here..." His voice trailed off as his lips met hers. Emerson closed her eyes, soaking in the kiss, the heat of his lips and hands, wanting to savor every second leading up to her announcement. She wasn't sure how things were going to be after it.

Just say it. "Speaking of that." But she hesitated. She didn't want to ruin what they had going. And the only way she wouldn't do that was to *not* say anything about the phone call from her boss and *not* get on a plane tomorrow leaving him. But she'd never be able to continue pretending it didn't happen.

Nick looked at her curiously, his head slightly tilted, his hair falling over his forehead. She reached up and twirled a lock between her fingers. "My boss called this morning."

He tensed as soon as the words were out. His fingers tightened on her hips, and it looked like he was holding his breath. Same. She felt the same. Just saying it aloud brought back the visceral reaction she'd had when she saw Mr. Samuelson's name on her phone screen.

"There's been a situation. One of my colleagues was fired this morning. Charged with misconduct. My boss wouldn't explain any of the details, just said the police were arresting him."

A furrow settled between Nick's beautiful eyes. Eyes that weren't focused on hers anymore. Was he pulling back already? Protecting himself?

She trudged on, needing to say everything.

Her voice might have squeaked when she said, "He wants me back tomorrow."

# Chapter Twenty

Nick wasn't sure he'd heard her words correctly. There seemed to be a buzzing in his ears. But the look in her eyes, the sadness he saw in the swirling mix of blue and green, confirmed what she said.

*He wants me back tomorrow.*

"He wants you back tomorrow," he repeated the words. His voice sounded odd. He couldn't believe this was happening. They'd just had their first amazing night together and he'd already been planning for another.

But this changed everything.

Emerson's words only clarified for him what he'd suspected since Saturday night. His feelings for her had advanced to a whole new level. He'd been falling for her, for her smile, her laugh, her generous heart, but the second she'd said the words *He wants me back tomorrow* his heart stuttered, constricted and fell over the edge of whatever precipice it had been balancing on.

Emerson's eyes looked sad as she nodded, her gorgeous hair sliding forward over her shoulders. Nick forced his fingers to loosen their grip on her hips. One hand rose, feathering his fingers through her silky strands. He remembered that she'd said she liked it when someone did that. He liked it too. He couldn't get enough of her. Here he'd been making a plan for wooing her over the next two weeks and suddenly, she was leaving tomorrow.

"Nick," her voice cracked a little, "I know this is sudden. I was completely caught off guard." The truth of her words was written all over her face.

"This isn't the military." Nick shook his head, still confused over her boss's highhanded declaration. "You're under no contractual obligation to return at his command, are you?"

She frowned up at him. "It's my job, Nick. I've been with this company for eight years. If I don't go back tomorrow it's just as good as quitting," she declared, and with her posture erect and her jaw locked, she pushed out of his arms, putting space between them.

Already distancing herself?

He fisted his hands around the edge of the desktop to keep from reaching for her. If she needed space, he wasn't going to force her to be within touching distance. "That's a very admirable quality. But you have a choice, Em. There's always an opportunity to walk away. You can say that you've had enough, and you want something different. There's no shame in that."

Emerson moved around his desk and paced the open space in front of the window. The view of the bay beyond the window drew his eye. The sun shone on the calm waves as they lapped at the sandy shore. The temperature would be over seventy today and he'd been hoping to talk her into getting on a paddle board this afternoon.

The silence was making him crazy. They both had too many thoughts rushing through their minds. But since she wasn't talking, Nick felt he had to. "Yes, you'd be leaving them in a bind, with one man down already, but there must be other employees eager to rise in the ranks. Some that would love to fill your position."

A disgruntled groan escaped Emerson's clamped-shut lips. She stopped pacing and pressed her fingers into her eyes, rubbing them, sliding her fingers over to her temples, massaging them next. He wanted so badly to replace her hands with his and ease the tension he could see filling her head. This sudden change in plans was overwhelming to her, and he could relate.

His eyes roamed her body, from the top of her head down to the sneakers on her feet. Her legs were braced, her spine straight, her neck stiff, lips pinched. She looked more like she did when he'd first seen her at the Keel & Rudder. Just the thought of going back to her old life was stressing her the hell out. Couldn't she see that?

"Em, they will survive without you," he urged. Nick stepped around the desk, closer to her, but he didn't crowd her. He desperately wanted to pull her into his chest and wrap her up in comfort. Seeing her so stressed was killing him. "But will you survive going back into that work zone with it now even more stressful than it was when you left?" His words were soft but emphatic.

Emerson turned toward him, her gaze meeting his. "Nick, I—"

The jingle of the front door opening cut off her words. Voices filled the silence in the shop, and Nick remembered he had scheduled rentals today since it was Spring Break. Releasing a deep sigh worthy of an award, he leaned forward and kissed her forehead, his lips lingering against her skin as he said, "I'm not walking away from this. But right now, I've gotta run."

He felt her breath huff out against his neck in what may have been a chuckle. "I know you're busy. I'll talk to you tonight," she added, pressing her nose into his neck. Her lips touched his skin briefly before she pushed past him and out the door. The jingle of the bells over the door sounded a few seconds later.

Nick knew there was a lot more talking that needed to happen, but right now, he needed to focus on this job, not his heart.

Stepping out into the shop, with Styx following at his heels, he greeted the group of high school kids milling about looking at the shirts and hats. He received a few waves in return and could hear excited squeals from the girls when Styx ran over to them. She was going to get all the pets this morning.

"Good morning, y'all. You picked a great day for this." He shifted fully into his outdoorsy-guy mode and got to work pulling up their registrations, mentally preparing himself to gather the boards and paddles since he was the only one in the shop today. Spring Break was in full force, and he'd given Terry and Jazzy a few days off so they could enjoy their break before coming back to work.

Nick wished he could lead this group in a lesson and be out on the water with his thoughts. He found that to be one of the best places to do his thinking. Too bad he couldn't put a sign on the door and go for a paddle. Nope. He'd have to compartmentalize all the random Emerson thoughts zinging around his head for now.

After getting the kids all squared away, he said, "Okay, y'all follow me and I'll get you set up down on the beach front. Everyone have sunscreen and water?" Lots of heads nodded in response. "Bathrooms are here." He pointed to the left before scooping Styx into his arms for the jaunt down the back steps leading below the building. Nick made small talk, asking them about what school they went to, if they'd paddled before, and whether they liked Auburn or Alabama.

At the bottom of the steps, he set Styx on her feet. Since she was still working on traversing the steps, he decided to carry her so they wouldn't hold up the kids.

Nick enjoyed the kids' banter as they gathered near the equipment storage cages under the building. They seemed like good, competent pseudo-adults, so he decided they could be trusted with his equipment. Using a key from his key ring, he opened the lock on the paddle board storage cage. "Guys, y'all load the boards onto this pull cart." He moved the cart out so it could easily be loaded. "And girls, y'all load up the paddles."

Once everything was in order he offered to pull the cart across the parking lot for them, but one of the guys said he'd do it. Nick nodded and sent them on their way. "See you in three hours."

He sure hoped he had a ton of customers today otherwise he'd go crazy if left to his thoughts for that long. The end of the workday couldn't come fast enough.

***

"Woman, where's the fire?" Callie shouted as she exited the kitchen door onto the back deck.

Emerson looked up from the table and felt her shoulders relax. Callie would be able to talk her through this and help her make it make sense. "I got here as soon as I could. I had to wait until after my meeting to leave the school. Hi, Aunt Carolyn." Callie leaned down and hugged her shoulder, pressing her blonde head to the top of Carolyn's. Her light pink dress matched the shade of Carolyn's shirt like they'd been bought together.

"Hi, sweetie." Carolyn reached up and patted Callie's hand. "Emerson has some news she'd like to share, so I'm going to leave y'all to it." When she sat forward to shift her chair back from the table, Callie helped her, and supported her arm while she stood. "Thank you, Callie."

"You're welcome, Aunt Carolyn." Emerson took another sip of her sweet tea while she waited for Callie to take the vacant seat. A chuckle escaped, almost causing her to snort sweet tea out of her nose, when Callie slapped her palms gently on the table, her bracelet full of science-specific charms like beakers and microscopes clanking against the glass top, and demanded, "What's the news?"

Emerson shifted in her adjacent chair, her gaze locking with her cousin's. Seeing love and concern in her eyes, she decided to just drop the bomb. "My boss wants me back in New York tomorrow."

Callie's expression was comical. She could win an award for the fastest expression changes in ten seconds. Her eyes, eyebrows and mouth went from curious to furious along a meandering route passing through surprise and shock first. "What? Why? How?"

Emerson ran her fingers through her hair and sat back in her chair, pulling her knees up to her chest. "So many questions. I had them too. He said there was a 'developing situation' this morning and that my asshole colleague had been fired and was getting arrested at the time of his call."

"What?" This time her question was a near shriek. Her eyes bulged, and she couldn't stop moving her hands. Being a teacher, Callie tended to talk with her hands a lot, but right now, they didn't know what to say.

"Yep, totally out of the blue. It came as a complete shock. The phone call, but also the firing. I had no idea." She paused, listening to the cry of the laughing gulls near the end of their dock, as her mind replayed her boss's words. Then she shared, "I told Nick already."

"Oh, how'd that go?" Everything seemed to quiet down with that statement. Like she was nervous to ask.

Emerson reached out to touch her glass, turning it with her fingers. It slid easily on the condensation puddle on the tabletop. "I went to his shop to tell him in person. I explained the call, its suddenness, and my obligation to my job."

Callie's long hair slid over her bare shoulder when she nodded. Her light pink dress was sleeveless and showed off Callie's muscular arms. "You do have an obligation. Out of a sense of pride and responsibility. You've worked there for how many years now?"

"Eight years," Emerson supplied.

Callie's lips pursed as she seemed to ponder her next question. "But you don't have a contract, do you?"

"Nick asked the same thing. No, no contract. But I can't just *not* show up tomorrow. They need me. They expect mc to fulfill my job description...and there have always been unwritten expectations. With any job, I imagine. You'd know this as a teacher."

Callie nodded emphatically. "Absolutely. You have to be able to go with the flow and be a team player. I admire that about you, Em. But I also know what we've talked about. Remember the panic attack?" Callie's hand pointed out to the water's edge where Emerson had nearly lost it just a few days ago. Oh, she remembered it well, thank you very much. Then Callie brought that hand down to grasp hers on the tabletop. "Remember we talked about your health and your happiness. About having a chance for love, if you stayed here."

"I've been doing nothing but thinking today." Emerson sighed, rubbing her temples for the hundredth time that day. A *chance for love*. She felt a twinge in her mid-section at those words.

Must be the butterflies in her stomach. "The call this morning just threw a bomb on all my casual thoughts and shook everything up. The visceral reaction I had to seeing my boss's name on the caller ID was really the clincher."

"The clincher?" Callie repeated, tilting her head in question.

"So here's what I'm thinking," Emerson drawled. "What if...what if I return to work, help get the shit-show straightened out and," she paused for dramatic effect, as well as to garner the courage to say the next words out loud, "then give my notice?"

That statement was met with silence. Birdsong in the distance was the only sound.

Not what she'd been expecting.

It was the first time she'd said the words out loud. They sounded different than in her head.

Louder.

Stronger.

More real.

More absolute.

If Callie's facial expressions were award-worthy before, this reaction would come in a very close second. Elation lit her eyes and flushed her cheeks. She must have needed time to process the words, just like Emerson. "Really? You mean, you're actually listening to me? You're really considering moving home?" Her voice rose with each of her questions.

Callie jumped up before Emerson could answer any of them, her chair screeching along the deck boards, and rushed around the table to throw her arms around Emerson's neck. She laughed and swayed in her cousin's embrace.

"Am I crazy?" It was a legitimate question. She felt wild inside with so many thoughts and emotions swirling around that it was hard to concentrate on one thing for long.

Laughing, Callie fell into the chair beside Emerson, keeping hold of her hands. Emerson sat up, dropping her feet to the deck, and held onto them tightly. The joy in Callie's eyes warmed her heart. "No. I think it's the best idea. I've missed you, and I'm thrilled you'll be so close again."

Emerson's smile matched the wattage of Callie's. It was so big her jaw was starting to hurt. "I've missed you too. I've missed my family. More than I realized. Probably because I didn't let myself think about them too much. I was where I thought I wanted to be and that was that." Emerson gestured with her hand straight ahead, away from her body as she spoke. "I kept my head down and stayed focused on my career, not doing much else."

"I hate the reason behind you coming home, but I'm so glad your sudden departure from New York helped break the routine of you working yourself into an early grave."

Emerson agreed. When she'd been in the thick of it, for over a decade, she couldn't see it. It took coming home to a completely different habitat to see what life in that fast-paced world had been doing to her.

"When I came here, I was completely on Team New York. I knew I was heading back once I got Mom settled. But after a week or so I started processing the words you were telling me. I noticed the changes. I was more relaxed, sleeping and eating more. The constant ache in my shoulders had lessened. I was smiling more," she added with a telltale smile.

"So much smiling," Callie added with a chuckle in her voice. "And you're so welcome for inviting you on the kayak trip that day. It got you in front of Nick again and gave you a chance to talk to him. I'm guessing he's responsible for most of your smiles since you've been home."

Emerson confirmed her statement with a grin. "He is. But so are you, Cal. And Mom. I love her stubbornness and her tenacity. She is going to hold onto her routine for as long as she can, and I admire that."

"You are both very strong-willed women."

"Said the kettle," Emerson scoffed.

Callie laughed and tossed her a wink. "We come from good stock. Oh, Emmie, I'm so happy about this. Ecstatic, really. Did you tell Nick this news?"

"No, we had only just gotten started talking about the phone call when he had customers come in. I told him I'd talk to him tonight."

"I know he's going to be so happy with your decision. Y'all are so cute together." Callie laughed and stood up. "Let me get some sweet tea so I can hear all the juicy details about your sunset sail."

# Chapter Twenty-One

Nick had worked himself up over the last several hours. He'd held on until the shop officially closed even though he'd wanted to flip the sign and duck out early. He was so revved up, so eager to hear what she was planning to do.

The thought of her leaving and going back to New York, without any idea if or when she'd come back home to visit had caused an ache in his chest. An ache that had spiraled out from there, until he could feel it in his limbs. It had become obvious to him throughout the day that he couldn't let her leave without telling her how he felt. That he'd fallen in love with her.

Completely head over heels.

After leaving the pizzeria on Sunday, he'd started dreaming up all the adventures he'd wanted to take her on over the next two weeks to show her how beautiful this place was and make her want to live here.

Make her want to stay. With him.

Then, bam! His heart had thudded in reaction to her words, racing one hundred miles an hour and it hadn't really slowed down much. He needed to see her, to hold her in his arms, to ask her how she felt about her summons. Because that was exactly how he thought of her boss's words. He understood they were going through some shit up there, but he couldn't believe the man's audacity.

His stomach knotted with anticipation.

He pulled up in front of her mother's because there was an SUV in the drive he didn't recognize. Images flashed through his mind of them in this very same place last week. It had been the first time he'd had his hands on her, tracing her soft, smooth skin, feeling her pressed against him. He'd been so damn hard he could have busted through his shorts. He'd wanted inside her so badly. He'd wanted their clothes off, wanted them skin to skin.

Thinking about that now wasn't a good idea. He needed to clear his head and adjust his shorts before heading inside.

Nick took a deep breath and got out of the truck. He held Styx's leash and allowed her to meander to the door, following her nose. It gave him a couple extra minutes to get control of his emotions.

He rang the doorbell and stepped back, waiting. The knots in his stomach pulling tighter as every second passed. Surprise lifted his eyebrows when Callie answered the door.

"Hi," Callie greeted, stepping out onto the porch. "I've gotta run. Emmie's in the backyard. She said for you to come on through the kitchen. Oh, look at this sweet pup," she crooned, squatting down to pet a dancing Styx. "She looks just like my Goose did when he was a baby. Aww, thank you for the kisses. Now, Goose is going to wonder who I've been seeing." Rising to her feet, she laughed and waved as she strode down the front steps to her SUV. "Have a good night," she called out.

"Goodnight," Nick murmured, confused by her happiness. Wasn't she upset about Emerson leaving tomorrow? Nick stood frozen in his spot a moment longer, glancing at her retreating back then towards the open front door. Looking down at Styx, he said, "Let's go find out our fate, Styxy."

Nick followed the path he'd taken the other night from the front door. Passing behind an armchair that faced the TV he walked through the large case opening into the kitchen. The back door to the deck was open and he tugged gently on Styx's leash to get her to follow. She'd had her nose to the ground under the table, probably helping sweep up crumbs left behind by Emerson's sister's kids.

The kitchen door opened onto a large deck that covered the length of the house. Colorful pots of blooming flowers lined the edge. A section of the backyard close to the house was fenced off. He could see an array of flowers blooming there.

His eyes drifted out from the yard to the waterfront and the bay beyond. The view was unbelievable. My God, what an incredible place to grow up. The setting sun cast an orange glow on the land. It glinted off Emerson's hair where she sat in a swing that hung from one of the Live Oak trees that flanked the property.

She twisted in the swing toward him when she heard Styx's yips and waved to him. Styx got so excited when she spotted Emerson, she stood up on her hind legs tugging at the leash. Nick unclipped her and followed behind her as she ran down the steps. She took a tumble down the second to last one, but that didn't slow her down. She stood up, shook her ears to right herself and took off across the lush, green grass, straight to the woman who held his heart.

Emerson leaned down and scooped Styx up into her arms and welcomed all the puppy's kisses. Nick's heart swelled so much it pushed against his ribs. His girls. What a beautiful picture they made silhouetted by the golden glow of the sun. Nick's steps faltered when his brain flashed a brief image of Emerson in that same swing holding a child in her arms instead of

Styx. A smiling, laughing baby. Was it possible? Did they have a chance for forever, for a family?

Nodding his head, bolstering his confidence, he continued forward, determined to make it so.

"Hi," Emerson laughed while dodging continuous Styx kisses. "Thank you for coming over."

"Hi," he returned, stopping in front of her, taking in every glowing inch of her. The sun was only minutes from setting, and it lit her eyes like the hottest blue flame. "I wanted a chance to finish our conversation."

"Me too." She lowered Styx to the ground then put her hands on the ropes. "Push me?"

Her smile was radiant. He really didn't know what was going on here. First, Callie was happy. Now, Emerson. Was she that excited about going back to her life? From how she'd acted this morning, he'd thought she didn't want to go. Maybe something else had happened. Maybe her boss called her back and told her to finish out her month, that they could handle the chaos on their own. Maybe.

"I'd be happy to." Nick moved behind her and took hold of the ropes above her hands, pulling her backward into the air before letting go. She flew forward, her hair trailing out behind her. Her long legs encased in a pair of shorts the color of watermelon stretched out, then tucked under her as she came back to him.

This reminded him of when he was younger. There'd been a park across from the pizzeria/apartment in Jersey. He and Tony had spent many an hour competing to see who could swing higher. Then that competition had morphed into who could jump out of the swings at the highest point, and then who could jump the farthest. Somehow, neither had ever broken anything, which was a damn miracle for all the spills they'd taken as kids.

As she went higher, Nick had to reach up and push against her lower back, his large hands splaying over her luscious curves as well. She giggled and he thought the sound could have been angels singing from the heavens.

Yep, he could definitely see himself swinging a baby out here or pushing a toddler on the swing. Again, he couldn't help but think, what an amazing place to grow up. The long dock reaching out over the water had a slide off the side. He could imagine lots of squeals of joy, big splashes and fishing right there off the dock.

"Em, this place is amazing."

She turned her head to look at him over her shoulder as she swung back towards him. "Incredible, right?"

Nick caught the ropes and carefully pulled her to a stop. He stepped in front of her and threaded his fingers through her hair, feathering the strands, letting them land back against her shoulders. "Yes, incredible. This you is completely different from the earlier you. What's changed?"

Emerson sighed and he had to talk his heart into not constricting at the sound. She stood up from the swing and took hold of his hand, leading him toward the dock. Styx was nearby, her front paws digging for treasure in the dry sand. Then she buried her nose inside. Coming up for air, she looked up at them with a smiling, sandy face when they passed by.

Nick laced his fingers with hers, admiring her smooth skin, and the strength in her grip. Gulls cried out, fighting over a fish one had hanging out of its mouth. Pelicans bobbed on the surface of the water just beyond the end of the pier, stretching their beaks straight up in order to swallow their dinner. A Contender sped by with fishing poles strapped in for the return trip home.

Being here with her felt like they were back where they were Sunday morning after their sailing trip. After the night they'd shared learning each other's bodies, each other's likes and needs. It felt as if this morning hadn't happened. As if she hadn't dropped the going-back-to-New-York bomb on him out of nowhere.

A slight breeze ruffled his hair, shifting hers along the shoulders of her white T-shirt as they turned to step onto the wooden boards of the dock. The boards creaked beneath his sneakers as he strode beside her in silence. It was a natural silence. A peaceful one. Nothing strained, even though he felt things were unresolved between them. Right then, with the sun about to dip below the horizon, the breeze on his skin, the lapping of the waves nearby, and her hand surrounded by his, he was in heaven.

She turned her smile towards him and confirmed it. This was his heaven. Here with her. On the water. In the sunshine and the fresh air. He couldn't ask for anything more.

Well, the only thing he would ask for was for her to stay here with him. To take a chance on him. So, he spoke first, needing to get the words he'd been thinking about all day out before she told him her plans.

Nick stopped walking and turned towards her. The sun glinting off a sea glass pendant laying against her chest drew his gaze and he reached up to trace the beautiful piece, a nearly perfect match to her eyes. Eyes he focused on now as he said, "Emerson, your happiness has grown since the first day I saw you at the Keel & Rudder." He sure as hell was the happiest he'd ever been.

His heart was triple-timing right now, the pulse in his neck practically vibrating. Worry over her decision was the main cause. But more importantly because she was in his arms again. He laid his palm over her heart, thrilled to feel hers beating at the same pace.

"You've changed so much since that day." He lifted his hand from her heart and brushed his fingertips across her shoulders, pushing her hair behind her back. His fingers wrapped over her shoulders and massaged them. "Your shoulders aren't so stiff. And you're rarely without a smile now. You realize it's this place, right—" He raised a hand to the house, then the swing and the water beyond. "—that's making you so happy."

He paused, bringing his focus back to her eyes. "Emerson, don't you feel it? Don't you feel like you're back where you belong?" Even he could hear the emotion flowing through his words. His heart was in his throat, constricting his airflow. His stomach was back to being in knots.

Because this was it.

This was him putting himself out there.

This was him hoping she'd see what she'd been missing and what she'd found since coming home. This beautiful place, this serene habitat. But also, him, and their relationship.

Emerson's eyes glistened with tears and her lips curved into the biggest smile he'd ever seen on her face. "I do." She reached up and cupped his cheek, her thumb tracing lightly over his bottom lip. It took everything he had in him not to suck her thumb into his mouth, but he needed to concentrate. To let her talk. "Yes, I do. This place isn't the only thing making me happy though. It's also you."

She threw her arms around his neck and pressed her lips to his. Nick lifted her off her feet and devoured her lips. She met him at every angle, deepening the kiss. His heart was singing. He felt her words deep in his soul. His mind played a trick on him, and he could see them on this very same dock, at sunset, saying "I do" to each other.

Pulling back, he had to hear her say it again and make sure he'd heard her correctly. "You're staying?"

Emerson's eyes were dazed from their kiss. Blinking them, she focused on his and then did the exact opposite thing he'd expected.

EMERSON SHOOK HER head. "No, I have to go back—but," she quickly added when he frowned, "but, I'm going to give them my notice once I help them get settled. I can't just leave them in a bind. I can't just walk away. That's not who I am."

The tautness she'd felt in the muscles beneath her hands went slack with her words. It was like she'd taken the wind out of his sails. "But, Nick, I will be back. I've been away too long as it is. And you're right, this is where I belong. Right here," she paused and rose up on her toes. Placing her lips ever so softly against his, her eyes open and gazing into molten honey, she whispered, "With you."

Those butterflies she'd felt in her stomach earlier now had the zoomies. The tingling sensation radiated out from her core, sliding along her nerve endings. This was right. This was what she'd been waiting to feel. This sense of being home. Yes, she was standing on the dock at the house where she grew up, but it was different now.

This sense of being home had everything to do with this man whose body fit perfectly against hers.

Whose arms were wrapped securely around her waist.

Whose lips were tasting hers.

She needed this man in her life. Needed his touch, his lop-sided grin, but most especially, his heart. And his lips. Don't forget his lips. He did incredible things to her with those lips. He made her *feel* incredible things with those lips, and these strong hands that held her so tightly could heat her skin in an instant but also provide her with so much comfort.

She needed him. She needed all of him.

Pulling back slightly, breaking the kiss, Nick suggested, "Let's sit. My damn legs are weak." She chuckled. Hers were too.

He took her hand and led her to the side of the dock where they could keep an eye on Styx who was still digging in the sand and appeared to be chasing a ghost crab. When she sat down, her legs dangling over the edge of the boards, Nick wrapped his arm around her back, pulling her into his side. With his head resting atop hers, he confessed, "I was so ready to argue with you, to fight for you. To demand that you give us a chance."

Heat began to swirl outward from deep within her stomach, a lovely sensation spreading out to every inch of her body. This. This was why she wanted to stay. Needed to stay.

This feeling.

This man.

This moment.

"I want that chance." Emerson gave his leg a squeeze beneath where her hand rested, her fingers then wrapping around the hem of his shorts to keep her hand still. There was a golden glow coming from the horizon as the sun dipped below it. It made his eyes look even more like honey. "I just have to get things settled first. But they will know when I return that I won't be there much longer. It could be two weeks; it could be a month. Either way, I've made my decision and being here with my family, with you, that's where I want to be. Need to be."

Nick leaned forward, resting his head against hers, his lips meeting hers in a lazy, precious kiss. "I need you, Emerson," Nick whispered. "*Mi sto innamorando di te.*"

Lordy, his voice. It was so deep, so rich, it oozed like honey through her ears and slid along her veins. His words sounded so beautiful, but she had no idea what he said.

Looked like she needed to start her Italian lessons soon.

At her questioning look, he took pity on her and translated. "I'm falling in love with you."

"Oh, Nick, say it again in Italian." She turned her body, drawing her knee up, and placed her hands on his face, loving the feel of the stubble under her palms. Her thumb touched his lip as he spoke.

"*Mi sto innamorando di te.*"

Emerson's heart swelled. "Beautiful. I'm gonna need you to record that for me so I can listen to it every time I feel down about not being here with you."

Nick kissed her cheek and spoke into her ear. "I've got more for you. *Voglio passare il resto della mia vita con te*—I want to spend the rest of my life with you, *bellissima.*"

Emerson gripped the front of his shirt, his breath fluttering over her skin as his words flowed through her, marking her heart, claiming it as his own.

"I want that too, Nick. Coming home has woken me up, made me realize I was missing out on so much in my life. That I wasn't really living. Being with you has brought me so much joy. I can't wait to see what is still to come." She kissed his lips, her eyes searching his. "I love you, Nick Valentino."

Nick's laugh was loud and deep and warmed her heart as he tackle-hugged her, pulling her back with him onto the dock, her body resting on top of his. "I love you, Emerson Taylor."

Emerson's smile grew bigger, she had no idea how that was even possible. With her arms wrapped around his neck she lowered her smiling lips to his laughing ones and sealed their declarations with a passionate kiss.

Which was lovingly interrupted by puppy kisses.

Nick laughed and grabbed hold of Styx, pulling her into their embrace. "Expressions of love and sloppy, wet kisses from my girls. I couldn't be happier."

# Acknowledgements

I had some wonderful helpers and inspiration for this book. First, I want to thank Butch Starnes for teaching me how to sail, in person twenty years ago and more recently with a refresher course on paper. Any mistakes during the sailboat scene are my own. Second, I want to thank Mendel and Carrie for the brainstorming sesh about dog names. Styx is a cute one! I saved the best for last—thank you to my sister Jill for always supporting me by reading through my stories and offering helpful critiques. You are the best, Jill!

I want to extend my gratitude to all those who have read my books. Bonus points to those who have reviewed them so that others can find out about them. Thank you all.

Happy reading!

Ivy

# About the author

Ivy Beck enjoys writing Contemporary Romance and Romantic Suspense with emotion and humor woven throughout. Her former life was spent teaching marine science along coastal Alabama. She switched to raising kids and editing for several New York Times bestsellers a few years ago. The kiddos are older now giving her time to let her creative mind wander. Ivy loves her boys, her pets and spending time outside. She loves kayaking and hiking. The water and the woods are her happy places. She lives in south Alabama with her husband, two sons, two dogs and one cat, and spends most of her day being a mom taxi. Which, surprisingly, is a really good place to think about the next chapter of her current WIP!

# Also by

Check out my website for more details on each book, plus, a free short story.
www.ivybeck.com

***

Heartstrings: Lanie runs from the greatest love she's ever known, only to find Sean again in another city. Will this second chance bring them back together forever?

***

Snapshot: A small-town photographer is targeted. The newest hire on the police force fights to find the unknown enemy, while also fighting his feelings for her.

***

Lucky Girl: Joni swears off workplace romance, but five minutes into the first date she's hooked. Unfortunately, Luke's personal baggage threatens to end things before they even get started.

***

Unexpected Arrival: A Steamy Novella  Angelina Cruz is waylaid by a snowstorm in Alaska. She finds help from Noah Bishop, a native who just happens to own the newest hotel establishment on the island.